DIME IF I KNOW

A CLEOPATRA JONES MYSTERY

DIME IF I KNOW

MAGGIE TOUSSAINT

FIVE STAR

A part of Gale, Cengage Learning

GALE
CENGAGE Learning®

Detroit • New York • San Francisco • New Haven, Conn • Waterville, Maine • London

25.95

GALE
CENGAGE Learning®

LIBRARY OF CONGRESS CATALOGING-IN-PUBLICATION DATA

Toussaint, Maggie.
  Dime if I know : a Cleopatra Jones mystery / Maggie Toussaint.
  — First Edition.
    pages cm
  ISBN 978-1-4328-2718-2 (hardcover) — ISBN 1-4328-2718-9 (hardcover)
  1. Single mothers—Fiction. 2. Women accountants—Fiction. 3. Maryland—Fiction. I. Title.
PS3620.O89D56 2013
813'.6—dc23
                             2013008359

First Edition. First Printing: August 2013
Find us on Facebook– https://www.facebook.com/FiveStarCengage
Visit our website– http://www.gale.cengage.com/fivestar/
Contact Five Star™ Publishing at FiveStar@cengage.com

Printed in Mexico
1 2 3 4 5 6 7 17 16 15 14 13

This book is dedicated to Ben Phillips and Hunter
Adams.

ACKNOWLEDGMENTS

Former police detective Lee Lofland provided insight into evidence and arrests. Critique partner Polly Iyer was instrumental in helping the book shine. Thanks to beta reader Craig Toussaint for that last comb-through. The nod for moral support goes to friends and family near and far. Any mistakes or errors in this book are mine and mine alone.

CHAPTER 1

Sunlight feels different in October. Thinner. Paler. Cooler. Unwanted change rides on the biting wind. In general, change doesn't suit me, but this fall I want something different. The idea began as a whisper skulking around the edge of my summer thoughts. As weeks passed, the notion solidified. Points pro and con volleyed through my consciousness, occupying more and more of my waking hours.

"Cleo?" my golf pro boyfriend asked. "What were your swing thoughts on that shot? Did you mean to hit a duck hook?"

Rafe Golden's voice drew me back from my musings. I could give him the answer he wanted to hear. I could pretend to be paying attention to his golf lesson, but I wouldn't lie to him. Instead, I leaned on my six iron and studied him. "I was thinking about something else. You."

Heat burned in his eyes, but his tanned face remained the epitome of professionalism. "The mental side of golf is as exacting as the physical. Great golfers go through the same preshot routine before they strike the ball as amateurs do. Settle your thoughts, and let muscle memory guide you."

I nodded, breathing in his just-showered scent, treasuring the sexy twinkle in his dark eyes, the languid grace of his lanky frame, and the baritone timbre of his voice. I was so gone on him it was pathetic.

"I can do better." With that, I whacked a few more dimpled balls, some on target, some on tangents, but mechanics like stance, grip, and swing plane didn't hold my attention today.

My name is Cleopatra Jones, Cleo for short, and I'm crazy about my golf pro. When I'm not with him, I fantasize about the magic of his touch. When I'm with him, reality more than matches my fantasy. Who'd have thought I'd ever have a hot affair?

Not bad for a thirty-five-year-old divorcée and mother of two teens.

Not bad at all.

But trouble lurked in paradise.

I'd begun hearing wedding bells. Rafe had been clear from the start that this was an affair. I didn't want to jeopardize my excellent fringe benefits with talk of lasting commitment. Except I couldn't stop thinking about how nice it would be to have him as a fixture in my life, how nice it would be to wake up next to his smiling face every morning.

I wanted more than great sex and sneaking home in the middle of the night. I wanted to have this settled. To not worry about date clothes or morning breath. To be the upstanding citizen my late father expected me to be.

"Cleo?"

Uh-oh. I'd drifted off again. We'd been at this for thirty minutes, and if I kept stinking up the course, the club's owners would surely fire Rafe for being the worst golf instructor in the known world.

I shot him a guilty smile. "I'm sorry. That was a terrible shot."

"You seem distracted."

"I am." I did a quick calculation. "We've been at this a while now. I've had a dozen lessons, and I'm not improving. You're a great instructor, I know you are. I saw what you did with Lorenzo Baker's swing. But we should face facts. When we're together, I can't focus on golf."

He grinned like the Cheshire Cat. Electricity snapped in the air between us. My thoughts veered to the last time I ran my fingers through his strawberry blond hair, to when his six-foot frame had been riveted on giving us both pleasure.

I punched him playfully in the shoulder. "I'm serious as a heart attack. Around you, everything shorts out, and my swing thoughts vanish."

His eyebrows waggled. "I'm sure with enough repetitions we could groove your stroke."

"More repetitions and I'll drive away your paying customers. A lousy player like me isn't good for your professional image. I should take lessons from another golf pro, say Fred over at the city course, or Bobby at that new place over the mountain. At least then there wouldn't be any physical distractions."

"Those guys? No way. Fred's fourth wife just left him, and he'd put a ring on your finger in a heartbeat. Bobby's always bragging about his sexual conquests. Nope. I don't want you going to them for anything, least of all a swing tune-up. We can keep working on it. In fact, I insist that you remain my golf student." He edged closer. "There's nothing I like better than our private practice sessions."

Heat steamed off my face despite the brisk temperature of the October day. We'd practiced my swing plenty in his bedroom mirror, but clothing had been optional. "Stop, please. I can't be thinking about that now. It's broad daylight."

He edged closer on the pretext of examining my club grip. His voice dropped to an intimate caress. "Why not? I think about it all the time."

A chill tangoed down my spine. My mouth went dry. I thought about *it*, too. About how nice *it* was. About how special he made me feel. About a life centered around the two of us.

Like that would happen. I had Responsibilities and Obligations. Children I dearly loved. And Mama. Couldn't forget her.

"You're incorrigible," I said.

His warm breath feathered the side of my face. "Guilty."

"You make me feel like a teenager."

"God, I hope so. You're coming over tonight, right?"

I laughed, slow and sultry, now that the balance of power had shifted. "I'm not the one who got us all hot and bothered on the driving range."

"Want to head to my office? Jasper won't disturb us, not if he knows what's good for him."

"Ooh." The thought of his assistant pro walking in on us cleared my head. I stepped back a few paces to minimize the testosterone-induced fog. "We definitely have to wait until later. I've got puppy duty this afternoon. Oh, and tomorrow I can't do lunch because I'm helping Jonette with her campaign. She wants to finalize the details for her mayoral fundraiser."

"Does she have a chance of winning?"

"Hard to say. People either like Jonette, or they say she's got too much baggage. She entered the race to make a point with our pompous mayor, which she's made, so she feels successful already. Darnell stepped on plenty of toes as mayor, and White Rock will hurt him."

"Good point. That residential development is going nowhere fast. He should've hired a professional to manage the White Rock property before the bottom fell out of the economy."

"As his accountant, I advised him of that very thing, but Darnell likes to hold the reins." I brightened. "Jonette has a radically different management style. She delegates like crazy."

"Does this mean you'll be mayor pro tem if she wins?"

"Lordy, I hope not."

At a faint buzzing sound, Rafe pulled his phone from his trouser pockets, studied the number displayed, and grimaced. "Sorry. I have to take this."

"No problem. I'm packing up anyway."

"Don't leave. I'll only be a minute."

He walked over to the ligustrum hedge, leaning into the phone for privacy. My curiosity spiked. Rafe always took his calls in front of me. Who was on the phone? My thoughts detoured to a worst-case scenario. A hurt family member. An old girl friend. A newer girl friend. A younger girl friend.

I sighed. It was a miracle that Rafe Golden dated me. Women threw themselves at him. Only he was very adept at not catching them. I couldn't remember how many times I'd pinched myself to make sure his interest in me was real.

Me. An accountant. Dating a professional athlete.

The very idea made me smile. I tucked my club into the golf bag, sauntered around to the front of the cart, and waited for my fellow. I was a lucky woman indeed, and it was about time I caught a romantic break. This relationship with Rafe felt right, even if I longed for marriage, and he liked the status quo.

Rafe slid in beside me and wheeled the cart around in a tight circle. I gripped the side of my seat to keep from being spun out of the vehicle. "Gracious. Is there a fire?"

"What? Oh. Sorry. I was in a hurry and wasn't thinking. Something's come up. I have to cancel tonight. All right if we move our hot date to tomorrow night?"

"Sure." His worried expression fanned my fears. "Did you hear bad news? Is one of your golf crew injured? Can I help?"

"Nothing to worry about. I'll take care of it."

His rigid posture and white-knuckled grip on the steering wheel told another story. What the heck? My curiosity and suspicion accelerated from zero to sixty in the blink of an eye.

CHAPTER 2

Men.

My insides bubbled as violently as the soup kettle on the stove before me. Rafe and I had dated exclusively for months. I thought I knew him, but did I really? He refused to talk about his family and now this. He'd blown off dinner and more from me tonight with no explanation.

On a Saturday night.

Date night.

Ugly suspicions colored my thoughts.

Who'd called him? What had they wanted? Why hadn't he told me what was going on? He owed me more than a "Sorry, I can't make it," didn't he?

Wait.

Was I thinking like a girlfriend or a wife? Damn. I was over-reaching. I had no right to vent wifely outrage or expect too much from our relationship. How depressing. Being a girlfriend had more gray areas than being a wife.

I grabbed a long-tined meat fork and poked a red-skinned potato. When that slid in easily, I checked the meat. The tines of the fork went right into the meat, too. Perfect. At least cooking was one thing I did well. I turned off the burner and moved dinner to an unheated area on my stovetop.

To silence my jealous leanings, I filled my lungs with the hearty smell of the meat and vegetable dish. Nothing signaled the changing of the seasons to me like a pot roast. Something about the stick-to-your-ribs aroma put me in mind of jumping into piles of leaves and nesting on the sofa with a thick throw and a good book.

One of these days, I'd read a book from cover to cover again. As it was, I was lucky to read a chapter at night before I fell asleep. But I couldn't complain too much. I loved being an accountant and spending time with my two kids. With the Saint Bernard puppies and Madonna, their mom, living in my house, I had my hands full.

I turned my attention to the double batch of corn muffins. They'd crowned up nicely, so I popped them in the oven to bake. Glancing out the front window, I saw my daughters, Charla and Lexy, playing with the puppies.

Now that Moses, Arnold, and Ariel were five weeks old, I hoped housebreaking was next on their list of doggie accomplishments. Seemed like we were always cleaning up a puddle or worse in the house.

With a chocolate cake on the sideboard and a tossed salad in the fridge, I joined the girls on the lawn. Arnold barrelled over to greet me, all paws and nose on my pant leg. His tail wagged his entire body.

Lexy shook her finger at me, her green eyes flashing fire. "Don't reward him for that. Only reward him for things he does right."

My youngest was thirteen going on thirty. I smiled at her knowing tone. Never mind that I'd raised two great kids, she believed I knew nothing about parenting puppies.

"It's okay. I want to play with him." I patted my thigh. "Come on, Arnold, come say hello."

Laughing, I let him scramble over me, enjoying the many licks on my face. Hearing the laughter, Ariel bounded over. Soon the girls and Moses joined me in a big pile of puppies and children. What a perfect family moment.

"They're so adorable. Can we keep them?" Charla asked, her red curls as saucy as her personality. At fifteen, she cared less about logic and more about wish fulfillment.

Lexy nodded eagerly. "I could train them for shows."

Moses bottomed out on my leg. I gave him an assist. "Jonette has her pick of the litter, and the other two will go to good homes. That's been our plan from the start."

"Yeah, but if one goes to Jonette, it's still sorta ours," Charla continued. "Madonna's really your dog. If we kept the other puppies, one could be Lexy's and one could be mine."

We'd inherited the mama dog this past summer. I'd learned the hard way that having two dogs this size in our house was not a good idea. Even so, I hated to be the heavy here. I'd much rather be the fun mom that always said yes.

Except the accountant part of my brain wouldn't shut down the computations of triple food bills, triple vet bills, triple pet care responsibilities. Cha-ching. Cha-ching. Cha-ching. Walking Madonna was akin to steering a supertanker. I couldn't imagine walking multiple supertankers.

"They're cute, but puppies grow up and so do teenaged girls," I said. "Once Jonette makes her choice, we'll find homes for the remaining puppies."

"I have to interview the prospective owners," Lexy said. "These puppies deserve the very best."

As I nodded in agreement, Mama's Olds shimmied into the driveway. Instinctively, we each grabbed a puppy. Mama popped out of the car like a mini-tornado and hurried over to us. I hadn't seen that much pep in her step in months. Maybe years.

"News," Mama said, waving her arms. Her shock of short white curls bounced with every step of her classic navy pumps. "I have news."

Her bright red face alarmed me. Was her heart medicine in her purse? I scrambled to my feet. "Let's go inside and get you seated first. Then you can tell us your news."

Her smile stretched from ear to ear. "Ain't nothing wrong with me, but I'm partial to a little coddling now and then. Lead on, McCleo."

Moments later, we sat around the kitchen table and gazed at Mama expectantly. Delilah Sampson might have been sixty-two, but she knew how to hook an audience. "Well?" I asked, puppy in my lap.

"Well, nothing. It's swell, that's what it is. Absolutely, magnificently swell."

"What's going on, Grammy?" Charla asked.

"I never thought I'd be saying these words out loud again, but here goes." Mama stopped for a breath deep enough to jostle the triple-stranded pearls at her neck. "I'm getting married."

I jumped and nearly upended little Moses. "What?"

"Who?" Lexy asked.

"Where?" Charla asked.

"You heard me," Mama said. "I'm getting hitched. To Bud. He asked me, and I said yes."

I felt the weight of Charla and Lexy's gazes. "Tell us the details," I added, torn between needing to know and remaining blissfully ignorant of the particulars.

"I've reserved Trinity Episcopal on Saturday, three weeks from now. Father Tim agreed to marry us."

"Three weeks. That's soon," I managed, thoughts spinning.

"It won't be a huge occasion. I thought family and a few close friends would attend. A quickie wedding is all we need; it isn't like I'm a blushing bride. The bloom has long fallen off that azalea."

"Mama," my tone sharpened, "there are impressionable young girls in this room."

"They know more about sex than you think," Mama quipped.

"When I was their age, I knew what was what."

Charla looked like she had something to say. I caught her eye and shook my head. "Be that as it may, I'd like to keep this conversation smut-free."

"You would," Mama said. "Pity."

"What about wedding clothes?" Charla fluffed her red hair. "Where will you get your gown? How will we get everything done in three weeks? Jocelyn Brown's sister took a whole year to plan her wedding."

"I'm sure there's a dress in my closet that would work just fine," Mama said. "I'm too old to make a big fuss about this."

"I'll take the wedding pictures," Lexy offered. "I've learned a lot from taking yearbook photographs."

"Lovely idea," Mama said. "Tag, you're it."

The myriad details of planning a wedding worried at my peace of mind. I couldn't wrap my brain around everything that needed to be arranged. "What about food for the reception? Flowers? A cake? These people are booked a year in advance around here."

"The church ladies will handle the food. Francine and Muriel are going to make one of their red velvet cakes. And flowers make Bud sneeze. I'll buy fake ones from the craft store."

She'd told her best friends before she told her own flesh and blood? I summoned what passed for a smile. "Sounds like you have it all worked out, Mama. That's good."

"I don't want to hurt anyone's feelings, but Bud and I want simple. No attendants, no groomsmen. That way it won't cost anyone an arm and a leg to come to my wedding."

"That wouldn't keep us from coming, Mama. You have your wedding any way you want it to be. This is your day."

"What about a ring?" Lexy asked. "Did Mr. Flook give you a ring?"

Mama beamed and pulled a glittering rock out of her

oversized purse. The solitaire diamond and white gold setting looked high end. "He did. Isn't it gorgeous?"

Charla grabbed for the ring and slid it on her finger. It was too large for her, but her expression of feminine delight hit me hard. How long before Charla sported a wedding ring? She was fifteen now. I'd been married and a mom by twenty. She had only a few more years before college and then she'd be off living by herself. She'd be hearing wedding bells of her own soon.

"The ring is lovely," I murmured as both Lexy and I tried it on. Mama plunked the ring on her finger. It sparkled as her hands fluttered through the air as she described Bud's traditional proposal.

Gazing at Mama's radiant face, I dismissed my reservations. "You and Bud deserve the best. I'm happy for you."

And I was.

But a part of me acknowledged the naked truth. Her gain contrasted with my loss. I'd settled for less than I wanted with my golf pro. Hot affairs were exciting, but there was always that element of doubt in the back of my mind.

Where was Rafe, and what was he doing?

CHAPTER 3

My fingers gripped the steering wheel when Rafe's voicemail clicked on again. "This is Cleo." I grimaced at the razor-sharp edge to my voice. With Rafe sneaking off last night to do God knew what, I wondered how many women left him messages. I didn't want to be mistaken for another woman.

I cleared my throat, trying not to sound as desperate as I felt. "I called to invite you to dinner tonight. I have news to share, news I need to tell you in person. Call me."

With that I hung up. I'd phoned him at bedtime last night, before early church this morning, and now, at midday. All the calls had gone to voicemail. Where was he? Normally he worked at the golf course on Sunday. I'd checked the club, and his Jaguar wasn't there.

Lord.

Had I crossed a line? Was I turning into a psycho girlfriend who had to know where my boyfriend was every minute of the day? *Now, now,* I told myself. This was genuine concern. It wasn't like Rafe to be out of touch for so long.

I had to face facts. He was an adult. He hadn't been missing twenty-four hours. I should put his whereabouts out of my mind and start on my other projects for today.

Like helping Jonette with her mayoral campaign.

I exited my sedan and entered the Tavern, the Hogan's Glen watering hole where Jonette worked. Her boyfriend, Dean, owned the seventies-style bar. Both greeted me warmly. Jackson

Browne crooned a song about pretending, and I took my cue from the singer. I could pretend everything was all right.

"Are we plotting world domination today?" I slid into the booth across from Jonette, who looked young and hip in a bright-pink blouse and black slacks.

She thumbed through a sheaf of papers. "I wish."

Dean brought me a glass of water and pulled up a chair. Today his long hair was clubbed back in a ponytail. In his black T-shirt, jeans, and boots he resembled an aging rock star.

I smiled my thanks at him and nodded at Jonette's stack. "What's all that?"

"Crapola from the Internet. Whose bright idea was it to fish for issues? I've got more issues here than I care to know about. Each voter wants their pet project guaranteed, and then they'll vote for me. No way I can please everybody."

"Right," I said. "Trying to please everyone is a recipe for disaster." I stopped to clear my throat. "And, fishing for issues was your idea. You wanted to know what 'the people' thought."

Dean's head came up, and relief shone in his eyes.

"The people are crazy," Jonette said. "Here's one asking the city to buy Crandall House and turn it into a museum and interpretive center. Where would I get the money to do that from the city budget? Maybe if I stopped trash pickup for ten years or so I could swing it, but everyone would be unhappy about rotten garbage in the street."

Crandall House had been built two centuries ago by our town's founding father. Now the family descendants lived elsewhere, and they wanted a small fortune for the house.

"Yeah. Big-ticket items like that need to go on the back burner," I agreed. "You need to take on a few lesser causes that mean something to you. Read me the topics from the other emails."

"A guy wants me to drill more wells because we'll run out of water if any of the White Rock houses ever get bought. Here's a guy wanting me to legalize medical marijuana."

"That one gets my vote," Dean said.

"Here's one from that grumpy lady over on Third Street," Jonette continued. "She wants speed bumps installed on her street because folks drive too fast past her place. And here's someone asking if we can't get three weekdays of trash service for the price of two." Jonette thumbed through a few more pages, and her face lit up. "Yes! Found it! This is the issue for me. We need to establish a dog park in the city. I need a place for my puppy to play."

"A dog park would be nice," I agreed. "Pet owners should have a place where pets can romp off the leash."

"I can't imagine anyone getting upset over a new dog park," Dean said.

"Looks like I've got my first agenda item," Jonette concluded.

"We're coming along. Tell me about the event next week. You're holding it here at the bar?"

"Yep. Figure most folks know we're dating, and they know where the bar is; might as well take advantage of that to get them here."

"What can I do to help?"

"Select a menu of food we need to serve. Something classy but cheap."

"I can do that." My face heated. "Oh. I almost forgot. I've got news. Big news."

"Rafe proposed?"

"Nope." I waited, drawing the suspense out. I wasn't Delilah's daughter for nothing.

"Charlie proposed?"

Charlie was my ex. He'd recently moved next door so that he could spend more time with our girls. So he *said*. "That doesn't count. He proposes every time he sees me. That's not news, and you know it."

"Oh!" Jonette's eyes danced. "It's your mother, isn't it?"

I nodded. "Yep. Bud proposed. She accepted. They're getting married in three weeks. I'm getting a lawyer in my family."

"Wow."

Jonette's eyes met mine. "Wait a minute. How long have you known about this?"

"Less than twenty-four hours, but Muriel and Francine knew first," I said to soften the blow. "They're organizing the food for her reception. Say, that gives me an idea. I wonder if they'd do the food at your fundraiser. It could be a trial run for their new catering business."

"We don't have much money," Jonette cautioned. She chewed her lip a moment. "Maybe my campaign committee could chip in to finance the snacks. Then we could spend the rest of the campaign going door to door to beat that rat-fink Darnell."

"I'm good for twenty bucks," I said. "And maybe Francine and Muriel would do it at cost if they could hand out brochures for Two Sisters Catering."

"Yeah, yeah. I'm okay with them networking at my party. Let's see. If you, me, Dean, and Rafe chip in twenty each, that'd give us eighty. Would Charlie cough up twenty for the fund-raiser food?"

"Charlie would do it. He'd think that would earn him a spot in my good graces. But, Rafe . . ."

Jonette grabbed my hand. "What? What aren't you telling me about the golf pro?"

I pulled away from her, hugging my middle. "It's probably nothing."

"You're not acting like it's nothing. What did he do?"

"I don't have any idea what's up, but my imagination is running wild. He got a call yesterday morning during my lesson and cancelled our date last night. I can't find him anywhere today." My lip trembled. "He's not returning my calls."

"Bastard." Jonette nudged Dean. "Go beat him up, honey."

Dean froze.

"What?" Jonette zeroed in on her boyfriend. "You know something."

"I shouldn't say."

"You should," Jonette insisted.

"Yes, please," I urged. "Any information is better than nothing. I don't know if he's hurt or dead or just a jerk."

"There aren't too many red Jags in the county. I recognized his car at first glance."

Jonette smacked her open palm on the tabletop. "This is worse than trying to get information out of Cleo's mom. Where was he parked?"

Linda Ronstadt belted out a song about being cheated and mistreated. My heart raced as I waited for Dean to spit it out. It had to be another woman. Nothing else would make Dean so hesitant, right?

"I gave Tucker Harris a ride home last night at closing time. Turns out his wife threw him out of the house, so he's living over at the Catoctin View Motel."

What was Rafe doing on that side of town? Rumor had it prostitutes worked out of Catoctin View. Another rumor said a drug ring used the premises for pharmaceutical transactions. Any way I looked at it, Rafe's presence at a seedy motel a little past two in the morning wasn't a positive thing.

"Bastard," Jonette repeated with vehemence. "Two-timing, sneaking, thieving, shithead of a loser. You demand he get tested for sexually transmitted disesases, Cleo. Don't let him near you unprotected until he gets a clean blood test. What am I saying? Don't sleep with him ever again. Let's do a Lorena Bobbitt on him. He deserves having his privates hacked off for catting around. Son of a bitch."

His likely betrayal cut me to the quick. "I can't believe he went out and paid for sex."

"We don't know that he got laid," Dean warned. "All I said was his car was there. He could have loaned his car to a friend. The car could've been stolen. There are many perfectly good reasons why his car might be at the Catoctin View Motel."

Instead of cheering me up, Dean's assertions plunged me into a volatile mood. Right or wrong, Rafe had concealed his actions. He didn't want me to know.

I wasn't important enough to rate an explanation.

I deserved more than that.

CHAPTER 4

Other than a quick buss on the lips, Rafe remained distant throughout dinner, confusing me further. I passed the green beans topped with peanut chocolate candies down to my ex-husband, Charlie, who'd invited himself to dinner once he sniffed my chicken and rice casserole. This whole business of him living next door was entirely too convenient for him for my liking.

Which is why he became my neighbor, to remain underfoot until I forgave him for his adultery and second marriage and welcomed him back into my bed. Not happening. I wouldn't be so gullible ever again, which made me wonder why I sat here pretending everything was fine with Rafe.

"More chicken and rice?" I asked, passing the serving dish down to Rafe.

"Thanks." He spooned another large portion on his plate and wolfed it down.

Men who drove fancy sports cars probably expected more out of Sunday dinner than a casserole, congealed salad, canned green beans doctored up by Mama, and store-bought rolls, but he wasn't complaining. Worse, he acted as if nothing was wrong.

"There's this new guy who wants to be on the yearbook staff," Lexy said when I asked her about her week at school. "He's a photographer like me."

"Is he cute?" Charla asked, vibrating with enthusiasm. "Is he a freshman?"

26

"He is in my grade. You may have seen him. He wears dark framed glasses and has really short hair. He had on a button-down collar dress shirt on Friday."

Charla made a dismissive gesture with her hand. "Major geek. Don't waste a minute on him. You'll never fascinate him as much as the mysteries of the universe."

"He's an excellent photographer. His pictures really grab you. Everyone on staff couldn't stop talking about his pictures last week."

"You take good pictures, too," I said. One of the puppies over in the puppy box started yipping. I shushed him. "I'm sure there's room for two top-notch photographers on the yearbook staff."

Silently, I urged Charlie to chime in and support his youngest daughter, but my ex-husband was lost in his own world. Some things never changed.

"Mom, our cheerleading captain has the cutest little car. It's pink. Who knew they made pink cars? I want one like Liz's car, only I want mine to be purple. That'd be way cool."

I scooped up a forkful of chocolatey and peanuty green beans. "Got news for you, dear. Your car is a classic color. Gunmetal gray to be exact."

"Oh, Mom. Not the beast." Charla's horror radiated from every fiber of her being. "You can't be so cruel as to make me drive the Gray Beast. Everyone has already seen that car."

"It's a survivor, and survival's what I want for you."

At the scrape of a fork, I glanced over and saw Rafe's plate was empty again. "More?"

He sat back in his chair, patting his flat abdomen. "No, thanks. I'm good. It was delicious."

"I'll say," Charlie chimed in. "Marry me again, Cleo. I can't live without your chicken and rice casserole."

Rafe glared at Charlie. As the testosterone level in the room ramped exponentially, I sought a way to diffuse the situation. A brawl between my lover and my ex-husband would ruin my day—and everyone else's, for that matter.

"Can't do it, Charlie," I said. The puppies starting yipping again. Their mother shot me a look of exasperation and slunk out of the room. "Chicken and rice comes with an expectation of fidelity."

He gave me his best my-shit-doesn't-stink smile. "You can't keep holding that against me. What do you say to forgiving and forgetting?"

"Nope. I have a policy about that. No do-overs."

"Drat. I'll have to change my name and romance you from scratch."

Before I could throw him out, Mama and her fiancé arrived. She'd met Bud Flook through Daddy, and Bud had been in love with her ever since. He waited throughout her long and happy marriage to my father, and now he'd finally gotten the girl of his dreams. I couldn't be happier for them.

"Hello, hello!" Mama breezed in, waving her diamond-clad hand through the air so that the stone flashed when it caught the light.

Rafe stood to give her a kiss. Charlie lumbered to his feet and did the same. "That's some rock you got there, Delilah," Charlie said. "You found a sugar daddy?"

"Better than that. I got me a husband-in-waiting. Bud and I are getting hitched at Trinity Episcopal in three Saturdays. Everyone here is invited to the wedding. No invitations will be sent."

Charlie nodded. "Gotcha."

Rafe inclined his head in Mama's direction. "Congratulations to you both."

"You gonna dance at my wedding?" Mama asked, staring directly at Rafe.

"Wouldn't miss it for the world."

"Well, then. That's all right."

After dinner, Rafe and I escaped to the porch swing while the kids did their homework and Charlie did the dishes. Rafe glanced at me under his lashes when I sat down in the far corner of the swing instead of snuggling up to his side.

"Is something wrong?" he asked.

"You tell me."

"Nothing's wrong on my end. Why don't you tell me what's bothering you?"

"You've heard the expression 'once bitten, twice shy'?"

He nodded.

"Charlie's adultery hit me hard. I've made no secret of the fact that you're the first person I've seriously dated since my divorce. I learned my lesson. I won't tolerate infidelity or lying in a relationship."

His expression sobered. Did he know where I was going with this? Did I know? Yes. I did. "You want to tell me why you cancelled our date last night?"

"I told you. Something came up. It was personal."

"You went to the Catoctin View Motel."

His jaw dropped. "You know about that?"

"I do. I can think of one very good reason a man would visit a motel known to be a hangout for prostitutes."

"It isn't what you're thinking."

"What is it?"

"I went there to help a friend. I promise you, that was the extent of it."

"I want to believe you, but you're holding back from me. Why does it have to be like this between us? Why didn't you return my calls last night or this morning?"

He rose and paced the porch. With his long legs, he was back in no time. "I was busy."

"Too busy to send me a text message?"

"Drop it, Cleo. It doesn't concern you. You're crowding me."

I leaned into his personal space. "That's what Sampson women do. We don't back down from a messy situation. You want to sleep with me, you get the whole me, not just the fun anatomical parts."

"What's that mean? You saying you won't sleep with me?"

"I'm saying you aren't being open with me."

He looked away, then rubbed the back of his neck. "Come home with me, so we can be alone. I feel like everyone's listening to us out here."

"I don't care if God himself is listening. I care about getting a straight answer from you."

"You're not going to tie an apron on me and change me. This is who I am."

"I'm not trying to change you. I'm asking you to be honest with me."

"You're confusing me."

Glancing over, I saw Madonna's nose pressed up against the dining room window, looking out at us. She barked loudly. The puppies joined in the chorus, adding to the din in my head. What a crappy Sunday.

"Welcome to the club. Where's this going, Rafe?"

"Does it have to be going somewhere?"

That hurt. I studied him for a few beats before I answered. "Yes, it does."

Silence engulfed the porch. "You're changing the rules on me."

"I'm being honest about my feelings. I care for you, but I don't think I'm cut out for a long-term affair. It feels like something is missing."

"I need you tonight. Don't shut me out."

"You're shutting yourself out." I rose and squared my shoulders. "I expect the truth from you."

Rafe glanced down at his shiny Oxfords. "Did you ever wonder who you'd be if you'd made different choices in life?"

"Not really." If I'd overlooked my husband's adultery, I'd still be living with a cheater. If I'd never married the bastard, I wouldn't have my beautiful daughters. I'd made the only choices I could make.

He shot me an enigmatic look. "There's no point in digging up the past. I've been faithful to you. You have to believe that."

"Let's take the night to think on this." Trust without verification wasn't the Sampson way, but Rafe expected it. My expectations ran along the lines of trust but verify.

We definitely weren't on the same page.

CHAPTER 5

I opened the office of Sampson Accounting alone on Monday morning. Mama slept in after her big evening of telling everyone about the wedding. I, on the other hand, yearned for the escape of work. With that thought, I locked the door behind me and started the coffee.

After a restless night, my feelings about dating hadn't changed. I believed that a person dated with the ultimate goal of marriage, or at least this person did. Everything I knew about Rafe led me to believe he'd be a good husband, despite the fact he preferred having an affair. He'd been honest about his intentions all along. I'd been fooling myself thinking I didn't need a wedding band.

Now that I'd accepted my true goal in dating was marriage, should I stop seeing Rafe? Continuing to see him would prevent me from meeting other men.

Which sucked because I was in love with Rafe.

How many women had fallen into this trap of thinking it would all work out in the end? That their boyfriends would come to love them as much as they loved them? I was college-educated. Smart. I owned a business. But my track record with love was rotten.

I should talk to Rafe about my decision, but I couldn't. Not yet. Would he call me this morning to apologize for being a jerk last night? I clung to that faint hope.

Business was slow at Sampson Accounting, the two-person

firm I owned, and had been slow ever since the quarterly taxes were paid on September fifteenth. Usually I had homeowners' association finances to audit or new clients to interview. Today I had nothing except stacks of filing I didn't want to do. Instead, I turned my computer on and flipped through my emails.

At a knock on the door, I rose from my desk and hurried across the reception area. A thick fireplug of a guy in a shiny suit glared at me. He'd been my Sunday school teacher for years, and he'd always been a big brother figure to me. He'd also fussed at me for meddling in his business a time or two.

I opened the door and waved him in. "Detective Radcliff. What can I do for you today?"

He edged past me. "I need your help."

"Come on into my office and let's talk. You want some coffee?"

"Sure."

I poured two cups and carried them to my office. He accepted the steaming beverage, but set it down on my desk, his expression grim. I said, "For goodness sake, Britt. What's wrong?"

"Melissa's sister is in trouble."

Melissa was Britt's wife of twenty-five years. She was also the mother of his two grown sons and his surprise of a daughter. Melissa had a heart of gold, which she needed to put up with Britt's hardheaded nature. She'd sent over the most delicious chocolate cake I'd ever tasted after Lexy was born.

"What can I do to help?"

"The IRS sent Zoe a bill. Seems her no-account husband hadn't filed taxes in years. Now the rat-bastard is dead, and she's flat broke. Melissa wants me to take out another line of credit on our house to pay the bill, but I already took one out to set the boys up in their busted plumbing business. I don't know what to do."

While I couldn't untangle a knot of love, I knew all about knots created by the Internal Revenue Service. "I can help her with the paperwork she needs to file, and we can ask the IRS to put her on an installment payment plan until she gets caught up. She'll need to come in here and sign a consent form so that I can find out what the IRS knows."

"I can have her do that, but I'll be up front with you. She has five young'uns by that dead SOB, and if she loses her house, Melissa's already told her she can move in with us. I need you to fix this. Do you ever do any clients pro bono?"

Steam curled from my coffee mug. "Not as a rule, because it takes food out of my family's mouths. My finances are pretty lean. I want to help you, but resolving her tax crisis will eat up a chunk of my time, time that could be spent on paying customers."

"Could you do it on the side, then? Work on it when you don't have a paying client? Or would you cut your rate for her? I wouldn't ask if it wasn't a dire need."

My business instincts screamed *no*. Billable hours were the lifeblood of small businesses. But truthfully, I had time on my hands. And Britt had kept me out of trouble many times. I owed him a favor or two.

I nodded. "I'll do it because you asked, but don't let a soul know I'm helping her for nothing. I can't afford for the word to get out that I'm a soft touch."

The tension eased from Britt's face. "Thanks. I owe you."

"Tell her to come on by and give me the particulars. Like I said, I need her to sign that form to get the ball rolling."

"I will." He edged toward the door, thought the better of it, and came back. "You still seeing that golf pro?"

Alarm clamored through me at Britt's narrowed gaze. His pointed tone suggested his inquiry wasn't casual. "What? Is he hurt?"

"No. Nothing like that. But there's something off about his story."

"What story?"

"Haven't you heard? A woman named Starr Jeffries was murdered on the other side of town Saturday night."

"I saw something on page three of today's paper about a woman being shot, but I didn't read the story. What does that have to do with Rafe?"

"He's a person of interest in my investigation."

I couldn't draw a breath. Dean had been right. Rafe was up to no good on the other side of town. My hand went to my quivering stomach. "You're kidding."

"I don't kid about that kind of stuff. Stay away from him until I figure this out."

"Wait. Don't go yet. You can't leave me hanging like that. How is he involved?"

"Witnesses spotted his car at the crime scene. Not many red Jaguar convertibles park at the Catoctin View Motel."

Loyal to a fault, I sprang to his defense. "That's hardly a smoking gun. It's a public lodging. Other people own cars like his. Even if his car was parked there, he didn't murder anyone. Who is this woman? What do you know about her? How does she know Rafe?"

"I can't discuss an active case with you. I bent the rules to tell you I was looking at him, but it seemed fair to warn you since you're helping me out with Zoe."

With that, the detective left.

I reached for the phone. Called Rafe. Got his voicemail.

My fingers tightened around the phone. Where the hell was he? Why wouldn't he take my call? The message I left was short and sweet. "Call me."

CHAPTER 6

By the next morning, my nerves still hadn't settled, so I drove to the golf course to find Rafe. His car wasn't in the parking lot. Undeterred, I hurried into the brightly lit Pro Shop. Rafe's whipcord-thin assistant, Jasper Kingsland, slid off his stool behind the counter and snapped to attention.

"Where's Rafe?" I demanded, leaning over the counter.

Jasper took a step backward, bumping into his stool. "He's not here, ma'am."

"I can see that. I need to talk to him. It's very important."

"He called in sick today, Mrs. Jones. I don't know anything more than that."

"What about his golf lessons? Does he have any scheduled today?"

"He told me to cancel everyone."

"Damn."

All this avoidance and absenteeism didn't sound like Rafe. He was in trouble. I knew it, sure as I knew my name. If Britt was looking at him for murder, Rafe needed a good lawyer. Fortunately, a lawyer was about to marry into my family.

Today was Tuesday. The senior men's league played golf on Tuesday. Inspiration struck. "Is Bud Flook on the course?"

"Yes, he is. The seniors teed off an hour ago, shotgun start."

"I need a golf cart."

"You can't go out there if it isn't an emergency, ma'am."

36

"You're going to have an emergency if you don't hand me a cart key."

Wide-eyed, Jasper reached under the counter for a cart key and dropped it on the counter. "Take it."

I grabbed for it. "Thanks."

As I strode out, I heard Jasper mutter, "Gotta stay away from redheads." Though I normally would be insulted by such a sexist remark, I let it go. This couldn't wait another minute. Britt had a very narrow focus when it came to suspects. If someone connected to one of Britt's cases acted oddly, Britt interpreted that behavior as an indication of guilt.

In fact, the detective operated under the mode of "guilty until proven innocent." Given Rafe's odd behavior right now, I had no doubt Britt would come after him like a vengeful bloodhound. That wasn't fair. I'd solved several of Britt's cases, and I wouldn't let Rafe be railroaded on the guilty train if he didn't deserve it.

I bounced along the unpaved access road that ran behind numbers one, three, and five. The maintenance crew used this rutted lane for their equipment, but so did the ladies when they needed to use the bathroom in a real toilet back at the shop. Sometimes a portable toilet wouldn't do.

I zipped past three foursomes before I found Bud's group putting out on number five, a dogleg par four. I waited in the shade by their carts until they finished.

As Bud strolled back to the cart, his bushy eyebrows shot up when he saw me standing beside his golf bag. "Cleo! What a surprise." His stride faltered. His sharp eyes searched my face. "Delilah's okay, right?"

"Yes, Mama's fine. I'm sorry to bother you, but I need to talk to you about an urgent matter. Would you ride with me to number six?"

He nodded to his playing partner, Bert McGowan. "I'll catch

up in a minute, Bertie."

He settled next to me, questions in his eyes. I waited until his buddies pulled away. The next group began hitting their approach shots to the green. With balls dropping all around us, I had to talk fast. "I need to hire you."

"You're in legal trouble?"

"Not me. Rafe is. Or he will be. Britt thinks he's involved in something bad. I don't believe it, not for one red-hot minute."

"What does Rafe say about all this?"

"Who knows? I can't find him this morning, but that doesn't change his innocence. Would you be his lawyer?"

"Criminal law isn't my forte."

"But you helped Mama."

"I'm in love with your mother. Of course I'd help her."

"I'm in love with Rafe, and you're the only person I trust to help him."

"I don't know anything about the case."

"You know Rafe."

He sighed. "This is very unusual. Usually a client retains my services, not his girlfriend. I don't know if Rafe already has counsel."

"I can't leave this up to chance. My gut tells me he needs us both. If I've overstepped, I'll still pay you for your time. I need this for my piece of mind."

"You going to marry this man?"

Breath stalled in my lungs. Bud's generation came hard-wired with certain expectations. "He hasn't asked me to marry him."

"Joe wouldn't approve of you shacking up indefinitely. Me, either."

I swallowed hard, knowing he was right about my late father. "Rafe's coming around to the idea of marriage," I hedged, hoping with all my heart that visualizing marriage to Rafe would make it so. The imaging strategy worked for golf shots; whether it worked for marriage proposals remained to be seen.

"Truth is, he isn't ready to commit yet," I admitted. "He has family issues. Won't even talk about his relatives, but I'm working on that. Will you help him?"

"I'll look into it as a personal favor. I wouldn't do this for anyone else."

Overcome with relief, I hugged his neck. "Thank you. Thank you so much."

He patted my back, and I was surprised at the tears that formed in my eyes. "It's okay," he said. "We'll get to the bottom of this. We'll bring your young man up to scratch."

Embarrassed, I blinked away my tears. "As soon as I find him, I'll make sure he calls you."

Bud nodded. "Now, if that's settled, I'm in the middle of a round of golf."

"Gotcha. That bunker on number six is sneaky. It's hard to hit the green if you catch the sand trap. Aim left."

"Good advice. I've been in that trap a few times myself."

"You sure this is legal?" Jonette glanced around the entrance as I stuck my key in Rafe's door lock.

"I'm not breaking in," I whispered. "I have a key."

"Still, Britt is a stickler for the rules. I don't want him on my back again."

"Britt won't know about this, Rafe either. You're supposed to be giving me moral support in my hour of need. Don't add to my nervousness."

"You should be nervous. We're about to snoop through your boyfriend's house."

I unlocked the door, and we stepped inside. "He needs our help. He's in trouble."

"Nice place," Jonette said, looking around. "I don't understand why you can't ask him what this is about."

"I've asked him, but he's a brick wall."

"Look at this leather furniture. And these paintings." Jonette lingered in front of my favorite painting, a stunning portrait of a little boy flying a kite in a storm. "Are these real oils?"

"A decorator did his place for him."

"How does he afford this? We looked into getting a leather recliner for Dean. Couldn't swing it. How does Rafe manage such luxuries on a golf pro salary?"

"I don't know. There, I've said it. I'm blinded by sex, okay? I should have asked him a lot more questions, should have pushed harder earlier in our relationship for answers to things that didn't make sense. But I didn't. Now, I'm hoping it isn't too late."

"What are we looking for?"

"I'll know when I find it."

"That certainly narrows it down."

I motioned Jonette into the living room. "Snoop."

Ten minutes later, we'd rifled through the books on his bookshelf, the junk drawers in the kitchen, the bathroom medicine cabinets, and his desk. His laptop must have been in his car because it wasn't there. He didn't have a calendar in his house, but I remembered he kept track of appointments with the calendar inside his cell phone.

I hadn't found stacks of love letters from his past. No traces of another woman anywhere. No traces of me either, but that was my fault. I wouldn't leave so much as a toothbrush over here, because I couldn't pretend I lived here. Not when I had two teens, a neurotic dog with puppies, and a mama who needed full-time supervision.

"Got something," Jonette said, entering his bedroom carrying an old shoebox.

"Oh?" I came up too fast from under his king-sized bed, the bed I'd shared with him on numerous occasions. The room spun lazily and dark specks danced in my field of vision. I sat down on the carpet until my equilibrium returned a few moments later.

"Found this box in the guest-room closet under a stack of old golf shoes. He really needs to throw some of those shoes out. They reek big time. Anyway, this box contains pictures."

My pulse quickened. Pictures were good. "Let's take a look."

Rafe appeared in most of the photographs, as if someone else had taken them and given copies to him. "Who are these people?"

Jonette sorted through a handful on her lap. "I don't know, but that tall blonde, she's an Ice Queen if I've ever seen one. This young man now, he's certifiably hot. If not for Dean, I'd go after this guy if I had half a chance. Uh-oh."

When she stuffed the picture back in the pile, I reached for it. "Let me see."

"Nope. You don't need to see this one."

"Gimme."

When she didn't move, I reached over and grabbed the entire stack. Seconds later, I had the picture in hand. Rafe had his arm around a tawny-haired woman. The photographer had captured a telling moment with this photo, one of Rafe gazing at this woman with so much love, it burst out of the two-dimensional image.

"Uh-oh is right. Who is she?" I turned the picture over. It was dated seven years ago, but there were no names, no anything.

"Don't know." Jonette dove into the box again, this time finding a picture with a woman wearing a metallic name tag. "Here's another looker. Ashley Webber. This is a fancy design place, like that ritzy center down in Bethesda."

"Must be his decorator. She's attractive, too," I glumly observed.

"We knew he had a life before he moved to Hogan's Glen. He knew plenty of attractive women. Big deal. The pictures aren't important to him, or he wouldn't have hidden them away."

I saw a flash of red outside the window. Rafe's car. My lungs froze. It was one thing to snoop, but it was quite another to get caught. I had to act fast or there'd be hell to pay.

I grabbed up the pictures and shoved them back in the box. "God. Rafe's here. Put these back, and flush the nearest toilet before you join me in the living room. I'll tell him we stopped by to see him, and you had to pee."

CHAPTER 7

My stomach burned.

It churned.

It wanted to find a new home.

I understood completely because I'd rather be anywhere but in Rafe's house at the moment. Would my rash actions irrevocably harm my relationship with Rafe? Would he view my intrusion as a breach of trust?

I didn't know, but I wouldn't cower in fear either. I opened the door before he inserted the key in the lock. "Welcome home."

"What are you doing here?" he asked.

My plan was to welcome him with a kiss, but he brushed past me, eyeing his place furtively. His negative reaction worried me. Did he have something to hide?

How odd. Doubts crowded my head. How well did I know this man?

"You weren't answering my calls, so Jonette and I rode over here to see you."

"Jonette's here?"

I winced at the strain in his normally resonant voice. A toilet flushed on cue. "She is. She had to pee and couldn't wait. I hope you don't mind that we came in."

"This is my place."

"Yes, it is." My explanation would test the bounds of our relationship. I fortified myself with a deep breath. "But I'm not a stranger. We're involved. You gave me a key, remember?"

"I don't like being caught off guard like this."

No kidding.

Granted, my motive for being here wasn't pure, but his edgy reaction to my presence put me on notice. It seemed I wasn't as welcome as I thought. "I apologize for the intrusion. Usually I would call first, but I have been calling and calling, and you don't pick up. I'm worried about you. Really worried. I feel there's distance between us that wasn't there before. What's going on? Why won't you take my calls?"

"It's personal."

Jonette appeared in the hallway, glanced at our faces, and continued toward the front door. "Hi, Rafe. I'll wait outside for you, Clee."

Silently, I thanked her for her perception. It was bad enough having this conversation with Rafe, but these things couldn't go unsaid any longer. I didn't need an audience to witness Rafe dumping me.

Which I was pretty sure would happen in the next sixty seconds.

He stood ten feet away and hadn't touched me once, which was uncharacteristic for him. I wanted to touch him, but I feared being physically rebuffed. I had my pride, too. "I'm sorry if I overreached, but I want to help you. It makes me crazy knowing you've shut me out. I care about you."

"I don't want you involved in my problems."

"That's the point I'm trying to make. You say they're your problems, but they're our problems. I thought we were building something special together. I thought we were a couple. I thought you had feelings for me."

His unsmiling face tightened into a hard mask. "Drop it, Cleo."

Like a person standing in the receding surf, I felt as if grains of sand were washing from underneath my feet. Even though I held firm against the tide, I lost valuable ground. "I can't."

Neither of us moved, and the gulf between us widened. I shivered. I'd tried to be supportive and that hadn't worked. I'd tried to snoop and that hadn't turned out so well either. Might as well lay all my cards on the table.

"Detective Britt Radcliff told me about the homicide at the Catoctin View Motel," I said. "According to him, witnesses placed your car there the night Starr Jeffries was murdered."

"Don't."

"Don't what? Don't help you? I love you, Rafe. I want to help. Why do you keep shutting me out?"

"Because . . ."

"Because what?"

"Because I don't want you to get hurt. I want to keep you out of harm's way."

The chill in my bones eased. "Are you in danger?"

"I don't know. I'm not sure what's going on."

"Let me help."

He rubbed his temples as if he had a pounding headache. "There are things about me you don't know."

"Believe me, I already got that. I can help, I know I can, but you have to explain what we're up against."

With that, he glanced away, over toward the darkened kitchen. I sensed valuable seconds ticking off my life clock. What could be so terrible that he couldn't speak it aloud? Was he a killer? Did he have a secret alter ego?

"Starr's a woman from my past," he stated in a flat tone.

I released the breath I'd been holding. Finally. A morsel of information. "Friend, family, or something else?"

"We were involved for a while, but it didn't last."

"I see," I managed, but I died a little inside. Was Starr the blond beauty in the picture he'd gazed at with rapt adoration?

Had she broken his heart into a million pieces? Much as I wanted information, I couldn't wheedle this out of him. Twice I started to speak and stopped. Finally, he spoke.

"Starr was fragile," he admitted. "We kept in touch through the years. I visited her last Saturday evening. She was alive when I left."

My temptation was to stick my fingers in my ears and shout *la-la-la* so I couldn't hear Rafe talking about being with another woman. The tension in the living room thickened until I couldn't draw a breath into my lungs.

What could I say?

Beating around the bush wasn't my style. Even so, my nails pressed into the meat of my palms. "Did you sleep with her on Saturday?"

His head came up, and his jaw dropped. He met my level gaze. "No. We're not friends with benefits."

Thank goodness for that small favor. He hadn't cheated on me, and deep in my gut, I believed him. I hoped lust wasn't blinding me again.

I took my first deep breath since he'd entered the living room. My head cleared, and I realized I needed to prepare him for the rest.

Hands clenched together in front of me, I spoke from my heart. "I've been down this road before with Britt Radcliff. He's like a heat-seeking missile when he's after someone, and he's definitely after you."

"Let him come. I didn't do anything wrong."

"You don't understand. Britt's tunnel vision narrows the scope of his investigation. He won't be looking at anyone but you. He thinks your car at the motel room is incriminating." I swallowed wrong, coughed a few times, and blurted out the rest of it. "That's why I hired a lawyer to look after you."

Rafe's blond head bobbed. He scowled at me. "You did? Who?"

CHAPTER 8

The hair on the back of my neck ruffled. Rafe didn't challenge any of my assertions. He jumped right over the incriminating evidence and the dogged police pursuit and went straight to the lawyer. My hopes plummeted. I was so mixed up, I couldn't keep my signals straight, let alone his.

Guilty or innocent?

"Bud," I said, looking past him at the beautiful artwork in his living room. "I hired Bud Flook to be your lawyer. Before you say anything, I know he's not a criminal lawyer, per se, but he got Mama out of hot water, and that's saying something. Bud is a good lawyer, and a good man. I've known him all my life. He's trustworthy, diligent, and he knows the law. Say something, please."

"I don't need a lawyer. I haven't done anything."

His curt tone irritated the crap out of me. "Even more reason to hire a lawyer. Does Bud suit you? Assuming you *need* a lawyer, of course. Or did you have someone else in mind?"

Rafe jammed his hands in his pockets. "I agree with you, your soon-to-be stepfather is a fine man. If I need a lawyer, Bud suits me fine."

Whew. Thank goodness. "I'm worried about you. There's so much about this case I don't understand. Anything you can tell me will be a help."

"There's nothing to tell. Starr needed a friend. I tried to be that friend. I didn't kill her. She isn't, I mean, she wasn't a well person. She had . . . issues."

"What kinds of issues? Gambling? Drinking? Drugs? The mob? What?"

"Nothing like that. It was more internal."

"Illness?"

"Not really."

I huffed out another breath. "Playing a game of twenty questions doesn't help either of us. Why don't you tell me what was wrong with her?"

"It feels wrong. I don't kiss and tell."

I took a step back. "You kissed her?"

"No. That was a bad analogy. Or something. God. Do we have to do this now? Can't we leave it for another time?"

Another time. That meant he would see me again. He wasn't dumping me. Giddiness whirled through my concern for his well-being like a little kid on a merry-go-round. While I savored the thrill, I got right back on track.

"We need to be proactive on this," I said. "No telling when Britt will make his move."

"I'm not afraid of the cops."

No worries there. I was scared enough for the both of us.

Outside I heard a car door slam, followed by the sound of raised female voices. Not a good sign. I moved toward the bay window. A tall, statuesque blonde, not the adored woman in the picture, towered over Jonette. Behind her was a Bentley with a suited female chauffeur standing at the ready.

What now?

My heart somersaulted as I ticked off each perfect feature. The blond woman had a flawless complexion, with the right touches of makeup here and there, and a thick chin-length bob that looked high maintenance. Her neutral tailored skirt, jacket, and dyed-to-match pumps screamed money and chic boutique.

"Who is that?" I shrilled.

Rafe edged up behind me and groaned. "Trouble."

"Her name is trouble?"

"That's what I call her."

"Don't get mysterious on me. I'm your girlfriend, for crying out loud. Who is the woman in your yard? I have a right to know."

"Regina. Her name is Regina, though we call her Reggie because her initials are REG for Regina Elizabeth Golden."

"She's a relative?"

"My sister."

"You've never mentioned her before."

"I try not to think about her. You'll understand why in a few seconds. Brace yourself. Here she comes."

The front door opened, and we turned as one. Regina stalked in like a panther on speed, Jonette trotted at her heels. The chauffeur lagged a safe distance behind.

"What's going on, little brother?" Regina said. "Why is there a loose woman in your yard and another one in your house? You into threesomes now?"

Rafe ignored the jab from his sister. "Cleo, this is my sister, Regina. Regina, Cleo. I see you've already met Jonette." He turned to the chauffeur and introduced her to me as well. "It's good to see you again, Mary."

Mary nodded but didn't speak. What must it be like to work for Rafe's abrasive sister? That's a job I wouldn't apply for.

His sister arched a slender brow. "You've gone to the dark side? No more platinum blondes for you?"

I bristled at the caustic remark but remembered my manners. Mama would be so proud of me. "Won't you come in and have a seat? May I get you something to drink?"

Regina sank into a leather chair and purred. "Scotch, rocks, please."

"Jonette? Mary? Either of you like something to drink?" I

asked, glad for the chance to keep my hands busy.

"I'll take a glass of water." Jonette plopped on the leather sofa.

"Nothing for me, thank you," Mary said softly. She melted toward the exit.

As I fixed three waters and one scotch, Rafe asked his sister, "What brings you out to Hogan's Glen?"

"You won't come see me, so I had to come out here."

Rafe didn't follow up. The silence built like a summer storm.

"Have you been here before?" I asked, handing her a drink from a tray.

"Yes. I've made the trip before, trying to get Rafe to cease this golf foolishness and come back into the family fold. But he never listens to me."

I sat with Jonette on the sofa. Rafe lounged by the bookshelf. Was that so he could move fast if his sister pounced?

"I've found Rafe to be an excellent listener," I said loyally.

Regina downed the scotch. "You must be his new bed partner. Don't get too comfortable in that role. He'll replace you next week. Always easy to get laid if you're a Golden, right, little brother?"

"That's enough, Reggie. I'm not coming back with you."

"Pity. With that handsome mug, you'd be a rainmaker at Golden Enterprises." She heaved out a non-dainty breath. "Some cop up here has been sniffing around the firm and asking a lot of questions about you. Thought I'd offer the corporate legal department for your defense."

"Rafe's already retained a lawyer," I said.

"It's not like my brother to be proactive." Regina eyed me with a calculating glare. "I'm impressed."

"Cleo hired the lawyer for me, but I won't need one," Rafe said. "I didn't do anything lawyer-worthy."

Regina flipped her wrist in a careless motion. "Regardless, we have a dozen lawyers on retainer. You can have your pick of the lot." Her voice sharpened. "Ditch the hayseed lawyer."

Her insult shredded my patience. She could be rude to me, but she had no right putting Bud down. "Rafe's lawyer is no hayseed."

She lasered me with a steely glare. "I wasn't speaking to you."

"Play nice, Reggie, or leave my home," Rafe said.

"Winners don't play nice. Losers do. Come home and be a winner."

"Rafe is a winner," I protested, rising to my feet. "Furthermore, you're making him uncomfortable with your remarks."

"You know how to pick 'em little brother." Regina rose with predatory grace and strode toward the door that Mary held open. Regina's heels clicked a rapid beat on the hardwood floor. She paused in the threshold, making sure she had everyone's rapt attention. A sly look crossed her face. "By the way, Hill and Tiffany are an item now."

With that, she sailed out of the door, which slammed behind her. The jarring sound echoed through the condo.

I turned from the window and gazed at Rafe, questions burning in my brain. Poor Rafe looked, for want of a better term, shell-shocked. I was surprised drool wasn't dripping out of his slack-jawed mouth.

Dang, with family like Regina, who needed enemies?

CHAPTER 9

Jonette lounged on Rafe's leather sofa, water glass in hand. "Your sister doesn't like you very much."

"I agree, though my guess is Regina dislikes anyone who doesn't do her bidding." I turned from the bay window to face Rafe, who still leaned up against the wall.

"My sister is highly focused," he said.

Jonette drained her glass. "No point in sugarcoating the facts. She's a bitch on wheels."

"High heels," I said.

Rafe and Jonette looked confused, so I pointed out the obvious. "She's a bitch in high heels. It takes talent to storm across the floor on those four-inch spikes. I couldn't do it."

My friend snorted. "I'd like to see you try." Her face lit up. "We should have high-heel races at my election party this weekend. That'd show old lard butt I'm not afraid of his good old boy network. I'm winning that mayor seat from him."

"Good idea. Hang on to that thought for later." I crossed to Rafe's side of the living room and took his hand. "You okay? That was intense."

"My sister would take over the world if she could."

"No wonder you struck out on your own." His skin felt cool to my touch, but his fingers tightened around mine. Thank goodness my nurturing instincts hadn't failed me. "I have to ask. Is she always like that? Does she ever let down her guard?"

"Rarely. She's been demolishing the competition for years.

53

She always has to be the best."

Questions crowded my head. I wanted to ask them all, but should I? His sister's visit had been unpleasant. Rafe might need time to regroup.

But his reaction to her parting words had been so strong. I couldn't wait on his recovery. "Who are Hill and Tiffany?"

He gazed down his tan trousers, all the way to his spotless Oxfords. "Hill's my brother."

When he didn't say anything more, I had the option of dropping it. The words came out anyway. "And Tiffany?"

He stiffened. "My ex-fiancée."

I mentally reeled. He had a fiancée in his past. The image from the picture cropped up in my head, and I knew Tiffany was that woman. He'd loved her enough to want to marry her.

My face heated.

He'd loved her.

Before I could utter a word, Jonette jumped up and grabbed my arm. "We have an appointment in town. If we don't leave right this second, we'll be late. We have to leave right now."

"I-I-I need to talk to Rafe," I managed to say. "Take my car. He can drive me home."

Jonette tugged harder on my arm. "No can do. Your presence is required. And we're late. Very late. If we don't leave right away, the entire free world will self-destruct."

"We'll talk later," I said to Rafe as I kissed him goodbye.

He didn't say anything, which disappointed me. He barely acknowledged my kiss, which hurt. As Tuesdays went, this one earned the distinction of being Terrible Tuesday.

While we walked out, he stayed put. I tried not to take his inaction personally, but darn it, it was personal. He needed help, but he couldn't ask for it. He had deep, dark secrets and a sister who was a flesh-eating piranha.

"A dollar for your thoughts?" Jonette asked as she sped out

the driveway.

"Isn't the phrase a penny for your thoughts?"

"You look like you have more than a penny's worth on your mind. Come on. Tell me."

"Where to start?"

"I'll start. The sister's a bitch."

I nodded. "Of the highest order. Probably whelped in a den of wolverines." I paused to glance over at Jonette. "What did you talk to her about outside?"

"She tried to intimidate me. She said vagrants weren't allowed on private property."

"Yikes."

"I didn't let her have the last word. I told her she'd missed the turn for the shark tank."

I snorted. "You didn't!"

"I did. You can't give bullies an inch, because they'll wad it up and stuff it down your throat."

I wish I'd seen Regina's reaction to Jonette going toe-to-toe with her. That must have been something. Jonette took the next curve too fast. I braced against the door, the air from the half-opened window ruffling my hair. Afternoon shadows flickered across the road. Pungent evergreen scent filled my lungs as we drove past the Christmas tree farm. Normal things.

The tightness in my chest eased. "I was worried you would fight her."

"I would've clawed her eyes out if she weren't so scary."

"She was scary. Poor Rafe. I bet he slept with a weapon under his pillow when they lived in the same house. I know I would."

"His brother's a low-life. Why is he messing with Rafe's old flame?"

My mood tanked again as I connected the dots in this murky picture. "I have a feeling Tiffany's the blonde from the picture. He loved her, Jonette."

"So what? Something split them up, because they didn't get married."

"Even so, he's not over her. He reacted when I asked him who she was."

"That doesn't mean he loves her. He might hate her now. Some men do that. They go from loving someone to despising them in the same breath. They won't even speak their former girlfriend's name."

"Good try, but I'm not buying it." I picked a piece of lint off my trousers. "Thing is, he's been pulling back from me for a couple of days now. Something is up with him, though he won't admit it."

Jonette swerved around a dead skunk. The pungent odor filled the car, and we rolled down the windows all the way to clear the air. If only Rafe's problems could be dealt with so easily.

"Men," Jonette said. "Can't live with 'em, can't live without 'em."

"Why can't he tell me what's going on? Why does he have to be all strong and silent? I hate it when he's stoic like this."

"What are we going to do?"

"Not much we can do, unless I hold him down until he spills the complete story of how he pissed off his big sister and lost his fiancée. Much as I'd like to resolve his past issues for him, it might not be in my best interest for him to be around this Tiffany again."

I rubbed my face. "It's so frustrating to have only a bit of the story. How can I help Rafe if he isn't forthcoming about what happened? Maybe I shouldn't stick my nose where it doesn't belong, but I care about him. I don't want Britt to railroad him into a murder charge. I need a fresh angle to investigate. Right now we're stuck."

"Let's get unstuck. That's why we went to his house. Put

aside your personal feelings and get serious about this murder investigation."

"We know names now. The dead woman from Rafe's past is Starr. His sister is Regina, his brother is Hill, and the family firm is Golden Enterprises. I can't believe I didn't check him out when we started dating, but I've been so busy living in the moment and enjoying his attention that I dropped the ball. Even though he didn't want to talk about his family, I should have done some digging on my own. But maybe it's just as well. Regina is so forceful, I might have turned tail and run."

"Golden Enterprises. I know that name from somewhere." Jonette snapped one set of fingers as she thought. "Wait, I got it. I've seen that firm in the society pages of the Washington paper. They host red carpet charity benefits. I forget what they do. Banking or something like that."

My head was clearing now that I wasn't seething with jealousy. "Investments, I think. They manage several mutual funds and similar investments. I never connected Rafe to Golden Enterprises before. You'd think a hotshot amateur detective like me would have picked up on the silver spoon in his mouth."

"His family money would certainly explain the nice furnishings and the primo car. He's probably loaded."

Loaded with charm and secrets. I aimed to learn those secrets. "Speaking of his furniture, I'd like to have a talk with his decorator, Ashley Webber. She's another name we learned today. I'd like to know if she has any other ties to him. What about his old girlfriend? Should I track her down?"

"Let's wait a bit on her. She's already jumped into his brother's arms. If Rafe finds out we're snooping, it will seem less invasive to have talked with his decorator than his former heartthrob."

Though I wanted to grill Tiffany and ask why they didn't

make it, Jonette's head was clearer than mine. "Good point," I admitted.

"Meanwhile, we can comb the news feeds for more info about the dead woman. How did she become Rafe's friend? One would think people from his past could afford swankier accomodations than the Catoctin View Motel."

"Rafe isn't a snob about friendships. He knows us, doesn't he? We're definitely not from the money crowd."

"There is that," Jonette conceded. "It feels good to work with you on a case again, Clee. I enjoy digging into people's lives. What's our first step?"

"Online research. My first step will be the computer in my office. I need Ashley Webber's address and phone number. I'll schedule a design consultation with her."

"Great. That means I can play with the puppies before I go back to work."

"You made your puppy selection yet?"

"I was thinking Arnold because he's so outgoing and inquisitive, like me, but then I think Moses is such a cuddler, I should take him. And then I think they're both males who will hump anything that moves. I should stick with beautiful Ariel, but I don't want to say no to the guys. I can't make up my mind."

"What will Dean say when you bring three dogs home?"

"He already said no. I will be forced to decide, but I'm not there yet. I love all of them."

"You need to choose, because I have to advertise the other pups. Charla and Lexy are lobbying hard to keep the others. I can't have three of those giants in my house either."

"It would be easier if they weren't so cute."

I silently agreed, but cute only went so far, like charm. My thoughts boomeranged to the murder and my boyfriend. He couldn't have done it, right? I wanted to believe him, and I said I believed him, but a solid alibi would make me feel a lot better.

No question in my mind that Rafe had grown up with lots of advantages. He had money and upper-crust connections. He had good looks and charm. Had he traded on these assets to dispose of a problem from his past?

CHAPTER 10

"You've seen my work at the Washington Design Center?" Ashley Webber sounded as surprised as I felt. The trip down I-270 to her firm inside the Washington Beltway seemed farther than the physical miles I'd traveled. The buildings were bigger, ritzier. The people talked the same, but they dressed as if they lived in a different world.

I'd worn my ivory blouse and taupe slacks to meet Rafe's interior designer, but in this uptown setting of gilt accessories and antiques, I felt underdressed. Ashley's dark hair was pinned up into some sort of "prom do," all shiny and curly. Jeweled clips sparkled in her hair. Her sequined gown was fancier than any prom dress I ever wore. I couldn't imagine getting so dolled up for work every day.

As it was, I hoped my deodorant held out. I'd changed in the locker room at the golf course after my usual disastrous round in the Ladies' Nine Hole Golf League this morning. I'd nibbled on granola bars and sipped bottled water in lieu of lunch, so the sparkling water and fresh-cut veggies with creamy dip offered by the designer were quite welcome.

"I saw your work at one of your clients' houses." Picking up another small carrot, I glanced around, first seeing the framed magazine covers behind her curved-leg desk, then my gaze traveled down to the desk itself. With brass hardware and decorative molding, that gleaming inlaid desk probably cost more than my car when it was new.

Ashley thought I was gawking at the items on the wall. "I write for those magazines. Publicity drives clients to my doors, and you can never have enough clients, now can you?"

She obviously hailed from the moneyed crowd, probably didn't have to work to keep a roof over her head. Even so, my smile warmed. I didn't want to like her, but I did.

"Clients are the lifeblood of any business," I agreed.

"What business are you in, Mrs. Jones?"

"Please, call me Cleo. I'm an accountant."

"You must have a great head for figures. I'm wonderful at measurements and spatial placements, but put a tax form in front of me and my eyes cross." Ashley laughed in a manner that had me smiling. "Enough about me. You're here to talk about changing your personal space. First, let me reassure you that you've made an excellent choice. I'm a member of the American Society of Interior Designers, and my work has received international acclaim. Please tell me about your project."

I studied my sensible shoes for a moment. This was the tricky part. "Unfortunately, I'm not here about a design commission, though I wish I could afford you. I very much admire your work. I live out in Hogan's Glen, about forty miles from Bethesda. You designed the interior of a friend's home, Rafe Golden."

"I did." Ashley's smile dimmed. "I don't understand. What is it that I can do for you?"

"I'm trying to help Rafe. His name has come up in a police matter. He won't divulge his association with the person in question, and I'm worried his silence will be misconstrued."

"Rafe's in trouble? Does his sister know?"

"I met Regina yesterday. She said our local detective contacted her."

"Reggie doesn't tolerate dissention. If I know her, she's

phoned the governor to get that cop fired."

"That should be interesting."

"Reggie is—well, for want of a better term—overprotective of her family. She and Rafe, though, that's surprising."

"It is?"

Ashley's eyes narrowed. "I'm a business professional. I don't gossip about my clients."

"I'm not after gossip. I'm seeking background information. If I could learn more about the homicide victim, perhaps I could suggest a motive someone else might have had to kill her."

"Murder?" The designer shuddered. "This is about a murder?"

"Yes. I'm desperate to learn more about the connection between Rafe and the murdered woman."

"Who are you again? What is your relationship with Rafe?"

"We're seeing each other. Socially."

"I see."

Ice dripped from her words. A lesser woman might have walked away from this fishing expedition, but I couldn't let Rafe down. Knowledge was the best way to break down a wall of ignorance.

"I didn't know Rafe had money when I met him. He's the golf pro at my club. Our friendship developed into something more, though where it's going I can't say." Oops I didn't mean to say that. Now I sounded like a gold digger. Heat flooded my face. "I care about him, and I don't want anything to happen to him."

"I appreciate your good intentions, but I don't gossip about my clients," Ashley said in a crisp tone. "If you want details about his past, ask him."

"I have." I sighed. "He won't talk about it."

"Good for him." Ashley stood. "Excuse me. I have to cut this short. I've an appearance as the fairy godmother in my daughter's school play."

That explained the fancy outfit. I withdrew a business card from my purse as I rose. "If you think of anything that might help, please call me."

Ashley gazed at the card in her hand for a long moment. When she glanced up, her eyes misted. "Be good to my cousin."

Her cousin.

That fit.

As I drove home, I pondered the new information. Rafe's sister was politically connected. She zealously protected the family name. From what Ashley implied, Rafe and his sister didn't see eye to eye, which I'd already observed.

All in all, my trip was a bust. Except for learning Rafe's beautiful cousin was loyal to him. I moved into the left lane to thread my way through the rush hour traffic on I-270 northbound. Helping Rafe was harder than I thought. I was short on leads, even shorter on suspects. I had no idea who shot Starr.

I could only hope Regina's protests spurred our police force to widen the investigation for Starr's killer. Yeah, right. Like that would happen. Britt was as dog-headed as I was. If anything, pressure from his superiors would backfire. He'd focus his attentions exclusively on Rafe after the interference. Worse, he'd push to close the case to keep his boss off his back.

The chances of Britt backing away from Rafe as his chief murder suspect were no better than they were of Mama cooking normal food for supper.

"Want to go out for dinner? My treat." My tight grip on the phone belied my casual-sounding offer. Truth be told, Rafe never let me pay for anything on our dates.

My leg jiggled in my office chair. I jammed both shoes hard on the floor as I waited for Rafe's response. The familiar sights of file cabinets, computers, and stacks of unfiled folders in my utilitarian space did little to ease the tightness in my chest.

There was so much I wanted to discuss with Rafe, so much I wanted to share with him about my last few days. He'd avoided me at the golf course this morning. Even Jonette had noticed his absence.

"Not tonight. I'm tied up," Rafe said.

He sounded so tired, so defeated. I leaned into the phone. "Rafe, please. Let me in. I can help. Whatever it is that's bothering you, I'm here for you."

"It's better this way."

"Better for whom? Not for me."

"I need to work through this alone. You have your daughters to consider, and your business. I don't want to cast a bad light on your personal or professional reputation."

"I'm not worried about my reputation. My daughters are fine. They've survived much worse than a bad light shining on them."

"I'm not your ex-husband. I can clean up my own mess."

I bristled at his surly comment, but I understood his desire to handle his own problems. Rafe wasn't the type of guy to rely on anyone. He relied on himself. But I wanted him to trust me with this. I needed him to trust me.

For that reason, I resisted the urge to fill in the silence. Charlie had done a number on me, not once, but twice. I never thought of my ex and Rafe in the same breath. One was my past and one was my future. I hoped.

"I didn't kill Starr," Rafe said.

"I believe you."

"Thanks. Stay out of this. For your family's sake. For me."

The phone clicked in my ear. I stared at my desk. He was right. My livelihood mattered. I couldn't afford to throw it away, but I wouldn't let Rafe sink either.

I had his back.

CHAPTER 11

Arnold chomped down on my finger. My eyes watered at the sharp pain. I reclaimed my digit and tapped the puppy lightly on the nose. "No biting."

Undeterred, he latched onto the hem of my blue jeans and tugged. His startled reaction when I didn't resist knocked him back on his haunches so that he looked like a rearing pony. I laughed, awakening his sister, Ariel, who'd curled up in my lap. I gave her another cuddle and set her on the rug so that I could play tug-o-war with her rowdy brother.

After a day of wrestling with updated computer software and trying to figure out why the stupid computer wouldn't recognize the printer, I needed puppy therapy. Picking up a squeaky toy, I engaged Arnold lightly, taking care not to pull too hard and harm his puppy teeth. Ariel and Moses, who'd been chasing the dust bunnies behind the sofa, joined in the fun.

Despite talking to Rafe and his cousin, I had no fresh leads to help Rafe beat a murder rap. Today's newspaper offered me an opportunity to approach the problem from a different direction. Starr Jeffries' funeral was on Friday.

Tomorrow.

The lighthearted puppy antics took my mind off my troubles. Madonna lumbered over to drool on my shoulder, her maternal pride in her babies apparent in the way she mooned over them.

I stroked her face. "You're a good mom to look out for your little ones."

Arnold spied his mom and let go of the toy to nip at her heels. Madonna gave me a pained look, then hurried upstairs. I had no doubt that she planned to hide out on my bed. Initially, I'd discouraged her from sleeping with me. Saint Bernards were large dogs, after all, but I understood her need to get away. To have a space apart from the children. These days we shared the bed.

Which brought me back full-circle to my problem with Rafe, who wasn't sharing much of anything with me. He said he didn't kill Starr Jeffries. Someone killed her. Someone who wanted Rafe to pay for the crime. That wouldn't happen as long as I had breath in my body.

I wanted to wave a magic wand to fix everything. Failing that, I could plague Britt until he let something slip. I could contact Rafe's other family members in hopes they'd confide in me about Rafe and Starr. I could grill his assistant, Jasper, at the golf course. I could go to Starr's funeral.

Of my options, the last one held the most promise.

Puppies climbed on me and licked my face. I rolled on the floor with them, laughing. Charla breezed in from school on a whirlwind of teenaged angst. "Jackie has the coolest car ever, Mom. I need a cool car."

"You're getting my car." Soon as I buy a good used car for myself, I amended silently.

"Ugh. The Gray Beast isn't cool. Dad says—"

"Don't start with me on 'Dad says.' Dad doesn't keep his promises."

"He does now. He's changed. He told me so, and I believe him."

With that, she stomped upstairs to commiserate with her sister. I could've saved her a trip. Lexy was worried about the other photographer on the yearbook staff. She had no energy to spare for the "let's get Mom and Dad back together" campaign that Charla waged.

Moses and Ariel snuggled next to me while Arnold tried to leap on top of them. I positioned him beside his littermates, dividing my attentions between the three of them. Arnold wouldn't settle. He jumped on the others again, prompting them to chase after him.

There I was again. Alone.

Getting to be the norm for me these days.

The more I saw of alone, the less I liked it.

I caught the puppies and placed them in the puppy box for a time-out until after dinner. After all that romping, they ought to be sleepy.

I sighed deeply, filling my lungs with the mouth-watering aroma from the kitchen. It smelled like roasted pork. I could only hope that it wasn't basted with lime gelatin or swimming in blueberry yogurt. You never knew what Mama would mix together in the kitchen.

I followed my nose to the kitchen where Mama bustled around with a happy glow I recognized. She was in love. The big rock on her finger caught the light, reminding me that Mama's future looked bright. I was truly happy for her.

"Roast pork?" I asked, settling into a wooden chair.

"Pork tenderloin with an orange marmalade glaze."

"For real? It sounds so normal."

"I don't have to pinch pennies anymore. Bud's got more than enough money for the both of us. I thought normal might be nice for a change."

"You said normal was boring."

"I'm trying on normal. Never said I'd wear it everyday." Mama sat down beside me at the table. "What's bugging you?"

"Rafe."

"I thought as much."

"Has Bud said anything to you about Rafe's case?"

"A little, but I'm not supposed to tell."

"That's no good. How can I help him if you keep me out of the knowledge circle?"

Mama chewed her lip for a moment. "Bud says Rafe doesn't have a good alibi."

"Rafe says he didn't do it."

"Bud says Rafe's determined to keep you out of this."

I waved away that news. "Tell me something I don't know."

"Can't."

The front doorbell rang. "This discussion isn't over." I rose to answer the summons, knowing that it had to be a stranger or a cop. A friend would come to the kitchen door.

Tall and regal, Regina Golden looked down her nose at me. She presented an immaculate appearance in a chestnut-brown leather jacket, coordinating blouse, snug cream-colored trousers, and high-heeled boots. Behind her, the Bentley purred in the driveway. The female driver nodded to me.

Regina got right to the point. "May I speak with you?"

I knew this woman could shred people in a matter of seconds, and I didn't want the girls or Mama exposed to her. Heck, I didn't want to be exposed to her, but she was Rafe's sister. I stepped out on the front porch, leery of what she had to say. "Sure." I gestured to the rocking chairs. "Would you like to sit down?"

"No. This won't take long. Stay away from my brother."

I barred my arms across my chest, conscious of the fact that my jeans and floral blouse were dotted with puppy slobber and dog hair. "Why would I do that?"

"He doesn't want you around. He told me so."

Coming from her, it didn't sound like a generous act on his part. She made me feel as if I were inflicting myself on her brother. I hastened to clear the air. "He's protecting me, but I can look after myself."

Regina flicked her wrist dismissively. Diamonds sparkled on her fingers. "Ashley called me. You're interfering in our lives. Stop it at once."

"I'm not interfering. I'm trying to clear Rafe's name. What are you doing to help him?"

"I don't answer to you."

"Rafe's in trouble," I shot back. "He doesn't have an alibi."

"If you care so much, why don't you give him one?"

"I do care, but I won't lie for him. The best way to protect Rafe is to find out who killed Starr Jeffries."

"Damn Rafe and his plebian tastes. If he hadn't associated with the help in the first place, this never would have happened."

Her derisive tone made me wonder how she talked about me to others. I wasn't in her financial league, that was certain. "Playing the blame game never helps. Rafe needs help, not accusations."

"He won't use the company legal team. Said he prefers the geezer you hired for him. That's ridiculous. We need big guns to fight this kind of accusation."

Rafe's choice made me smile inside. It was a small victory, but joy surged clear to my toes. Regina might be his blood kin, but I knew my man.

"Finding out who killed Starr is the best way to prove Rafe didn't do it," I insisted.

"Stay away from my brother. You won't get a dime out of our family."

That did it. I worked my back teeth apart. "I'm not after your money."

Regina's face flushed red. She whirled to leave, and tossed me a parting salvo over her shoulder. "So you say."

So I know. My hands fisted as Regina's chauffeur drove them into the sunset. Miss High and Mighty thought she knew everything, I fumed. She didn't know me, or she wouldn't have bothered telling me to stay away from her brother. One sure way to get me to do something was to tell me not to do it.

I'd better iron my navy slacks after supper. Wild horses couldn't keep me away from Starr's funeral tomorrow.

CHAPTER 12

After three wrong turns, I arrived at the Parkerville Funeral Home at five after eleven on a cloudy Friday morning. The flickering neon sign by the squatty brick building tickled my funny bone. If you only read the illuminated part, you'd think this was the *kerville funeral ho.*

If it was me, I'd have that sign fixed.

According to the notice I'd found online in the *Montgomery County News'* obituary section, Starr Jeffries' memorial service started at eleven. Which meant I was late.

I buttoned my navy blue blazer as I hurried across the thinly populated parking lot. The lack of cars worried me. Didn't Starr have family or friends who mourned her passing? Was she a lost soul Rafe had taken under his wing?

From the obituary, I'd learned Starr was thirty years old and had lived in Madeira, Maryland, about eight miles west of the funeral parlor. That was all. There was no next of kin mentioned, no parents, no children. There'd been no occupation listed and no designation for memorial gifts. My heart went out to the woman, and I hadn't even known her.

She'd lived such a short time and had barely left a footprint to show she'd been here. I hoped more could be said for me when my time came.

Inside the funeral home, my eyes watered at the heavy floral scent. Since there were no cut flowers in the vicinity, I assumed the fragrance came from air freshener.

An older woman in a dark purple leisure suit hoisted herself up from her seat by the door when I entered. She leaned heavily on a wooden cane. "May I help you?"

"Starr Jeffries. I'm here for her memorial service."

She gave me a long look, the same expression Mama used when she disapproved of something. I bit my lip so I wouldn't apologize for being late. I'd never been here before, and I didn't see how my lateness mattered. Of course, if I had a GPS gadget, I could have come straight here. Maybe I'd get one for my next car.

"Follow me," the woman said as she limped off.

We traversed a brightly lit hall with only two closed doors at the other end. "I hate for you to walk this far for me. I can find it if you'll just point out the door."

"I'm old but I'm not useless. If I don't do my job, they're gonna fire me, so hush up and follow me."

I hushed.

Finally, she stopped and pointed to the door on the left with her cane. "That one."

"Thank you." I opened the door and slid inside before she ordered me around again.

In the room, two clumps of people gazed at a man in a shiny suit who extolled the power of Jesus to save sinners. He thumped his Bible and used sweeping arm gestures to emphasize his points.

I slid into the back row and tried to look inconspicuous. Did I know anyone? Quickly, I took an inventory of the occupants. Three gray-headed ladies. A bald guy with two squirming kids. A brunette about my age, and two Hispanic women.

Rafe wasn't here.

I released the breath I'd been holding. The youngest kid stopped kicking the support under her chair long enough to look over her shoulder at me. I winked at her, and her eyebrows shot up as if this was some wonderful new game.

The service leader moved on to talk about when we all lived in heaven with Jesus. I found myself checking the time, wondering if the minister had ever known Starr. None of the remarks seemed personal.

Worse, none of these people looked like murderers.

The door snicked open and a barrel-chested man swaggered in. Oh, no. I sank down in my seat, but it was too late. He'd spotted me.

Detective Britt Radcliff sat down next to me. He placed his arm around my folding chair and leaned in close. "What the hell are you doing here?"

"You shouldn't swear in a funeral home."

"Answer my question."

It wasn't so much his tone of voice as his stern face that prompted my whispered response. "I need to learn more about this woman. If she has ties to Rafe, I want to know what they are."

"This is a police matter," Britt growled in my ear. "You're not the police."

The preacher glared at us. I ignored the angry detective at my side and feigned interest in the service. Another ten minutes of fire and brimstone, and the man turned on a canned recording of a tinny piano beating out the notes to "What a Friend We Have in Jesus."

The people in the front rose. I stood, too. Britt caught my arm. "Do not make trouble. Pretend you're with me."

The brunette stood talking with the preacher, so we approached her first once the preacher moved on to shake other mourners' hands.

I didn't enjoy Britt telling me what to do. He could hang on to me all he liked, but I was free to say what I liked. "I'm sorry for your loss," I offered.

The woman scrunched up her face. "I don't know you. How do you know my sister?"

Britt offered his hand. "Britt Radcliff, ma'am, and this is my associate, Cleo Jones. My sympathies to you and your family. We drove over from the Frederick area for Starr's service today."

"You knew Starr?"

Britt nodded. "We recently became acquainted with her. We're terribly sorry her life was cut short. She had so much to live for."

"Well, I hate to speak ill of the dead, but if she was so stupid as to get herself killed, the least she could have done was to buy a life insurance policy to get me some money. Now I've got to raise her brat. Kids cost money. I can barely afford to feed myself, plus I had to pay for her cremation. Can't afford to bury her, so I'll take the ashes home with me. Just what I wanted, to keep Starr with me forever. It's ghoulish, I tell you."

The woman's words didn't ring true to me. "Do you need help clearing out her place?"

"Heck, no. I'm moving into that trailer of hers. Deer Pines Mobile Home Park over in Madeira is a sight better than the dump I've been living in. Her place is paid for, and it goes to Kylie and me anyway. Say, you want some punch and cookies? They've got both in the back."

"No, thanks. We've got to get back home. We only wanted to say goodbye to Starr." I started to turn away, but I glanced over my shoulder. "I'm surprised you didn't bring Kylie."

"Kylie's only five. Much too young to sit through a funeral."

"Good point."

Britt boxed me in at the Gray Beast. "You will cease and desist your investigation."

"I won't. You're looking at Rafe for the murder. He didn't do it, and I'm going to prove it. Someone else killed Starr Jeffries."

"He had the means and the opportunity, Cleo. Your boyfriend isn't the nice guy you think he is."

"You're wrong. He didn't have any reason to kill her. He wasn't involved with her. He told me so."

"People lie, especially desperate people."

"How do you know someone in that room didn't kill her? The sister was hiding something. It could be her. She profited from Starr's death."

"I don't have any eyewitness reports of her being at the scene."

"That doesn't mean she wasn't there. Any one of those people from the funeral could have been there. How will you eliminate them as suspects?"

"Legwork, but I don't need to be tripping over you."

"Don't you get in my way either. I plan to have a future with Rafe Golden."

"Not a good idea. I'd feel more comfortable if you stopped seeing him until this was over."

"When's the last time I did what you said?"

His face fell. "Never."

CHAPTER 13

Teeth clenched, I grabbed hold of a handful of dead zinnias and yanked them out of the ground. An explosion of rich dirt landed on my sleeves, my knees, my lap. I filled my lungs with the comforting smell, tossed the shriveled plants into my wheelbarrow, and reached for another cluster of brown stalks.

I'd been putting this chore off for days. Once I pulled out the annuals, it was an acknowledgment that fall was here and winter was breathing down my neck. I wasn't ready for the seasons to change. In fact, I wanted to turn the clock back to the halcyon days of summer.

Those golden moments with Rafe where I found love and allowed myself to be loved.

I thought I'd hit solid gold with Rafe, but now I doubted my judgment and his integrity. Not good. October was off to such a rocky start. I couldn't see my way clear to December; at least I wasn't sure if Rafe would still be in the picture at Christmas. How could I even think of a near-term relationship with him while he was under suspicion of murder?

I still didn't know what Starr Jeffries meant to Rafe. She wasn't his former fiancée; that was a woman named Tiffany who currently dated Rafe's brother. I'd learned Starr had a sister and a young child, and that both would live in Starr's trailer home in Madeira. Other than that, I had nothing.

I hated having nothing.

Would Rafe even remember he'd promised to show up at

Jonette's mayoral fundraising party tonight?

I yanked and tugged my way across the front of my house, wishing I could remove the deadwood from my life so easily, that I could just be done with it and move into my happily ever after. I needed to take action to make it happen, but how?

"Mom!" Lexy stomped down the porch stairs. "I need you."

"I'm right here." I rocked back on my heels and watched her approach. Ever since she'd started middle school this year, Lexy had worn a pale blue bucket hat everywhere, and today was no exception. The collar-length ends of her dark hair flipped out beneath the hat. She scowled as she plopped down beside me.

"What's on your mind?" I tugged off the leather gardening gloves and hoped it wasn't the puppies. Or her sister. Or her wanting me to date the football coach. Or something her father had promised and then failed to deliver.

"John Paul Delong, that's what."

For the life of me, I couldn't place John Paul Delong. "How can I help? What has he done to make you so unhappy?"

"He's pushing me out, Mom. Mrs. Sellers loves his photographs. She never picks mine from the picture cache. His pictures are taking over the yearbook, and he's a freshman like me. It isn't fair. I want you to fix it. Call Mrs. Sellers. Tell her not to shut me out."

Ah. The boy wonder photographer on the yearbook staff. Lexy's competition. It was coming back to me. I identified with Lexy's outrage. As her mom, I wanted to fix her problem. It would be so easy to call the school and burn into this Mrs. Sellers. But was that really the best thing for my daughter? No. As daily problems went, this one wasn't major. With luck, it would be a confidence-boosting opportunity.

"I could do that, but this is a problem you can solve," I said.

"I can't. Didn't you hear me?" Tears glistened in Lexy's eyes. "Mrs. Sellers hates my pictures."

I opened my arms to my daughter, and she nestled up close. She had a good cry, and I stroked her back, wishing I could wring Mrs. Sellers' neck. When Lexy calmed, I lifted her chin. "Life is a bumpy road, sweetheart. This is high school, so you don't want to call in your parents unless it's a big deal." She puffed up to speak, and I shushed her. "Wait, I'm not done. The reason I think you can handle this is because I saw firsthand how you dealt with Madonna's puppy birthing. When there's a challenge, you dig in and make it work. You can do the same thing with this kid. You can get your pictures in the yearbook."

"Not as long as stupid Mrs. Sellers is our advisor." Lexy toyed with a handful of brown grass she'd ripped from the ground. "She hates me and my pictures."

"That's emotion talking. You can do better than that. You're my problem solver. I know you can rise above this. What's your strength in this situation?"

"What do you mean?"

"You've taken wonderful candid shots of the puppies."

"I had time to take a lot of pictures of them. They're always around."

"Take more pictures of yearbook material. The more pictures you take, the higher the odds are of snapping a really good one."

"That's true." Lexy hugged me close. "Thanks, Mom."

"And if that doesn't work, then we'll talk again. Okay?"

"Yeah."

She scampered off, and I resumed my weeding, wishing my problems were as easy to solve. A dark shadow fell over me, and my heart lurched into overdrive at the thought of someone walking up behind me unannounced. I turned, not knowing who was there. With the afternoon sun behind the person, I couldn't make out a face.

Not good.

So not good.

I shrank from the intruder, scrambling away on hands and knees.

My ex caught my arm as I collapsed. "Easy, Clee. It's me."

Shrugging off his grip, I pressed a hand against my racing heart. I wanted to yell at him, knowing if I did I'd see his smug smile at having provoked a strong reaction out of me. Damn him. "Charlie, you scared the living snot out of me."

"Sorry, love." He nodded toward the house. "What was that all about?"

"Lexy is working through a problem at school."

Charlie's affable grin vanished. His affection for me may have wavered a few years back, but his daughters were the loves of his life. "Want me to step in?"

"No. I want her to handle it."

"She's a kid."

"She's a teenager, a hybrid between kid and adult. She needs the experience with conflict resolution, and she can take this guy."

"A guy is giving Lexy trouble? Who is he? I'll take care of him. It's my God-given right. I'm Lexy's father. You should've mentioned this before now."

"He's nobody, Charlie. Calm down. I only found out about the problem five minutes ago, so you're in the loop."

"I don't like anyone messing with my kids."

"Me neither, but this is the right call. If she can't resolve it, we'll both step in. Together. No head knocking and no threatening anybody, okay?"

"Together. I like that." He stepped closer, his gaze softening. "I'd like us to do more things together. We could leave the kids with your mom and Bud and head up to Deep Creek Lake for a few days, like old times. What do you say?"

I loved Deep Creek Lake. Our summer vacations there had

been a bright spot of our marriage. Trust Charlie to play the sentimental card when I was loaded down with worries about my boyfriend.

I retreated a few steps for good measure. "Did you forget I'm seeing someone else? There isn't an us."

"But there could be. I've been patient because our separation was my fault. I want there to be an *us*. I screwed up. Big time. I want my entire family back."

His cologne washed over me, tangy and oh-so-familiar. Tears welled in my eyes. I couldn't get Rafe to talk to me, and I couldn't make Charlie go away.

"What?" he asked. "What's wrong?"

I turned from him, blinking the tears back. "Nothing I can't handle on my own."

His hand rested on my shoulder. Heat and comfort radiated from his touch. "Want a hug?"

I stood my ground. "No. Please don't do this. I'm not your wife."

"You could be. I'll remarry you today if that's what you want."

I shook my head. "You had your chance. I don't trust you."

"We'll get past that."

"Dad!" Charla slammed the front door behind her and bounced down the stairs, red curls flying. She hugged us both, her brown eyes sparkling with joy. "I'm ready for my driving lesson. Can we take your car?"

Charlie took a long look at me. "No, we'll borrow your mother's car. That's the car she wants you to drive once you have your license. I want you to be comfortable driving it."

My daughter's face fell. "Can't we take your car?"

"Nope. From now on, we take the Gray Beast." He turned to me, handing me the warm keys from his pocket. "If you need transportation while we're gone, feel free to use my car."

I took the keys. Dazed, I watched them drive away. Temptation reared its ugly head. My relationship with Rafe was a certifiable mess. Charlie was right here, doing exactly what I expected him to do and more. He claimed to have turned over a new leaf.

It was wrong to trust him.

Wrong, wrong, wrong.

But I did.

CHAPTER 14

Charla and Lexy had insisted Jonette decorate the Tavern with streamers and balloons for her mayoral fundraiser. Looking at the bright clusters of red, white, and blue in the crowded room, I realized they'd been absolutely right. The decorations helped the bar look more like a campaign headquarters and less like a lonely hearts gathering hole.

Jonette glowed in a crisp white blouse and pressed navy slacks, conservative clothes by her liberal standards, but she carried the polished look off to perfection. Her jaunty brown bob was styled away from her face, and she'd ramped back the mascara about fifty percent. All in all, she looked like a credible public servant.

Which pleasantly surprised me.

Jonette had entered the race because Darnell had made her mad one time too many. Judging from the size of this crowd and the donations I'd collected this evening, she had a good shot at winning the office. Darnell must be sweating in his mayoral boots.

"What's our bottom line?" Jonette asked an hour into the event.

I patted the wooden donation box. "We've done quite well so far. Enough to purchase that radio spot you wanted and more."

"Cool." Jonette surveyed the crowd. "I don't even know some of these people. Isn't this amazing?"

"Let's hope they turn out on election day. You need these

votes and more to become mayor."

Jonette nodded, her gaze sweeping the room once more. She tugged my sleeve. "Looky there. Another miracle."

I followed her gaze to the lanky man with strawberry blond hair filling the doorway. Rafe. He'd come after all. My spirits brightened. I held still, almost afraid to breathe as he scanned the crowded room. When his gaze landed on me, his expression softened, and he started toward me.

"I didn't think he'd come," I whispered to Jonette. My hand strayed to my hair, smoothing it back from my brow. I tugged my blouse down, sucked in my tummy.

"He's here, and he's loaded." Jonette leaned close. "Make sure you squeeze a campaign contribution out of him before you hit the sheets." With that, she sauntered toward Esther Wilcox and greeted her like it was old home week.

My thoughts turned to the determined man headed my way. Rafe seemed happy to see me. I sipped chardonnay and wished I'd worn my new lingerie.

Rafe's red golf shirt reminded me of a famous golfer who wore red shirts on the last day of the tournament, the day he expected to win. Had Rafe's wardrobe choice been deliberate? Was he here to officially patch things up between us? The possibility tantalized me even though I was irritated with him for shutting me out of his life.

He stood before me and reached for my hand. Sparks flew up my arm, igniting the fire smoldering in my belly. Oh, yes, the chemistry between us hadn't changed. A small sigh of welcome hummed in my throat.

"Hey, you," he rumbled in his deep voice.

Overcome with emotion, I tugged him close for a kiss. To my delight, he obliged, putting his mind to it. My toes curled as the noisy din of the room receded. "I've missed you," I said.

"I'm doing my best to keep you out of harm's way, but I

couldn't stay away tonight."

"I'm glad you came. It means a lot to me. And Jonette. She wants your money, of course."

"Of course." He pulled a check from his pocket and stuffed it in the donation box. "Done."

"Thanks. Jonette's doing great tonight. I'm proud of her."

He nodded, but his face clouded.

"What? What is it?" I asked, sensitive to his darkening mood.

He exhaled slowly, as if he didn't want to say anything, which only made my trepidation worse. Terrible thoughts raced through my head. Had something happened to my girls? Was it his family? Did it pertain to Starr's murder? What was it?

"Please tell me," I said. "I'm going nuts imagining things."

He studied my face. "Starr's sister called me this afternoon. Said you were at the funeral today. You and a cop."

I hastened to explain. "I didn't go with Britt. We went separately and happened to sit together."

"I don't want you connected to Starr."

"I want to clear your name," I countered. "I want to know about your relationship with her."

"Starr is poison."

I set my wineglass down. "She's dead, and Britt thinks you shot her. Unless another suspect comes to his attention, you're all he's got."

"Good thing my girlfriend got me a lawyer." He edged closer, his lips nuzzling my neck as he spoke. "I don't want to argue about this. I've missed being with you. Can't we focus on us tonight? Come home with me. I need your strength and your loving."

I needed the physical release of lovemaking as much as the next person. More, maybe, because I was worried about Rafe going to jail.

Sex would be nice.

Sex wouldn't solve anything.

I hovered in that breathless void of uncertainty. Wanting everything to be open and honest between us. It aggravated me that I was torn between my physical desire and my need to know the truth. Was sex with a murder suspect right or wrong?

While my thoughts warred, a fracas started at the door. I glanced over to see Jonette's boyfriend, Dean, jostling with a white-haired man. "Damn. What's he doing here?"

"Who?" my boyfriend asked, craning his neck around to see.

"Darnell's here."

Rafe's arm cinched around my waist, and he turned to study the disaster in the making. "That can't be good."

Darnell faked right and lunged left, a move no doubt left over from his glory days on the high school football field. In any event, he outfoxed Dean and climbed up on a table. He raised his hands and shouted, "People! People!"

He clapped his hands loudly when it wasn't quiet enough to suit him. "Listen to me. Don't give a dime of your money to this pretender. You know what side of town she's from. There's nothing she can do for you that I can't."

I hid my face, embarrassed for the mayor. He'd been my client for years, and I knew when he got spun up about something, he couldn't back down. By taking him on, Jonette had threatened his power base. I prayed he hadn't stopped taking his meds.

A low rumble of masculine frustration filled the crowded room, sending waves of dread through me. Uh-oh. Roger Dalton. Jonette's third ex-husband. "Got that wrong, boy-o," Roger drawled in a dangerous voice. "There's nothing about you I want. But, Johnsy, she's one hot chick."

The entire room burst into laughter. Dean stepped between Jonette and the incumbent mayor, hands fisted at his side. "Get out of here, Darnell."

"Exactly my point," the mayor went on as if Dean hadn't spoken. "Hot chicks aren't mayors. Half the men in this room have sampled her wares. She's not mayor material. Never was. Never will be."

That was a low blow, even for a worm like Darnell. I wanted to squash him like a bug, but Rafe held me tight. "Let me go," I muttered in his ear. "I need to kill Darnell."

"Wait," Rafe said. "Let it play out. I know a thing or two about political situations."

"You miserable worm." Red of face, Jonette edged around Dean and grabbed Darnell's leg. "Get off the table, and get the hell out of here."

Darnell shook his leg but Jonette clung like a bulldog. "Don't be taken in by her pretty face, folks," the mayor said. "She'll tell you lies about me. I have a college degree and years of experience at being mayor. I'm a proven leader. She's nothing but an aging barmaid."

Dean grabbed hold of Darnell's other leg. "Asshole. Out of my place, or I'm calling the cops."

Fake laughter burst out of the mayor's mouth. "That'll play well in tomorrow's paper. 'Cops called to mayoral fundraiser' is a killer headline."

"Think you've got it figured out?" Dean snarled, tugging at the suit-clad leg. "The headline will read 'Drunken mayor disrupts the peace at opponent's fundraiser.' "

"The newspapers will print what I damn well tell them. Let go of me. I'll have your liquor license pulled and run the two of you bad seeds out of town."

Roger Dalton stepped forward, cell phone held high. "You may control the newspaper in this town, but you don't control the Internet. I uploaded your rant to YouTube and tweeted about it. Two dozen people have already seen it. This thing's going viral."

Darnell shrieked and lunged for Roger. Dean, Rafe, and a few other men in the crowd escorted the outraged mayor from the building.

I hurried to Jonette and hugged her. Her chin quivered. My eyes watered with sympathy, but I fought the tide of emotion. One of us had to be strong, and it was my turn.

"Some party," she said. "Where's the nearest rock? I want to crawl under it and not come out until after the election."

"Oh, no you don't. That's why Darnell came here. To bully you and to embarrass you. Instead, he embarrassed himself."

"All the things he said about me were true."

"Your past isn't news to anyone here. We all have pasts. We've all made a mistake or three. Look at how long I was married to Charlie."

"Hmm. Well. Okay, then. We'll soldier on." Jonette searched my face. "You and Rafe patch things up?"

I looked away, knowing I couldn't lie to her. "Not exactly."

"Holy mother of God," Jonette gasped. "Look what walked through my door. Meow. I've always had a thing for tall, buff, and gorgeous. A man with smoky eyes like that shouldn't be allowed to prowl the planet. Let's check him out."

My heels dug in. This was a bad idea. "I've got a boyfriend, and you do, too."

"Come on, it'll be fun."

She took off like a shot. Worried that this might be train wreck number two of the evening, I trailed after her.

Jonette pinned a Moore for Mayor button on the collar of the grinning man. "Jonette Moore. And you are?"

"Hill Golden, ma'am. Sorry to intrude. I heard my brother was here tonight. But I no longer care, not with two such pretty ladies at my side."

My brain caught up with the conversation. "You're Rafe's brother?" The man was drop-dead handsome. The way he smiled at me made me think I was the love of his life. My heart fluttered.

He shook my hand, caressed it a bit. "Call me Hill, sweet thing. I didn't catch your name."

"I'm Rafe's . . ." My voice trailed off, not sure how I should declare myself to his brother, remembering his sister thought I was a commoner. Sensing the awkward pause, I hurried to finish. "I'm seeing Rafe. Socially." Heat flamed my cheeks. Everyone knew socially meant having sex.

Hill whistled through his perfect teeth. "Rafe has excellent taste in women. You're his first redhead, by the way. And now that I've met you, I'm thinking red is the way to go. Why don't the two of us go someplace private and get better acquainted?"

Repelled, I drew back. "Eew No."

"That attitude is turning me on, Red."

"Don't call her that," Rafe growled as he joined us. "Leave Cleo alone."

Hill's expressive eyes lit with understanding. "Cleopatra Jones? I get it now. She's the one that's got big sis in such a swivet."

"Reggie sent you?" Rafe asked.

"She did. Here's her message, and I quote, 'Stop this golf foolishness and come home where you belong.' Message delivered. Now I'm ready to party. I see you've got dibs on the redhead. I call the smoking-hot brunette. I always did want to screw a mayor."

Steam shot out of Jonette's ears. "I'm not a mayor—not yet anyway—and I'm not screwing anyone."

Regret filled Hill's eyes, turned the corners of his mouth down. "Pity."

"Go home, Hill," Rafe said.

"Aw, bro. I just got here. What's the biggie?"

"You've got a girlfriend at home."

"You know about Tiffany and me?"

Rafe barely nodded his head.

"I love her," Hill said. "We're getting married, but I'm footloose tonight, and I love a party."

"Go home," Rafe repeated.

"Is there trouble here?" Dean asked, looking every bit the aging biker in his black-leather duds and red bandana tied around his head.

Hill's hands shot up, palms out. "No trouble at all, buddy. I'm admiring the scenery."

Rafe grabbed Hill by the collar. "Let me show you the door."

As they threaded through the crowd, Jonette grinned. "Every Friday night should be this fun. This is one helluva ride, isn't it?"

I felt nauseated after the high drama, but this was Jonette's party. "Sure."

Don McLean sang goodbye to his American pie, and I wondered if Rafe and I would end up saying goodbye. My chances of having a future with Rafe kept getting smaller and smaller.

Worse, I'd made no progress in coming up with another suspect for Starr's murder. No matter how I analyzed the data, I still had a murder suspect for a boyfriend.

Was I leaping to conclusions? Maybe Britt had rounded up a new suspect and Rafe was in the clear. If that was so, I could focus on our communication issues.

The only way to find out what Detective Britt Radcliff knew was to ask.

CHAPTER 15

At noon on Saturday, Britt hurried down the police station stairs onto the sidewalk where I waited. "Is that a milkshake?" He eyed the insulated cup with turquoise and peach midline stripes as if it were the Holy Grail. "Tell me that's from Honey's Ice Cream Shop."

"It is." I waggled a paper sack under his nose. The smell of fried food perfumed the crisp fall air. "This hamburger and fries are from the burger joint out on the highway."

Britt's face fell. "My wife has me on a strict diet."

"I know good and well that you only pay lip service to Melissa's good intentions."

He took another deep breath, licking his lips. "What's this lunch gonna cost me?"

I shrugged. "Can't two friends have lunch together?"

"Not if one is male and the other is female."

Despite his protest, I hoped he would eat with me. I angled toward the concrete picnic table on the wooded side of the parking lot. Heartlessly, I jiggled the bag a little to let more of the french fry smell out. Britt followed as if I were the Pied Piper, and I felt the pleasant buzz of satisfaction. So far, so good.

When I sat down at the table, the chill of the concrete bench seeped through my slacks. "You want these? Help yourself. Neither Rafe nor Melissa will assume the worst if we're sitting out here in the open in front of God and everybody."

Two cops pulled in the lot, waving at Britt as they headed into the station. Word of us sitting here would quickly spread through the department. Britt must know that.

I flattened the empty paper bag, dumped the fries on top, and took a fry. "Help yourself. I like 'em best when they're hot."

"What are you up to, Cleo? Is this a bribe?"

"No way. You have a solid, unimpeachable reputation. Like I said. We're old friends sharing an order of fries."

He snuck a fry. Then another. He looked longingly at the foam cup. "Is that a strawberry shake?"

I munched another fry. "Yep." I opened up the burger and shamelessly fanned the scent toward him. "I bought this food for you. Are you man enough to accept a peace offering?"

He grinned and reached for the burger. "I am."

I smiled. "We missed you last night at Jonette's fundraiser."

He bit deep into the burger and moaned with contentment. After he swallowed, he replied, "One of my boys had a ball game last night. Family comes first."

"Yes, it does." That was the understatement of the year. "Did Jonette press charges against Darnell?"

"She came down here to do that this morning. I talked her into filing an incident report instead. The public is wary of folks who bring charges against incumbents because it ends up costing the taxpayer. This way she has a record of the incident, which will nail Darnell's sorry hide to the wall if he crosses the line again."

A lone bird chirped in the nearby leafless trees, a single voice in a forest of forked branches. "He certainly wasn't thinking right last night. I've never seen him so agitated."

"Being mayor is all he's got. Jonette is a threat to his future, to his livelihood."

"He should have thought of that before he started acting like

91

an idiot. He's the reason Jonette decided to run. He kept picking on her every time he saw her. Her campaign is a direct result of his bad judgment."

"A man pushed to his limits rarely reacts well."

His cryptic words puzzled me. I wasn't sure if he was still talking about Darnell or if I should assume he was talking about Rafe. No point in waiting any longer when he'd given me the perfect lead.

"About that," I ventured. "I saw Rafe last night."

Britt shook his head. "I can't talk about the case."

"Did I mention your murder case or Starr Jeffries? No, I did not. You did."

Britt slurped his milkshake, ate another bite from his burger. His eyes rolled in bliss. "This is delicious. Way better than those veggie burgers Melissa's been feeding me. A man's gotta right to eat red meat. A man's gotta right to live."

"A man's got a right to live the way he wants. I agree with you a hundred percent. All men should have that luxury, even Rafe, who wouldn't harm anyone."

Britt stilled. "As your friend, I'm telling you the man's in trouble. Nosing around isn't helping him. Knock it off, and stay away from him."

"The two of you should start a band, because you're both singing the same song." I leaned across the table. "If Rafe wanted to kill someone, it'd surely be his sister. She's a hard person to like."

"I met Regina Golden. She's prickly all right. But she's not a suspect in my murder case."

"I didn't say she was, though I'm curious how you ruled her out." His jaw tightened, and I worried I'd pushed too hard. I hastened to smooth things over. "Regardless, I know it looks bad because Rafe was once involved with Starr."

"He was still involved with her. Phone records show they

talked monthly." Britt's face clouded. "Damn, you tricked me. Don't do that again."

Even though it wasn't good news, it was more than I'd had when we started this conversation. I grinned. "You volunteered that information."

"Don't do this. I'm building a strong case against Rafe. He did it. I will prove it."

"You've been wrong before."

He wadded up the wrapper from the burger until it was a marble-sized lump in his fist. "I understand you going to bat for Jonette and Delilah when they were in trouble with the law— you've known them all your life. But Rafe? You two have only been seeing each other for a few months. Walk away from him. Save yourself the embarrassment of his arrest."

"I can't. And I won't. It's not my nature to walk away from trouble."

"Trouble does seem to find you."

"I'm not afraid. Rafe's innocent, and I'll prove it."

"How?"

"I'm still working that part out."

Britt drained the milkshake with a loud slurp from the straw. "If you won't stay out of it, make sure you take someone along with you when you go places. At least then you'll have backup."

"I'll think about it." I searched his craggy face again. "Is there anything else you can tell me? Off the record, of course."

He set the wadded-up wrapper down on the table. "There is something I've been meaning to talk to you about, but the timing hasn't been right."

"I'm getting a lot of scrutiny on this case, so I can't say anything off the record, but I need to talk to you about two other things. First, Melissa's sister got a vomiting bug and can't come over for a few days. Melissa's staying with her to help with the kids. Zoe'll come visit you as soon as she's able."

"I hope she feels better soon. What else did you want to talk about?"

He wouldn't meet my gaze. "This other thing is harder to say. I've wanted to tell you for a few days, but the timing was never right."

Interest unfurled like a flag on a stiff breeze. "Oh?"

He looked away, staring at the tree tops and the thin clouds high overhead. "These things can be difficult. I'm not sure how you will react, and I want to make sure you know that I'd never do anything to hurt you."

Britt had kept an eye on me for as long as I could remember. He was the big brother I never had. Even so, he'd hurt me on a couple of occasions. "Besides arresting my best friend and Mama, you mean?"

"That was work. I didn't have any choice about that. This is different. I'm having a hard time saying this because I don't want you to get the wrong impression. I didn't ask for this. She did."

What on earth? "For Pete's sake, spit it out. I can't stand the suspense. Who are you talking about?"

"Delilah."

"Mama?" I clung to the concrete bench. It could be anything if Mama was involved.

He nodded. "She asked me to give her away at the wedding."

"Why?" Heat flushed my face as I realized my gaffe. But I didn't apologize because I wanted an answer.

"You'll have to ask her," Britt said.

My mood tanked. Was Mama trying to make amends for the nasty things she'd called him when she'd had a run-in with the law? Or was there another reason?

A secret reason.

I hated secrets.

CHAPTER 16

After lunch, I watched the puppies play on the front lawn. Ariel chased her tail. Moses stalked a dandelion or two. Arnold galloped back and forth between his littermates, plowing into them. Fur flew and little yips sounded as they worked things out. Madonna looked on with a distracted maternal air as she lay beside me in the grass, her large head resting on my leg.

What would it be like to be as carefree as these puppies? To not worry about meeting my family's basic needs or praying for their continued welfare? To live in this moment and trust that all the rest would take care of itself?

I couldn't imagine being so complacent. I didn't trust anyone else to take up the slack when my family needed help. Taking care of my loved ones rested on my shoulders. And Jonette was just as much family as my blood kin.

"Decide yet?" I asked her.

Jonette sighed with regret and leaned back on her elbows, watching the puppy show. "I'm torn. I love Ariel's independent nature. I love how Moses cuddles up to me. And Arnold, he's a bruiser like me, born to break the rules. How can I possibly choose when I love them all?"

"It won't be long now before we have to find homes for all of them."

"I know. I know. Dean's pressuring me to make a selection as well. He's ready to order a monogrammed puppy bed, and God only knows what else. What if I pick the wrong one? That will break my heart."

I understood about bad decisions. Once upon a time I'd been married to Charlie Jones. He'd ripped my heart out and trampled on it without a second thought. Since then, I'd moved on, but my ex had realized his mistake and turned on the charm.

I glanced at his house. His car was in the driveway instead of at the bank. Maybe he'd decided to take the afternoon off, too. Jonette and I had been out here ten minutes, and he hadn't bothered us. Maybe he'd finally gotten the message I wasn't interested.

Instead of feeling relieved, my stomach tightened. Change seemed to be my constant companion these days. Charlie was a jerk. I knew that, but what was Rafe? It worried me that I doubted the man I loved. It worried me more that I might have lousy taste in men.

Madonna whimpered softly as if she knew of my emotional turmoil. I petted her broad head until she calmed. I felt better, too. Ariel barked at a falling maple leaf, making Jonette laugh, bringing my thoughts full circle.

"Be bold. Make a puppy choice," I reiterated, grabbing up a handful of stiff grass and tossing it in the air as if I were judging the wind for a golf shot. Madonna eyed the bits of falling grass with apprehension. "The rest of us are stuck, waiting to take our cue from you."

"That's putting a lot of the responsibility on me."

A puppy tugged at my shoelaces. "Responsibility's a bitch, isn't it?"

My friend's gaze sharpened. "Are we talking puppies or something else?"

I could fob her off, but this was Jonette. If I didn't tell her what was on my mind, she'd nag it out of me. "Something else."

"And?"

Gulping a deep breath, I started with my least worrisome problem. "Mama asked Britt to give her away at the wedding, and he was worried I'd be mad. I'm not, but her choice surprised me. I never saw it coming. Heck, I didn't even think she'd want anyone walking her down the aisle. I thought she'd want to bask in the spotlight by herself."

"Your mom's always had a soft spot for Detective Dumb-as-Dirt."

"True. I asked her at breakfast about her rationale, and she gave me a frosty look as if I'd mortally wounded her by even mentioning it."

"You mad about that?"

"I don't have any right to be mad. She can ask whomever she wants. It isn't like granddad could do it. He's been gone twenty years."

Jonette glanced over at me, speculation in her eyes. "You'll have the same problem when Rafe asks you to marry him."

"That's not happening. Not in the near future. Maybe not in the distant future either." My stomach knotted tighter. "He won't let me in."

My friend nodded with understanding. "Men."

I sighed the air from my lungs, trying in vain to release my deep-seated fears. "Britt said Rafe was more than the victim's long ago boyfriend. According to Britt, they had been speaking by phone monthly." I paused to gather my courage. "He was still involved with Starr Jeffries while seeing me socially."

"Damn him. I thought he was a decent guy. I should've known better." Jonette sat up ramrod straight. "Did you get checked for STDs?"

I couldn't breathe. I'd been so worried about my hurt feelings that I hadn't considered any other angles of Rafe sleeping around. Because of my hysterectomy, we'd stopped using condoms after the first couple of times. I shivered. "Wouldn't I have symptoms if there was a problem?"

"Call your doctor first thing on Monday. Better to be safe than sorry."

"I'll do that as a precaution. I want to believe Rafe didn't cheat on me, but since I was oblivious to the fact that Charlie cheated on me for months during our marriage, I'd be a blockhead to trust blindly."

"Say no more. Men are scum. Except for Dean, of course." Jonette waited until a dump truck rumbled past on the street before she continued. "Who really killed Starr?"

"I don't have the slightest idea. Rafe doesn't want me to nose around, either."

"That never stopped you before. Besides, we don't know for sure he's innocent. He could be using you to look like he's a regular guy."

My spirits sank further. "It is a possibility."

"You must have some dirt on the other woman by now."

"Not really. She has a sister. And a kid. They're moving into Starr's trailer over in Madeira."

"What did her neighbors say?"

"I'm afraid to ask. What if they say Rafe's car has been over there many times? Where does that leave me?"

"In the market for a new boyfriend. But wouldn't it be better to know than to keep worrying and doing nothing?"

"You're right. I dread finding out, but I should go."

"We'll go together. This afternoon."

The puppies yipped and streaked across the yard, running full tilt for Charlie. I groaned inwardly. Trust him to turn up like a bad penny.

My ex scooped up all three bundles of fur and let them lick his face. "Hey, hey, hey," he said as he sauntered over to us. "How's it going?"

Jonette and I exchanged an "oh, no" look, but other than run inside, and we wouldn't do that, we had no option other than to grin and bear the unwanted intrusion.

He handed Arnold to Jonette, Moses to me, and he kept hold of Ariel. Figured he'd keep the female for himself.

"Ladies," he said as he settled on the ground on the other side of Madonna, close enough that I got a strong whiff of his aftershave, the brand he previously used for our romantic getaways. I was amazed he would stoop so low and even more amazed I wasn't repelled by his scent.

"Charlie," I answered.

"What are we doing?" he asked. "Watching the cars go by? Wishing we all had dates for Saturday night?"

"We're enjoying the puppies," I said, with a warning glance to my best friend. "Jonette doesn't know which puppy to claim."

"I want to make sure I get the right one," Jonette said.

"Arnold is the dog for you," he said. "He'll be happiest with your varied work schedule."

Jonette studied Charlie. "How do you know that?"

He shrugged. "Simple. Moses needs a full-time person to snuggle with, like Cleo here. He'll pine away if left alone for hours at a time. Ariel needs someone young and energetic to keep up with her. Arnold can self-entertain. He's happy to have people around or to be by himself."

His analysis was amazingly on point. I'd thought the same thing, but I hadn't been able to articulate it quite so succinctly. "You're good. Maybe you should have studied pet psychology in college."

"Nah. Financial matters are my strength. That's why Cleo and I get along so well. We have similar strengths."

We had gotten along well, up until the point of him screwing another woman in our bed. Old anger boiled up. Moses squirmed in my arms, and I clung to him and my temper. I wouldn't let Charlie goad me into an argument.

"How's the investigation going?" Charlie asked casual-like, rubbing Ariel's tummy.

Suspicion narrowed my gaze. "Why do you ask?"

"I'm here to offer my services."

"We're doing fine on our own," I said.

"Great!" Jonette said at the same time. "We need all the help we can get."

Charlie smiled at her, his dimples showing. "Where are we? Bring me up to speed."

"We're doing a recon this afternoon, asking around Starr's trailer park," Jonette said. "We need to figure out why someone wanted her dead."

Charlie finally glanced my way. "I could check out her financials."

Damn. "That would be helpful," I admitted with reluctance. "But won't that raise red flags with the cops? Surely they're looking into her money as well."

"I'm very good at what I do. No one will even know I was sniffing around." He released Ariel, who chased after a late butterfly. "Anyone else you'd like me to run? What about lover boy?"

Ice sleeted through my veins. "Rafe?"

"Yeah. I'd like to know if he's got financial ties to the dead woman."

"Me, too," Jonette said.

He had me at dead woman. "Me, three."

CHAPTER 17

As trailer parks went, Deer Pines Mobile Home Park looked presentable, though the sun-faded trailers were pockmarked with grime and hard wear. Clunkers and pickups were parked near the front doors. We drove down every street looking for the manager's office, but every block had the same tired and worn-out look.

"A sign would be nice, people," I said. "I was expecting an office with a vacancy sign. How do we tell who is in charge?"

Jonette pointed to a person shuffling around his postage-stamp yard as I slowed the Gray Beast for another right turn. "Let's ask that old dude over there."

Nodding, I pulled up next to the white-haired man in a dull brown jacket, baggy pants hitched to his ribs, and scuffed slippers. He eyed us with suspicion.

"Can you tell us where to find the manager?" Jonette asked.

He took a long drag from his cigarette before answering. "Manager ain't working today. The office is closed on the weekends."

"Darn." Jonette batted her eyelashes. "We heard there might be a place open here. That a resident who lived here passed away."

Usually men responded positively to Jonette's bedroom eyes and sassy manner. This guy didn't perk up one bit. Must be time to recharge his testosterone.

Time for me to try my luck. I leaned around Jonette. "We're

in a tiny place over near Frederick, and we read about Starr Jeffries in our newspaper. We're sorry for her misfortune, of course, but we need a bigger place to stay. Figured we'd see if her place was available."

"Nope."

I sighed with as much tragedy as I could muster. Even threw in a little shoulder action. "I thought sure we wouldn't be too late. This looks like such a nice neighborhood. Quiet and all."

"That it is."

Man, my luck was as bad as Jonette's. Why wouldn't this guy open up? I bet even his dentist had a hard time getting him to open his mouth.

"In case the other tenant backs out, could you point out the place for us?" I asked.

"No harm in that I suppose." He stubbed out his cigarette and approached my ancient sedan. He leaned into the window, his heavy gaze resting on our breasts. "It's the tan and white singlewide a block over on the right. Say, are you ladies looking for a little something-something?"

I choked out a denial. "Just looking for a new home. Men aren't our thing."

He licked his lower lip. "Darn. I always wanted to do a three-some with a red-hot mama and a steamy brunette."

I gagged on his unwashed body stench, and Jonette made a show of looking at her watch. "Can't stay. Gotta go."

The guy held out his hand. "I'll hang onto your phone number for the manager, if you like."

"Never mind." I edged back in my seat and shifted the car into gear, anxious to put distance between us. "If we can't get Starr's place, we still have to find a new place to live. We'll be back next week if we can't find an opening elsewhere."

I sped away from the curb, wanting to stomp on the gas and get far away from that lecherous old man. "Gross."

"He was. But you, my friend, were super at lying. He believed you and not me."

"How do you figure that?"

"He gave you the information we wanted, didn't he?"

"So?"

"He bought your story. Sure you wouldn't like a run at politics? You'd have everyone eating out of the palm of your hand."

"No politics in my future, except for helping you win your election."

"I appreciate the support. I know Darnell is one of your clients, and I hope you don't lose his business on account of me."

"I'm not worried about what Darnell does." I slowed in front of the tan trailer. There wasn't so much as a cigarette butt on the neatly manicured lawn. No flowers. No shrubs. Not a single toy. "Doesn't look like any kids live here. No bikes or anything."

"Maybe the kid is too small for bikes. Maybe crackheads steal everything in the yards after dark."

"Crackheads? Are you serious? There's no one here, except for that sleazeball. This place looks run down but not abandoned."

"You got me there." Jonette stared at the trailer. "Now what?"

I jammed the lever in park. "Now I'm going to knock on the door."

"Why?"

"Because that's what we came here to do."

Jonette followed me out of the vehicle, clutching her oversized purse to her tummy. "Let's do it."

"You got a gun in there?"

"Nope. Pepper spray."

"Isn't that illegal in Maryland?"

"I wasn't planning on announcing it to the world."

"Good. I don't want to have to bail you out of jail again. It'd look bad for the mayoral campaign." Despite our light and easy banter, my dry throat and somersaulting tummy told me I wasn't calm about any of this. If Starr's sister was home, I had no idea what I'd say to her. I needed to do something to feel like I was moving forward.

Heart thumping, I knocked on the door. There was no sound from inside. I waited a bit longer. Still nothing.

Jonette gazed at me expectantly. "Now what?"

Not willing to give up, I gazed up and down the empty street. What would the police do next? They'd canvass the neighborhood. I could do that. "Now we knock on a few more doors." With that, I took off for the nearest door quickly, before I lost my nerve.

"Wait. Is that wise?" Jonette asked. "We don't know anything about these people."

"They don't know us either." I marched up the steps of the house next door. A rust-colored sedan with a child seat in the back seat was parked three steps away.

A young girl with dark under-eye circles who looked to be Charla's age peeked around the edge of the door. "You cops?"

"I'm an accountant. Cleo Jones, and I'm here with my friend, Jonette. I've been making some inquiries about a client of mine, Starr Jeffries, and working on her estate. Do you have a minute to talk to me? Did you know Starr?"

The door opened a little wider. The young girl exhaled visibly. "I knew her. We were neighborly, but we weren't best friends, if you know what I mean."

There wasn't an ounce of extra skin on this young woman's frame. I wanted to take her home and fatten her up. Where were her parents?

Not my problem, I quickly reminded myself. I was here to

keep Rafe out of jail. "I don't have the name of Starr's next of kin."

The young girl relaxed more, her shoulders bowing down instead of up. "You mean Jenny?"

I fumbled in my purse for a pen and a scrap of paper. Found a receipt from a fast-food restaurant. I scribbled the name. "Does Jenny have a last name?"

"Kulp. Jenny's last name is Kulp."

"What's her address? How do I get in touch with her?"

"Don't know her phone number. She has a cell like me. Not a landline. Those are too expensive, you know? And they're not very practical. I can take my cell everywhere I go and use it, but what can you do with a landline except sit on your butt at home and wait for it to ring?"

"Do you have Ms. Kulp's address?" Jonette asked.

She cut her eyes over to Starr's trailer. "She lives next door. With Kylie."

Another name. My eyebrows rose in inquiry. "Kylie?"

"Starr's kid."

I nodded as the memory resurfaced. "That's right. I forgot about Kylie. How old is she now?"

"Five. Starr had a party for her a month ago and invited me and my baby over. There were five candles on her cake."

A baby explained the young woman's eye circles. This neighbor was proving to be very helpful. I probed again. "Anyone else come?"

"Nah. Just us."

"Starr didn't have any friends?"

"Not really. Her sister came by every now and then. And the guy in the flashy car."

Uh-oh. "Flashy car?"

"Red convertible and a growling engine. He came around once a month. Every time he did, Starr asked me to watch

Kylie. That's how I remember when he visited. Starr brought Kylie over. I watched Kylie some other times too, when Starr had too much to drink or wanted to go gambling."

The bad news kept on coming. Rafe routinely visited Starr. I wanted to fold up and cry, but I soldiered on, as if I hadn't heard the most devastating news of my life. "She was an alcoholic?"

"She hid it most of the time, but she always smelled like booze, even when she drank vodka. She kept saying one day her ship would come in. I wished she spent more time with Kylie instead of bitching about everything. Kylie is such a cutie. She always helped me with my baby."

As if on cue, a child cried in another room. The teen's face lit up. "I have to go."

"Thank you." I searched for her name but she hadn't said it. I needed her name for thoroughness. "I didn't catch your name."

The girl eased the door closed, but stopped when there was only room for her thin face to appear. "Maddy. My name's Maddy Trace."

"Thanks for helping me, Maddy."

"I'd do anything to help Kylie."

With that, the door closed in my face. I tried to speak and couldn't. I tried to move and couldn't. I shot a desperate glance at my friend. Jonette grabbed my arm, levered me into the passenger seat of the Gray Beast, and burned rubber out of Starr's driveway. The acrid scent stuck in my nostrils.

I kept thinking about Rafe and Starr. What was he doing with her? A woman who drank too much and didn't take good care of her kid. A woman who gambled away money. A woman who didn't buy toys for her five-year-old to play with.

Was Kylie Rafe's kid?

What kind of father only saw his kid once a month?

"There has to be a logical explanation," Jonette said on the expressway ramp.

Logic had no place in my ugly thoughts. "He's a cheater."

"You don't know that. Don't you drive to your clients' houses?"

I gave Jonette a wry look. "Somehow I doubt this drunken, gambling, child-neglector was in the market for golf lessons. I don't know any other way to interpret the facts. Rafe cheated on me. He's been cheating the whole time I've known him."

"Cut the guy some slack, Clee. Until you know what's going on, don't be so quick to judge. I've seen the way he looks at you. The guy's in love with you."

Her words rankled. "Listen to you. Since when are you the voice of reason?"

"I know." Jonette frowned and darted around a slower moving vehicle. "I hate it. I'd much rather manifest emotional outrage. But you're giving a good performance."

"Nothing about this is a performance. Rafe Golden has some serious explaining to do."

"You're telling him about our investigation?"

"He thinks he has nothing to worry about. I'll give him the opportunity to explain. He doesn't, and he's toast."

"God help us all."

CHAPTER 18

Vintage cars dotted the parking lot at Hogan's Glen Golf Club. Shiny chrome gleamed under the noonday sun, accenting lustrous garnets and midnight blues, dotted among the classic whites and stately blacks. As I circled through the forest of big fins and whitewalls looking for a parking spot, I remembered why these older cars were here.

Today was the day of the local car club's invitational Hit and Run tournament. A nasty shiver crawled down my spine. I didn't want anything to do with hit and run, even if it had nothing to do with a car accident.

I snagged an empty space at the far edge of the lot, grabbed the bag of lunch, and hurried inside before I lost my nerve. I'd come straight from church. My skirt and heels weren't golf attire, but I didn't have time for a wardrobe change, so this would have to do. A gust of wind caught the door, and it swung open with a loud bang.

Rafe and his whipcord-thin assistant, Jasper, glanced up in surprise. My golf pro's eyes warmed at once, which heated my blood. Stupid hormones. I was here on business, not for fun and games. "Sorry about that. The wind ripped the door right out of my hands."

Jasper nodded in greeting. "Hey, Cleo."

"Hey," I managed to say as Rafe bounded over and drew me into a spinning hug.

"You smell good enough to eat," he said as he nuzzled my neck.

The shivers cascading down my spine had nothing to do with fear and everything to do with passion. I steeled my resolve. I was here for answers, not a nooner. "That would be our lunch. I took the liberty of bringing something over."

"Lunch sounds great. Let's head back to the office." Rafe grabbed my free hand and tugged me past a grinning Jasper. "You're in charge for thirty, buddy. Don't screw up."

"I got you covered, boss," Jasper said.

We stepped from the carpeted and heated shop into the storage area of bare concrete floors and bags upon bags of members' golf clubs. "I hope you don't mind that I didn't clear this with you first," I said.

"I love the way you took the initiative here." He drew me into his office, locked the door, and gave me a thorough, claiming kiss. My thoughts pinged wildly.

He cheated on you.

He's not cheating now. He makes me feel good. He makes me feel alive. What would it hurt to enjoy what he's offering?

Make up your mind, Cleo. You either trust the guy, or you don't. Oh, God. I'm weak. I want sex, and I want it now.

I wiggled closer. He took that as an open invitation for more, and so did I. The man had great hands, after all. Despite the doubts I had about him, I loved him and he cared for me. We fought each other for the embrace. I couldn't get rid of his pants quick enough to suit either of us.

Then we were skin to skin, and my hands stroked him as he enjoyed my assets. "You do things to me, girl," he whispered against my throat.

"The feeling's mutual." I ran my fingers through his golden locks, down his muscled back, and clasped him close. Sensing my urgency, he slid into home base, and we gave ourselves to passion.

★ ★ ★ ★ ★

Reason dawned slowly, and I covered myself with my hands, blushing with the knowledge of what we'd done in his office. My golf pro caressed my skin reverently as I sat in his lap. "For the record, you can surprise me like this anytime you want."

"I can't believe we did that. Jasper is right outside."

"My assistant knows how to be discreet."

"Oh." His assurance sent my thoughts careening in a different direction. The direction I meant to pursue before we got naked. "You do this often?"

He leaned over and kissed the tip of my nose. "Not as often as I'd like. What's for lunch tomorrow?"

"Tomorrow?" I grappled with the notion of sex for lunch two days in a row. I hopped off his lap and began dressing.

"This is one appointment I'd never miss," he said, his voice in its lowest, sexiest register.

Doing my best to ignore his innuendo, I slipped the heels on my feet and straightened. "I came here with lunch and to talk."

"Lunch." He stretched like a cat and reached for his clothes. "Yeah. I could eat. What we got?"

I scanned the office for the food bag. It was over by the door, where we'd started. I retrieved the paper sack. "Meatball subs. Though I don't know if they're any good now that they are cold. The bread's probably soggy."

Rafe opened his sandwich wrapper and dove right in. "This is great. Thanks."

I was hungry, too, and I was hesitant to talk about the case when we were still in accord, so I ate my sandwich in silence. A few bites later, Rafe opened the mini-fridge under his desk that he kept stocked with bottled water. He handed me one and took another for himself.

We finished, gathered the trash, and tossed it in the garbage.

Rafe leaned back in his squeaky desk chair. "Talk."

How could I be tough and demanding now that I had sated two of my basic appetites? "You're driving me crazy."

His deep laughter rumbled through the room. "That's the way it works, sweetheart. You do the same thing to me. Although I'd be a lot less crazy if you brought me lunch every day."

Heat flamed my cheeks. "Good grief. I'm not talking about sex. I'm talking about the case."

"Pity." His eyes narrowed, and an odd tension filled the room. "What case?"

With the hair on the back of my neck stirring, I had no choice but to stand my ground. "Starr Jeffries. Britt needs to shift his focus to another suspect. Got any suggestions?"

"Britt can focus on me all he wants. I didn't do anything."

"You had a relationship with Starr."

"A long time ago."

"That's not what I heard, and if I heard it, the cops heard it as well."

His gaze narrowed. "What do you think you know?"

"You kept in touch with her. You went to see her. In the *now*. What's going on? Why won't you tell me the truth?"

"I haven't lied to you. Starr wasn't a part of my life. I felt sorry for her, if you want to know the truth. She was never strong. She had looks for a while, but those faded and so did she."

"You dumped her because she got old and ugly?"

"I stopped seeing her because she slept with someone else."

"She cheated on you?"

"Our relationship wasn't going anywhere. She wasn't truthful about much. It drove me crazy that she said what she thought I wanted to hear. She never sounded sincere. Finding out she slept around was all it took for me to walk away from an intimate relationship with her."

He caught my hands and kissed them. "I swear to you. Starr

was my past. She and I never swapped keys or much of anything else six years ago. I dated her for a few months, that's all."

I stated the obvious. "We've only been dating for a few months."

"Yes, but what we have is richer, deeper. Your words have the ring of truth. You're consistent in what you do and how you care."

"I'm an open book. You're not. There are secret recesses in your life. Places you won't share with me. Things about your family. Things about your personal life."

"I don't ask you about your married life or how many times a week you had sex with Charlie. That's private."

"You think this is about sex?" I hated that my voice broke.

"Isn't it? Aren't you upset because you think I slept with Starr while I dated you?"

"Yes. No. I don't know." I got up and paced the small office. "I want to keep you safe, to make sure you'll stay in my life, but I don't understand your ongoing relationship with Starr. If you cared so much about her, why didn't you go to her funeral?"

Amusement danced with sadness in his eyes. "My lawyer told me to stay away."

I sighed out my relief. "Thank goodness for that, at least. If Britt had seen you, he might have made another false assumption."

"I don't see why you're so wound up."

"Why did you go there, Rafe? Her neighbor identified your car and you. She said you visited once a month."

His voice roughened. "I told you to stay out of this."

"The fact that you won't tell me what happened is a big red flag."

"I don't want you anywhere near the investigation into Starr's murder."

"I'm trying to help."

"I don't need help. Everything is under control."

"Take off the rose-colored glasses. We're neck-deep in a suck-ing mud hole. Time is not our friend. In the absence of hard evidence, Britt will line up the circumstantial facts and move against you. That's how he operates."

"Trust me. Everything will work out."

"I can't leave it to chance."

"Promise me you'll stay out of it."

"I can't do that. I love you, and I don't want you to spend the rest of your life in prison."

"Leave it alone."

"We've already cycled through this argument. I won't leave it alone. Where does that leave us?"

"Stalemate."

"Not checkmate?"

"Is that what you want?"

"No."

"Stalemate it is, then."

My lips tightened into a thin line. I hunted for my purse, knowing if I didn't get out of here in the next thirty seconds that tears would start streaming down my face. We weren't broken up, but we were darned close.

"Cleo?"

"Yes?" I glanced up to see mischief in his dark eyes.

He stood between me and the door. "I'd like a pastrami on rye tomorrow for lunch."

"Tomorrow's Monday, your day off."

He smiled and glanced hopefully around the office. "I know. But we can still eat here if you'd rather come to the club instead of my place."

"I'd rather you tell me why you aren't worried about this murder investigation."

"Simple. I didn't do it."

"That's not how it looks."

He was silent for a bit. "Do you think I killed someone?"

I chose my words with care. "My heart says absolutely not. But my mind isn't convinced. You're withholding information, and it makes me uncomfortable to know you don't trust me. I don't know who killed Starr. The cops think you did it. I need to shoot holes in their theory. I need to know who wanted the woman dead."

"I don't want you involved in this."

I reached around him for the door. "Too late. I'm involved. Get used to it."

Somehow I made it to my car without crying, but once I was safely locked inside the Gray Beast, the tears wouldn't stop.

CHAPTER 19

Knowing that Charlie had the girls this afternoon, I drove straight from the golf course to my office. It was past time for some answers. Snooping through Rafe's past might be viewed as a breach of trust; however, I rationalized the action as client research. If I hadn't been flattered and blinded by his initial interest, I would have done this long before I ever sat in his flashy red sports car.

No point in beating yourself up over coulda-shouldas. The point is to move forward from where you are today. Now, more than ever, I wanted to make sure Rafe stayed out of prison, but I had to know what I was facing.

I searched online for newspapers in his home town of Potomac, Maryland, but other than learning I couldn't afford a parking space there, I didn't find any bad news about him or his family. After searching two weekly papers, I tried the Washington dailies to broaden my scope.

As if I'd hit the jackpot, the number of entries for Rafe's family kept racking up. His mother, Amanda Golden, spent much of her spare time serving on community boards, bettering the world, along with acting as CEO of Golden Enterprises. His father, Shep Golden, had retired from the family firm to sail and play tennis.

His sister, Regina, worked as chief counsel for Golden Enterprises, but she sat on several community boards as well. Younger brother Hill frequented the society pages with his new fiancée, Tiffany Ellis. Beautiful blondes, every last one of them. Not a brash redhead or a sultry brunette in the Golden crowd.

A chill shuddered through me. Nothing about my bright red hair came close to a soft yellow color. Would Rafe continue to thumb his nose at family tradition and date me?

I rubbed my throbbing temples. Why was I worried about hair color when the true problem was my perception of the big picture? I wanted us to keep moving toward a legal commitment. Rafe preferred having an affair.

Deep in my bones, I knew something was off between us. Rafe's actions to date had been consistent. Until recently, he'd been creative in ways to steal time alone. With Starr's death, that had changed. He'd changed. He'd become unavailable.

Why?

I dug a little deeper in my mental database, trusting my instincts to sort through the meager facts. Published reports indicated Rafe's family members moved in different circles. Other than the family business, they appeared to have little else in common and weren't shown together in any local news or society pages.

Had something devisive happened in their collective past? The idea felt right. Given the minimal data points, nothing else made sense. Still, searching public records was a long shot at best. Their discord could be from feuding over an inheritance or another private family matter. But it wouldn't hurt to keep looking.

Searchable newspaper features only went back so far online before I hit a dead end and needed to find a library and a microfiche machine to continue. That would be tedious and time-consuming. With Britt hot on the trail of Starr's killer, time was of the essence.

I had to keep moving forward on the case, but nothing I'd discovered so far was worth feuding over, nor was it worth killing anyone. After searching several more keyword combinations to no avail, I thought to search obituaries. Those electronic archives stretched back farther than the regular news stories. The surname of Golden cropped up often, though not as often as Jones. Even so, there were a lot of records to sift through.

That's when I saw the notice. Brenna Nicole Golden. Same parents, same brothers and sister. I rubbed the chill from my arms. One of Rafe's siblings died as a teenager.

The cause of death wasn't listed. I scrolled down to the end of the obit. None of the big-name charities was listed as a beneficiary either. I had no idea how this fourteen-year-old died. Using her name and death date as search terms, I found another article from the archive of a competing newspaper.

Brenna Golden died of an accidental gunshot wound.

What?

I tried to focus on what a teen's sudden death might do to her family. There would be sadness, of course. Perhaps anger, too.

Was the fatal injury self-inflicted, a misfire, or an instance of being in the wrong place at the wrong time? Any of those possibilities would be heart wrenching. Parents might blame each other. Siblings might be bewildered. Any or all of them might feel guilty and responsible.

Turning off the computer, I paced my shadowed office, turning the new information over in my mind. Rafe had never mentioned Brenna. He'd never hinted about a family tragedy.

On the other hand, Rafe was estranged from his family. Sure, he claimed it was because they didn't approve of his golf vocation, but what if that wasn't the entire story? In the course of my career as an accountant and two forays into homicide investigations, I'd seen broken families, families where hate and distrust thrived and took a dark turn.

I'd met Rafe's brother and sister. Hill seemed privileged and spoiled. Regina seemed intense and overachieving. Rafe fit somewhere in between his siblings. He had Regina's strong work ethic, but he also had a caring side she lacked. His fancy car and condominium were indulgences worthy of Hill.

I shook my head. The things I knew about Rafe Golden dwindled daily.

Rafe. How would he feel if I mentioned Brenna's death to him? Would he think I'd overstepped?

I walked some more, circling my desk, striding through the outer office, skirting the front door, and starting another loop. What to do?

Did Detective Britt Radcliff know about Rafe's sister?

Brenna's shooting would be on file. Britt was thorough. He would have found it. Which meant he had access to details I didn't have.

Realizing my mouth was dry, I stopped at the fridge and grabbed a water bottle. The cold liquid hit the bottom of my clenched stomach and bounced.

Decisions.

Did I let Britt trample through Rafe's past and reach the wrong conclusions?

One thing was certain. Worrying never solved anything.

I whirled, picked up my phone, and called Rafe at work. "We need to talk."

CHAPTER 20

Needing privacy, I stayed in my office while I waited for Rafe. If Charlie or Mama or the girls came home, they'd respect that I was over here working, even if it was a Sunday. I couldn't sit still, so I grabbed a bottle of window cleaner and removed a coat of grime from my office windows.

I squirted the blue liquid, wiped it off, and squirted some more. A pleasing routine, most of the time. Today it didn't slow the racing of my heart or the sick feeling in my gut.

Did I believe in Rafe?

I did.

But was that an automatic answer built of misguided loyalty?

Loyalty was important to me, but so was trust. Did Rafe trust me enough to tell me the whole story about Brenna? It bothered me that I couldn't anticipate his reaction.

Outside the open windows, a familiar engine pulled up and stopped.

A car door shut.

I tossed my wet paper towels in the trash. *Time's up. He's here.* I opened the door for my boyfriend, and he strode in, his brows beetled.

"What's wrong?" Rafe asked, taking my hand.

He leaned in to kiss me, and I gave him a quick buss on the lips and sidled over to pick up the obituary I printed out. "I found something."

"And?"

I needed to explain my train of thought first. I let out a deep breath and set the page down. "I wonder if it has any bearing on Starr's murder."

His face clouded.

Before he spoke, I quickly laid the groundwork for talking about his sister. "Britt is using every tool at his disposal, every police report he can access to make his case against you."

"So?"

"I found something online, which means he found it, too."

"You're talking in riddles. I didn't kill Starr. There are no police reports in our brief past. It wasn't like that at all."

"I wasn't talking about Starr." I retreated, needing space between us. God, this was hard. I cleared my throat. "I was talking about an incident fifteen years ago."

His tan face paled then burned bright. "Cleo—"

"I need to know," I interrupted. "I promise to keep the information private, but I'm concerned about the case Britt is building against you. And I, oh dear." I stopped to fan my face. "I noticed a gun was involved in this prior incident. I'm asking if there's any reason to believe the police might draw the conclusion that you are connected with the prior event."

"Damn it, Cleo. That was a long time ago."

My heart went out to him. I softened my voice. "If there's something in your past, in this incident about your sister or another incident that made it into police records, Britt will find it. I'm asking if any official record links you to another shooting."

He turned from me, staring out the window I'd cleaned. He didn't speak for the longest time. The silence ate at me, nibbling at my good intentions.

This was a huge turning point in our relationship, a point that needed an investment of trust from him to yield a fruitful dividend for our future.

"I loved my sister."

I took a step closer, hoping his response meant we were no longer at odds. "Of course you did."

"Brenna was full of life. She was into everything and everybody, like your Charla. I miss her. I was seventeen when she died."

I stayed my hand before it touched him. He needed to get this out. "What happened?"

"Her death was an accident."

"Was she playing with a gun?"

"Nothing like that."

"What was it?"

"There was a rifle range on our property. We had guns, all of us, though they were locked in the cabinet downstairs."

"I don't understand."

He turned to face me, his brown eyes dull with pain. "Goldens are outdoor people. We hunt. We fish. We ski. We boat. We golf. You name it, we do it. I know how to tango on a sailboat, to flush teal from a wetland, to carve a trail down a mountain of snow moguls. So did my sister. We had every opportunity."

"What happened to Brenna?"

"Her death was an accident."

"I got that part."

"We had a routine. On Saturday mornings, we kids went down to the range to practice target shooting. Hill and I arrived first that morning. Reggie came a few minutes later and said she couldn't find Brenna. Reggie thought she was with us. After waiting a few more minutes, we decided to shoot without her. How I wish we'd done something else."

The raw edge in his voice ate at my soul. "Rafe?"

He stared into the distance as if he was seeing the event play out on a big screen. "I shot first. Then Hill took a turn. Reggie went last."

"Go on."

"I can't." He hung his head. "It was terrible."

"Please."

He glared at me. "Brenna was behind the target, and we didn't know until the maid's husband found her later that day. We killed her. We killed our sister."

He finished on a broken whisper that tore me apart. A low crooning sounded in my throat. I ached for all of them. The sister who was slain. The children that survived. Poor Rafe. How awful. How horribly, terribly awful.

I finally found my voice. "I'm sorry."

"That was the worst day of my life. I can't forget it, and neither can my family. My father threw out every gun in the house. My mother can't look us in the eye to this day. Reggie blamed herself for not finding Brenna first. Hill and I should have gone to look for her; God, it was bad. It still is."

What a horrible burden to bear. I reached for him, and he came into my arms, trembling. Tears welled in my eyes. Poor fellow. If I could have turned back the clock for him, I would have.

"I'm so sorry," I mumbled into his golf shirt, knowing I was repeating myself, knowing words weren't enough, knowing I'd reopened this terrible wound and made him relive this awful day.

He held on tighter. "I never wanted to hurt anyone, and especially not Brenna. She was the best and the brightest of us all. She made the best grades in school, had the most friends, and won her sporting events. She was our future."

I felt for what he'd lost, but a sense of maternal justice wormed its way out instead. "Brenna may have been a superstar, but each of you kids was super in your own right. Your parents should have told you that over and over again."

"Not all families are as wonderful as yours."

Wonderful? We were controlled chaos at best, but love threaded through everything my family said and did. I didn't see a close connection between Rafe and his siblings, nor did he claim to have one.

I retreated half a step, as if we were dance partners, and held his gaze. "I feel like a heel for dredging up this painful memory. I wish neither incident had ever happened, but we have to think like cops. Your sister and Starr were gunshot victims. Both were female. Both had personal ties to you."

Rafe stabbed his fingers through his hair. "I don't own a gun. Believe me, I don't want to ever hold a gun again. Brenna's death was a terrible accident, and I didn't kill Starr. Don't you believe me?"

"I believe Britt will use this incident in your past to show you're proficient with guns. He might even say you have a history of violence. We have to be prepared for that."

"There's no connection between the two incidents. Why don't you believe me?"

"I believe you. I do. But I know what we're up against. Britt keeps moving toward a goal, and right now you're in his sights. With his law enforcement connections, he has the inside track on information. The only way to beat him is to join forces and hopefully get ahead of him." I shot him a sympathetic glance. "I know this isn't easy, but we have to explore every possibility. Will the forensic team find your fingerprints or DNA at Starr's place?"

He didn't answer, and I thought for sure he'd bolt. First, he stared at the floor then he walked over to gaze out the window I'd cleaned. What was going through his head? He exhaled deeply and spoke in a monotone.

"I went to see Starr that night, but I wasn't sleeping with her. I was helping her get her life back on track, but each month she had a new disaster, a new excuse why she couldn't get a job.

Once I gave her money, she kept telling me how much she needed my help, how she couldn't make it without me. I wanted her to be self-sufficient. She had such promise six years ago, but she quit trying to stand on her own two feet and felt like the world owed her."

"I've known people like that," I said, stepping toward him. "They aren't easy to help."

"Starr manipulated me." He faced me, his expression grim. "She knew which buttons to push to worm money out of me. I let her. Once I invested in her future, I couldn't pull the plug. I wanted her to turn her life around. Giving up on her would mean I'd failed. I'm embarassed to be such a patsy."

"You were her welfare program?"

He managed a wry smile. "Something like that."

"Any more surprises I should know about?"

"Those are my only two brushes with the law."

Sneaky. He avoided my question. "We'll get through this. Family and friends pull together in times of crisis."

"You don't know my family."

"I know me."

CHAPTER 21

Monday morning arrived with sagging skies and rumbling thunder in the mountains. Even though I popped a decongestant and an analgesic, sinus pressure built in my head.

Crappy weather and a crappy mood.

Monday wasn't my favorite day of the week by any stretch. It was the day the pile of bills loomed large, and prospects of income looked slim this time of year. As an accountant, the bulk of my business happened during tax season, from January through April.

Over the past two years, I'd picked up auditing work here and there, which had greatly helped my bottom line, but I needed a more stable income base. I glanced down at the request for an audit bid we'd received from the school board.

Mama leaned over my shoulder. "Look at that date. We can't do it."

"The March completion date isn't optimal, but landing this client is a big deal."

"Joe always declined all non-tax business during our busy season."

"Daddy did fine by the company, but times have changed. Fewer people seek out an accountant. They do their taxes themselves these days. Our net income during tax season has declined each year. We need other income."

"We can't possibly manage a group this big."

"First off, there's no guarantee we'll win the bid. Second, it will be a great opportunity. I've seen how the system works. Once we get our foot in the door with the county, they'll send other work our way. We might draw more individual tax clients from there as well. We already know tax season is busy. If we get this work, we'll schedule around it."

"How? We'd need to hire another accountant."

"Can't do that. We have to tighten our belts."

"Don't you give me that speech. I can recite it chapter and verse after hearing it from your father all those years. Thank God, Bud isn't so miserly with his money."

I exhaled a sigh of relief at the chance to change the subject. "Speaking of Bud, how are the wedding plans coming?"

"Great. I'll be a married woman in two weeks. All you have to do is show up."

"I wish you'd let me help more. I could make food or help with the flowers."

"Nope. Got it covered. Francine and Muriel are having the time of their lives with this. They hope to launch an event service if all goes well."

"Good for them." At the sound of a car engine, Mama and I both craned our necks over to the window. We both recognized the car. "Damn."

Mama hurried to throw the door open with me trailing behind. "Look who's here! My favorite detective. The one who threw me in the slammer not long back."

Burly as a bear, Britt Radcliff marched in. He blushed and fumbled with the folder in his hand. "Sorry about that, Dee. I have to follow the evidence." He glanced over at me. "You got a minute to speak privately?"

I drew in a cautious breath. The pressure in my sinuses increased. "Sure. Come on back to my office."

I angled over to the seating area around a small table and gestured toward a chair. "Would you like a cup of coffee?"

He nodded. "I could use a cup."

"I'll get it," Mama volunteered.

Suspicion crept in my head. What was she doing?

Moments later, she returned with a tray of three steaming cups of coffee. She dealt them out and plopped down in a chair.

I gave her a pointed stare, the one that said I meant business. "Mama?"

"Whatever he has to say to you, he can say to me. We have no secrets in this family."

I rubbed my pounding head. "You are the queen of secrets, so don't give me that. Britt asked to speak with me privately. This doesn't concern you."

"I'm not leaving. No telling what he's got in that folder of his, Mr. I'm-following-the-evidence. Who's to say he doesn't have a fast-food receipt that indicates we're both serial killers? Nope. I'm staying right here because Sampsons stick together."

I glanced at Britt. "Sorry. You know my mom. If you'd like to reschedule, I could meet you elsewhere in private."

Britt's steely gray gaze passed from me to Mama and back. Silence crackled in my ears like static on a radio. What was in that folder? I wanted to rip it out of his hands. But I also wanted him to pick it up and walk away. Whatever it was, it wasn't good news.

I sipped my coffee, willing the steam from the cup to work magic on my headache, wondering if I'd look back on this instant later as the moment before the storm. Would everything after this point in time be forever altered?

Britt opened his folder and withdrew a picture. He placed the photo in front of me. I glanced down, seeing the strawberry blond hair, the freckled skin, and molten chocolate eyes. It was a little girl. An adorable little girl sitting on a swing, laughing. Behind her was the landmark bell tower of Baker Park in Frederick.

"Recognize her?" Britt asked.

"She's cute as a button," I said. "I don't know her. Should I?"

"Look closer," he urged.

I picked the picture up and studied it. "There's something familiar about her, but I can't place it. She's what, four or five?"

"Five."

"For goodness sakes, don't hog the picture," Mama said as she reached over. The color drained from her face. "I thought Rafe didn't have any kids."

"Rafe?" I snatched the picture back. Now that Mama had pointed out the resemblance, I saw it. The hair color, the freckles, the eyes. Oh, God, she had his eyes.

My heart galloped wildly. "This girl is Rafe's daughter? I don't understand."

Britt sat ramrod straight, his gaze honed in on my face. "Her name is Kylie. She's Starr Jeffries' daughter."

"I've never seen her before in my life." Mama's hand rested on my shoulder, and I drew strength from that human tether. "What do you know about her? Where is she?"

"Starr's sister, Jenny, has custody of her," Britt said.

"What's this have to do with anything?"

"Kylie's last name is Golden. She's five years old."

I did the math. Rafe said he'd dated Starr about six years ago. The pieces fell into place. Kylie Golden, five years old. An adorable child. She could be his daughter.

Air stalled in my lungs. "Does Rafe know?"

"You tell me. Has he ever mentioned Kylie?"

"Never."

Britt reached for the picture, but I wasn't letting it go. "I need this."

"That photo is evidence."

"That photo is a time bomb, and you know it. You can't flash it around showing it to people, letting them think the worst of Rafe. Get him over here. Show him the picture. Give him a chance to explain."

I recognized the signature growl of Rafe's car outside.

Britt shot me a chilling smile. "You read my mind."

CHAPTER 22

Rafe opened the door to my office without knocking. His strawberry blond hair was mussed, as if he'd forgotten to comb it. He'd thrown on a tan windbreaker over a navy polo and khaki slacks. He stormed through the reception area and marched to where I stood. "You all right?"

I nodded, reaching for his hand. When he leaned in for a kiss, I whispered softly, "I didn't know anything about this."

He squeezed my hand. Together we faced the law.

"What's this about?' " Rafe asked Britt. "Why did you summon me here?"

"I have questions for you. Questions you need to answer honestly. Since you're dating Cleo and I think highly of her, I wanted her present when we talked."

"Is my integrity in question?"

"Your everything is in question," Britt said. "What was your relationship with Starr Jeffries?"

"She was a friend of mine."

"Did you sleep with her?"

Rafe's face darkened, and he jerked reflexively. "A long time ago. What does that have to do with anything?"

My fingers tightened around his, offering a port of calm in the storm. I edged closer to him, needing to offer him more. That little girl was precious, so clearly a Golden. Britt believed the worst of Rafe, but I wanted to believe the best. In all my dealings with him, he'd been fair and honest.

Britt pulled the picture out of his folder. "It has to do with this."

Rafe stared at the photo as if it were the eighth wonder of the world. He reached for it, holding it in his other hand, studying the picture. "Who is this? Wait. Are you telling me this is Starr's kid?"

"I am." Britt's gaze narrowed. "Is she yours?"

"No. She can't be mine. I always used protection with Starr, and we weren't together that long. She . . ." He paused momentarily. "She was seeing someone else at the same time. Once I learned that, I broke it off with her."

"This child resembles you. You had an intimate relationship with the mother. The evidence seems straightforward. You had a kid with Starr."

"This is the first I've heard of a child. Starr never mentioned her to me, not once. I never saw a child or any toys when I visited Starr."

"And yet you were in monthly contact for these last two years. Before you deny it, let me assure you we've pulled your phone records. We also know there are deposits to Ms. Jeffries' bank account that correspond with your visits."

"She couldn't get ahead of her bills. I helped her out. She told me she was taking courses at the college and that she was training to be a nursing assistant."

Britt stared at Rafe with a feral intensity. "There were no payments to any college in her banking records."

"I don't understand. I tried to help a friend who was down on her luck, and for that you think I killed her?"

"She kept asking you for more money, right?"

"Yeah."

"It wouldn't have stopped. She wouldn't stop bleeding you for cash until you had nothing left. Was she blackmailing you?"

"No, I gave her the money of my own accord."

"That's not how it looks. From my standpoint, you had motive and opportunity. Now that I've dug into your past, I know about your gun proficiency. That brings up the means."

"Don't be ridiculous. I'm not a killer. Starr was my friend."

"Let me ask her about that. Wait. I can't. She's dead. You killed her."

"No."

Ice in my heart, I stepped between the two men. "That's enough, Britt. He said he didn't do it."

Britt tried his withering glare on me. "They all say that. Step away from him."

I gave it right back to him. "I won't. You've got this all wrong."

"I've got a grand slam. Means, motive, and opportunity. It doesn't get any clearer than that in police investigations."

"You don't have one shred of solid evidence. This is all circumstantial."

"What I have is a compelling picture, and I'm not just talking about the secret baby. Golden was seen at the victim's lodging the night she died. His fingerprints are on the door and in the room. He grew up around guns, and he'd been a person of interest in a previous shooting death. Add to that his frequent communication with her and the routine flow of money from his account to Starr Jeffries' account. A good prosecutor can run these facts through a jury and get a guilty verdict."

"Except he didn't do it," I insisted.

"You can't be objective. You're too close to this. To him."

"I know how it looks. We've been down this road before. Rafe didn't do it. He's not a killer. What about Starr's sister? She inherited Starr's trailer and her kid. She has as much motive as Rafe, more, now that I think about it."

"The sister has an ironclad alibi for the murder. She didn't do it."

"She could have hired someone."

"Now who's grasping at straws? Step away from him."

"I won't." I hugged Rafe close. My voice trembled. "I won't let you take him."

"For God's sake, I'm taking him in for questioning, not exiling him to Mars. Let go of him, or I will arrest you for obstruction."

"Do it. Arrest me. I'll sue you to the Supreme Court and back."

"Cleo."

"Don't *Cleo* me. You can't be right. I know it in my heart. I don't care what your evidence says." Tears flooded my eyes, breaching my self-control.

"Easy, Red," Rafe murmured in my hair, his hands stroking my back. "I appreciate your support, but I'm not worried about a few questions. Your family needs you to stay strong for them. You've got puppies that depend on you."

I tried to bring my tears under control. "Puppies? You're bringing the puppies into this? Britt's dragging the man I love off for questioning, and you're thinking about puppies?"

"Be strong. Can you do that for me?"

"I can, but I don't want to be strong. Can't a girl have a nervous breakdown when she wants? Why do I have to always be the strong one? Why isn't it my turn to fall apart?"

"Cleo," Britt warned again.

Rafe kissed me lightly on the lips, wiping the tears from my face with his thumbs. With that he disentangled us and moved over to Britt.

My heart lurched. I hugged my arms close, not wanting to believe this was happening. How many times did I have to do Britt's job for him? Why didn't Detective Dumb-as-Dirt trust my judgment? I gulped in another ragged breath.

Britt held the door open and nodded to Rafe. "You got any parting words, Golden?"

"Yeah, I do." He turned to me. "Call Bud Flook. Looks like I may need his services after all."

CHAPTER 23

Not knowing if Rafe would be released or arrested, I prepared for the worst. I'd learned the bail bonding process when Mama had been arrested for murder. If needed, I had enough cash for the fee, along with tax bills showing the value of my business and my home. I would sign them over without a qualm.

That wasn't the hard part.

Waiting was the real killer.

Mama peered around a clump of officers passing through the Law Enforcement Center's lobby. "Any sign of our fellas?"

I slumped into the plastic chair next to her. "Not yet. I remember sitting here waiting for you for what seemed like hours."

"Why can't Bud walk out the door with him?"

"The police must be still questioning Rafe. How many times does he have to say he didn't do it?"

Mama tapped her foot on the tiled floor. "You think that baby is his?"

It surprised me that she'd be more interested in the child than in my planning to sign away our house for my boyfriend. Not that I wanted to have either discussion. "The little girl looks like Rafe, but he said she isn't his. I believe him, but the resemblance is uncanny, isn't it?"

"Sure is." Mama fidgeted with her pearls. "What's taking so long? I swear I could have bought a week's worth of groceries and three pairs of shoes by now."

"You're free to take my car and head out if you like. I'll catch a ride with Bud and Rafe."

"No way will you get rid of me so easily. Not with my house potentially up for grabs. I want to know what's going on, and Bud will be all lawyerly about privileged information and won't tell me diddly-squat. You're going to save him, aren't you?"

Uh-oh. Would she lay into me about the house now? I feigned ignorance. "Save Bud? I didn't know he was lost."

"Rafe. You're saving him, right? We know Detective Hardhead has once again rushed in too quickly. You'd think he'd have learned patience by now."

"Don't you worry. I'll figure out who killed that woman. Britt made a mistake. Rafe's a good person, even if he is a little stubborn about his family."

"That's a bad sign." Mama glanced up when the door opened and a vibrant brunette dressed in pickle green appeared. "Look what the wind blew in—Johnsy."

Jonette hurried over to hug us both. "Why didn't you call me? I went by the house to play with the puppies between shifts at the Tavern and your puppysitters told me Rafe had been arrested. Unfortunately, Muriel and Francine didn't have a single detail to relay."

"Because there aren't any. Rafe wasn't arrested. He's being questioned about Starr's homicide as a 'person of interest.' I'm glad you're here. I could use the company."

"What am I?" Mama asked. "A broken record?"

I covered Mama's clasped hands. "You're company, too. I'm glad you're both here. Poor Rafe. I wish I could be in there with him."

"He has Bud," Mama said, pride ringing in her voice. "Bud will get him out of there as soon as he can."

"What's this I hear about Rafe's secret baby?" Jonette asked as we all sat down.

Mama cackled. I silenced her with a sharp look. "Rafe says it isn't his child," I said. "Starr Jeffries, the dead woman, is survived by a five-year-old daughter, which I learned about at Starr's funeral, and which Starr's neighbor told us about when we snooped around her mobile home park. What we didn't know through all this, having never seen the kid, is that she strongly resembles Rafe. Given that coincidence, Britt is certain Rafe is a killing machine."

"Seriously? Rafe's ex-girlfriend's kid looks like him, Rafe denies fathering the kid, and you believe him?"

"Starr had a kid." I held her gaze. "Rafe says the child isn't his."

"A kid. If Britt's right about the paternity, Rafe could have a kid living with him in the next few days. Boy, how'd you like to wake up one day and find out you had a daughter you didn't even know about? That would be a serious shocker." Jonette stared at the bubblegum machine across the room. "The thing I don't get is how Starr managed. By all accounts, she drank too much and couldn't hold a job. How'd she support herself and a kid if she was a drunk?"

I hugged myself to keep from shuddering. I couldn't imagine what that cute kid had gone through in such an unstable home environment. I knew Rafe helped Starr financially, but I'd promised to keep that private. I tried to steer the conversation in a different direction. "What if the sister's a drunk, too? What will happen to Kylie? How will her father, whoever he is, respond? Do you think one of Rafe's male relatives is the father?"

Before she could answer, the lobby doors opened again, and Rafe's siblings swept in. Regina ignored us and marched straight to the plexiglass receptionist's window. "Release my brother Rafe Golden at once, or I'll sue everyone in this building."

Hill trailed behind her, a little pale around the gills. Regina's assistant, Mary, looked efficient in a conservative brown business suit. She stood behind her boss, pen and note pad at the ready.

The staffer behind the glass scowled. "Take a seat, miss. No need to sue anyone. He'll be out when the detective is finished questioning him."

"How do I post his bond?" Regina continued as if the woman hadn't spoken.

"He hasn't been arrested, so there's no bond to post. If he is arrested, Mrs. Jones plans to post his bail. There's nothing further you can do at the moment. Have a seat in the lobby."

Rafe's sister growled and turned on me. "What business do you have posting my brother's bail? Why didn't you call me?"

"I was with him when he was brought in for questioning. It seemed expedient to be prepared to take care of the matter myself."

"Where'd you get the dough?"

How rude. I struggled to hold my temper. If she wasn't Rafe's sister, I'd be tempted to forget my manners. "I may not be a Golden, but I have resources. Besides, Rafe isn't a flight risk."

"He isn't going to jail, I can promise you that. My legal team is on the way from Bethesda. I'm throwing the weight of Golden Enterprises behind Rafe's defense."

Last I heard Rafe didn't want her legal eagles on his team, but maybe being here at the police station had changed his perspective.

"Sure is a lot of squawking going on in here," Mama said. "Who let the birds out?"

My jaw dropped. This was no time for Mama to speak her mind. "Mama."

"I'm stating the truth. It sets us free, remember?"

"Let's try to cooperate here." I made the introductions. Mama and Jonette sized up the Goldens in glittering silence. I turned to Rafe's brother. "You doing all right, Hill?"

"Police stations bring back bad memories for me," he said.

"Nonsense." Regina flicked her slender, jeweled wrist. "That was all years ago, and this isn't even the same cop shop."

"Doesn't matter," Hill said, digging his hands deep in his pockets. "They all have an air of sameness. Would Rafe mind if I waited outside?"

"Of course he'd mind," Regina snapped.

"It won't matter to him," I answered at the same time. "He'll be touched you came."

Hill shot me a grateful smile, turned, and left the building. Regina glared at me. "He'll never grow up if you make it easy for him," she said. "Hill needs to get past those childhood fears."

"Not everyone has an iron will." *Or an iron bra,* I thought to myself. "Or the courage to face their fear on a moment's notice. I give him credit for walking in here when he knew it would be uncomfortable."

My comment earned me another glare. I concluded Regina liked having the last word. She was rude and domineering. A real head case with a bee in her tiara.

"No wonder Rafe doesn't want to be around his family," Mama whispered to Jonette loud enough for everyone to hear. "His sister's an Amazon on crack."

"I don't do drugs," Regina hurled at Mama. "And I eat white-haired ladies like you for breakfast."

"Oh, yeah?" Mama shot to her feet and pushed forward into Regina.

I caught my friend's eye. "Jonette, would you escort Mama outside for some fresh air? Please?"

My friend shot me a pained look but rose to her feet. "Come on, Delilah. Let's step outside."

"Forget that," Mama said. "I'm not going anywhere."

I couldn't referee a cat fight in here. My best chance at containing this volcano was to keep Mama occupied. "I would consider it a personal favor if you and Jonette would get me a chocolate bar from the vending machine by the door."

Bless her, Jonette took pity on me. "Of course we will. Anything you want." With a deadly glare at Regina, Jonette cupped Mama's arm and dragged her away. My temples throbbed with the strain of holding onto my composure. I turned to Mary and summoned a smile. "How have you been?"

Her eyes grew wide, as if in fear. There was a barely discernible head nod in Regina's direction along with a microscopic headshake. "Busy."

I got the message. Mary didn't speak freely in front of her boss. Great. Fresh out of ideas, I stared at my hands clasped in my lap. The door opened and closed with two uniforms entering the lobby. My hopes soared as they neared, hoping they were coming to ask me to step behind the locked doors for my own personal security, but no such luck. They continued through the lobby as if we were furniture in the room.

God, I hated waiting. I'd much rather be doing something. My brain needed to be active or my feet needed to move. One or the other needed to happen, or I would explode from pent-up energy.

"If I give you fifty thousand dollars in cash, will you bow out of my brother's life?" Regina asked.

Did Regina say that? I glanced over at Rafe's sister and replayed her words in my head. Yes, she did offer me money. How rude. How degrading. How impossible. "No."

Like a veteran poker player holding a winning hand, she didn't flinch. "I'll double the amount. A hundred thousand. Will you leave him alone for that much?"

Of all the nerve. I lurched into a fighter's posture, my weight balanced on the pads of my feet, my arms ready to swing. "Why are you trying to get rid of me?"

Regina leaned down and got in my face. "You're nosy and

pushy, and I want better for my brother."

The door opened behind me, but I didn't bother to look. I couldn't. This woman didn't intimidate me. "Nosy is who I am, pushy is how I am. If you don't like it, lump it."

Bud Flook cleared his throat. "Ladies?"

CHAPTER 24

Rafe hurried to my side. "Cleo?"

I hugged him close, relieved to breathe in his familiar scent, so very thankful he hadn't been arrested after all. "I'm happy to see you." His heart raced beneath my ear. I blinked back tears. "I'm sorry you walked into that ugly scene. I was provoked."

"What did I walk into?" he asked, his concerned eyes for me alone.

"Nothing, really. A misunderstanding."

He kept an arm around my shoulder and glared at the group around us. "Will someone tell me what's going on?"

"Your sister tried to buy Cleo off, that's what," Mama crowed as Bud joined her. "She insulted me and Cleo, and I'm sure she would have lit into Johnsy if she'd had enough time."

He made no outward sign the news affected him, but I felt his spine stiffen. I saw the micro-tick in his cheek. "You will apologize right now, Regina," he said.

"Honestly, Rafe, I don't understand why you want to slum with these people," his sister said. "They don't matter. They don't care about you. Mom and Dad sent me up here to bring you home."

"Regina!"

"Oh, all right. I'm sorry if I hurt your feelings."

"You may be in charge of operating Golden Enterprises, but you're not in charge of my life," he said. "Your interference isn't necessary or wanted. Go home, please."

"I'm supposed to bring you back with me."

"Forget it. My home is here in Hogan's Glen."

What would Rafe do next? Would he throw his sister out of the police station? Would he storm off on his own?

I knew about his low estimation of his family, but the mediator in me sensed an opportunity. If he turned his back on them now, he'd burn a valuable bridge. I didn't want him to feel he had to choose between his family and me. I wanted him to reconcile with his parents and siblings. They didn't have to be best buddies, but surely they could be civil.

There was nothing quite like the feeling that your family had your back. Rafe's estrangement from his relatives denied him of that source of comfort and encouragment. I couldn't have made it without my parents and that was a fact.

"We could drive to Potomac and reassure your parents that you're all right," I offered.

"I appreciate what you're trying to do, but it's a lost cause," Rafe said.

"Listen to Cleo," Mama said. "Family is important." She nudged Bud. "Tell him."

"Family is important," Bud parroted, a goofy smile on his weathered face.

"Nice to see your lawyer's got a flexible spine and an independent mind," Regina said.

Rafe tucked me closer under his side. "Play nice, or you aren't welcome here."

"Mary and I will wait in the car. When you decide what you're going to do, let me know ASAP."

Mary shot us an apologetic look before trailing after her boss. I drew a full breath for the first time since his sister stormed into the lobby. "She sure broadcasts her feelings."

"I thought she'd never leave," Jonette said. "What was it like growing up with a ninja assassin as a sister?"

"My sister is a complicated person," Rafe said in a flat voice. "We all are, but I won't make excuses for her rude behavior today. She was wrong to be so hurtful. I apologize for her callous remarks."

I blinked back more tears.

He smoothed my hair. "Bud told me of your plan to bail me out. I can't believe you were willing to put up your house as collateral. I'm touched by your faith in me, but I've been in a tight spot before. The way to survive is to keep your head down and stay off the radar screen."

I stepped back, appalled at his inertia. My gut kinked. "Maybe that worked for another situation, but you need more for this one. Britt is a freight train when it comes to a murder investigation. He muscles over everything and everyone. We have to be proactive. Sitting back on your heels will earn you an orange jumpsuit and a life behind bars."

He looked away, sighed heavily, and met my gaze head-on. "You're exaggerating to scare me."

"To see you standing here in the police station so calmly, I'm not sure anything scares you. If I were in your shoes, I'd be climbing the walls right about now."

"We're different people. I am concerned about the investigation, but justice will prevail. I have right on my side. I didn't do it."

I shook my head and pressed my hand against my writhing stomach. "You can't leave your fate in the detective's hands. Britt is wrong about who killed Starr, and I'm going to prove it."

He closed the gap between us and took my hand. "I appreciate your insight, but the potential danger worries me. You've had close calls before, and you can only cheat death so many times. Let the professionals handle this."

Jonette snorted. "The professionals in Hogan's Glen couldn't find a killer in a haystack. Or at least, they couldn't find him or her in time. Cleo's your best shot at clearing your name."

"I've got plenty of time," Rafe said. "Plus, I've got a great lawyer. I don't see the problem."

"The problem is that time is critical." I jabbed my finger in his unyielding chest. Jonette and Mama flanked my other side. I could see their heads nodding in agreement. Everyone seemed to be on board except Rafe. How could I make him understand? "Evidence gets washed away. Memories fade. People move or die. If you want a fair shake at clearing your name, we need to be proactive about this."

Rafe shrugged his shoulders almost up to his ears. "I hear what you're saying, but I don't have the same sense of urgency."

Lord, save me from dense men. "I have enough urgency for both of us. I've been to this rodeo before, and it ain't pretty."

"What rodeo?"

"Britt's wild bull express. It'll brand you as a marked man, and you'll be writing your memoirs in prison."

"I didn't do it," Rafe said.

My hands shot up in the air, and I groaned. How could he totally miss the point? I don't know how I could state my concerns any clearer. Was he being totally thickheaded, or was I speaking a foreign language? I glared at my boyfriend. All along I'd thought his laid-back personality was a plus, but now I saw it as a giant handicap. This was no time to sit on the sidelines. It was time to get in the game.

Jonette tapped on my shoulder. "Enough already. Can we leave?"

"I need ice cream and pie," Mama said. "All this stress is doing a number on me. Comfort food is exactly what I need."

"The pie shop it is, my treat," Bud said. "Who's in?"

Jonette and Mama chimed in. Rafe said nothing. My whirling thoughts strayed to his ballbusting sister out in the parking lot. I bet she'd never set foot in a pie shop.

"Cleo? You want pie?" Bud asked.

Rafe needed our help. If he wouldn't cooperate with my investigation, maybe he'd listen about his support system. "I do. But there's something more important to consider. An opportunity to mend fences."

"Are we still talking about the rodeo?" Rafe asked.

"We're talking about your family," I said.

Rafe paled.

Mama nodded her encouragement. "You're right. Nothing like a spot of trouble to bring out the best or worst in a family. You guys should hop in the car and go see his folks. If this doesn't bring them up to scratch, nothing will."

"Bad idea." Rafe backed up, his hands held high. "You've seen my sister. My family doesn't draw together in times of crisis. We scatter to the four corners of the earth."

Finally! A reaction. I could work with a reaction. "You need to rebuild this bridge to your relatives," I said. "We need to give them this opportunity to step up and support you emotionally."

At that, Rafe laughed. "Your heart's in the right place, but my family throws money at a problem. They don't dirty their hands."

"They will this time. Your reputation and your freedom are at stake."

People ebbed and swirled around us in the police station. I hoped Rafe would yield on this point. I couldn't carry the entire load here. We needed his family to be on board with my "free-Rafe" strategy.

He studied my face. "You're determined to do this?"

He hadn't said no. I clung to that fact. He might take this important step. "Absolutely. Family is important, and if yours doesn't come around, at least we tried."

"Then we take my car, and we come home when I say. Are

we agreed?"

I smiled. "Agreed."

CHAPTER 25

"Sure, Bud can stay in my room tonight, Mama. No problem."
I tried not to gasp into the phone at the sumptuous estates
outside my car window. It wouldn't surprise me if each home
had stables, airplanes, yachts, and a golf course or two in its
backyard.

Rafe slowed to turn into a paved drive flanked by towering
ivy-covered brick pillars. Ornamental pear trees arched over the
winding drive. Every blade of grass looked as if it had been
groomed to perfection. The lawn seemed to go on forever. Holy
cow. I'd entered the land of the rich and famous.

Belatedly, I realized Mama had been asking about dinner for
the kids, and I hadn't heard a word she said. "Whatever you'd
like to do is fine with me," I said, hoping Mama's suggestion
had been reasonable. "You're in charge until I get back tomorrow. I need to go because we've arrived at the Golden residence.
Thanks for watching the girls for me."

Rafe didn't veer onto the offshoot of the drive that circled to
the two-story garage. Instead, he followed the broader sweep of
the driveway, parking in front of the mansion like a guest. My
heart went out to him. Was he so worried about his reception
that he thought we might need a speedy getaway?

I glanced at his drawn face, and I couldn't hold back the tide
of remorse. He hadn't looked this grim in the police station. "I
shouldn't have pushed so hard. I apologize for insisting on
handling your family my way. We don't have to do this."

"We don't, but I've been thinking about what you said. I want to clear the air with my family as an adult. I need to see where I stand with them, once and for all. I've stayed away for years because I don't feel welcome here. My choices weren't their choices, and it hurt that they weren't supportive of the career path I chose to take. For so long, we've all danced around the disconnect. I'd like to have their emotional support, but truthfully, I don't know if that's possible."

I was so proud of him, I nearly burst with emotion. As we exited the car and trod the stairs, I wished we'd stopped to change clothes. Maybe a ball gown would be appropriate for this swanky address. Yeah, right. Like I had one of those in my closet.

A smiling housekeeper welcomed us. Light glinted off her owlish glasses. "There's my handsome golfer. About time you came home."

Her face looked so familiar, I nearly asked if I knew her, but Rafe clued me in during our introduction. "Florie is Mary's mother. She's been with our family for twenty-five years."

"Nice to meet you," I said. Florie's smile had been genuine, but she hadn't embraced Rafe. Hmm. I was trying my best not to make snap judgments, but I was a fish out of water here. In my experience, family hugged each other, particularly if they hadn't seen each other in a long time. Maybe the housekeeper didn't consider herself family.

A slim blond-haired woman in an ivory shell, knee-length navy skirt, strappy sandals, and a perfusion of light and dark pearl necklaces hurried toward us. Her heels clicked on the foyer's ceramic tile floor.

She had Rafe's forehead and his long-legged stride. Her tanned skin and expertly colored hair bespoke a life of privilege and wealth. I'd already met his sister so I pegged this person as his mother.

She stopped a few feet short of us, though her floral perfume surrounded us a second later. "Rafe, I left the banquet as soon as I could. The ladies' club honored me today as Woman of the Year for the D.C. metro area. I couldn't walk out on them when I was their featured guest."

I noticed they didn't hug, didn't kiss, and yet not only had Rafe been through a trying ordeal today, he hadn't been home in a while. Did these people have an aversion to touching?

"Hello, Mom. This is my friend Cleopatra Jones. Cleo, my mother, Amanda Golden," Rafe said.

Amanda sized me up with a dismissive glance and didn't offer her hand. Not wanting to be rebuffed, I kept my hands to myself. "Nice to meet you, Mrs. Golden," I said with a head bob of acknowledgment.

A booming male voice from a room down the hallway cut into my words. "Rafe, that you, boy? About time you came home. Come on in here and join me for a scotch. It's cocktail hour somewhere."

"Coming, Dad," Rafe said.

I didn't understand this family dynamic at all, but I followed Rafe into a beautiful room. Vibrant jewel-colored art graced the wall. Delicate crystal accented the sleek tables. The jewel tones repeated in the sofa and chairs, rich burgundys, golds, spruce greens, and acorn browns. All in all, the perfect foil for a family adorned with golden hair, brows, and lashes.

Shep Golden wore casual clothing with a yachting flair— white-soled leather shoes, pressed khakis, and an anchor decorating the pocket of his blue oxford dress shirt. His dark tan contrasted nicely with his rolled-up sleeves.

Unlike the housekeeper and Rafe's mom, Shep put his drink down and wrapped his son in a bear hug, then he did the same for me. "Hey, hey, hey," he said, chucking my chin. "I like the looks of this one."

The feeling was mutual. Shep's open arms were the welcome I'd been missing in this household. "Hey yourself, Mr. Golden. Nice to meet you."

"Shep, please. No formality in my den, or whatever they're calling this room these days."

Mary popped in the door. She still wore her suit and heels from work, her dark hair pulled back in a twist. "May I fix anyone a drink?"

"Freshen mine up," Shep said. "Anyone else?"

"Gin and tonic for me," Amanda Golden said. "Don't forget the lime this time."

Regina trooped in with her cousin Ashley. "Red wine for us," Regina said.

"I'll help Mary," Ashley offered, placing her purse on a corner of the bar.

Regina scowled at her companion. "Suit yourself."

"Thanks for the offer," Rafe said. He turned to me. "What will you have?"

"Water," I said softly. Though I wanted this to work for Rafe's sake, I needed to stay alert and focused in this crowd of strangers. They might be Rafe's family, but the vibe I was feeling wasn't positive. Parking by the front door had been an excellent idea.

"A water for Cleo, and I'll have a diet soda," Rafe said as we sat on the couch. I hoped this visit would be in his best interest. Hoped that the worst was behind him.

"To what do we owe this honor?" Shep said after Mary handed the drinks around.

"Rafe was taken to the police station for questioning today," Regina said. "He came home to admit he was wrong for breaking out on his own. He's crawled back to use our legal team to extricate him from this debacle."

"Actually, I came here to let you know I was all right," Rafe said. "I have retained independent counsel, and I won't need the Golden legal team."

Shep swirled the scotch in his glass. "Our lawyers never lose. Sure it's wise to keep them out of it?"

"I've got this, Dad," Rafe said, gulping down his soda. "I didn't kill anyone, so the incident will fade from memory as the police continue with their investigation."

"If they questioned you today, chances are you're still a suspect," his mom pointed out. "Our legal team can determine the best plea for you and get you the best deal."

"I'm handling it my own way, Mom. I have every confidence in my attorney."

"You and your plebian tastes. No offense to you, dear." Amanda shot me a wry smile before shaking her finger at Rafe. "That's what landed you in trouble, associating with people like Starr Jeffries. Thank God you didn't marry her."

Rafe's chin went up. "Starr was a nice girl who never caught a single break in life."

"She associated with the wrong people and came to a bad end. You can do better that that. You *are* better than that."

"I'm no different than anyone else, and neither are you. Dad inherited the company and the money from his family. The rest of us live off the largesse. We're parasites."

"Watch your mouth. I won't tolerate disrespect. My conduct is exemplary. I wasn't questioned for murder," Amanda added in ringing tones.

"I didn't do it."

Regina came forward from the wet bar, raising her wineglass as if making a toast. "Well now, isn't that special? Either the evidence is wrong or you're lying to us. Which is it?"

"Leave your brother alone." Leather creaked as Shep shifted in his chair. "Everyone's overlooking the fact that this turn of events brought Rafe home. Stay the night, son. Let's put this unpleasantness aside and enjoy the evening. You might even decide to come back to Golden Enterprises. The CEO job is yours anytime you want it."

The look of alarm on Regina's face was genuine. "Not so fast, Mr. Chairman of the Board. We had to economize to keep everyone at the firm. You didn't want to fire anyone."

"So?"

"As Chief Operating Officer, I'm privileged to know the financial details of the company. If Rafe comes back, someone else will lose his job. Maybe two someones, to cover the cost of his salary."

"I'd fire every person on the payroll if it brought Rafe home for good," Shep said. "The company is important, but it isn't family. I want my son here, and I don't care who knows it."

Over at the wet bar, Mary knocked over a full glass of something, dowsing the front of her white blouse. Her face flushed as she sopped up the mess. "I'm sorry for the disturbance. Please excuse me while I change my clothes."

Lucky her, getting to escape the edgy tension in this room. Reggie and Amanda vibrated with it. Shep, who I'd dismissed as being clueless, wielded the power. The family money came through Shep. Since the others deferred to him, I assumed he controlled the money.

Rafe's assessment had been correct. The Golden family enjoyed wealth and privilege, but they did it at the whim of Shep Golden. Interesting twist.

"Did I miss anything?" Hill breezed around Mary, hugged Ashley, who was mopping up the mess at the bar, and turned back to us. "Is the great white hope moving home and making everyone's life perfect?"

"Lay off the sarcasm, Hill," Rafe growled. "I don't want anything from the family. I thought by coming here I could clear the air."

"The air's fine. Got a new cooling system not too long back," Shep said. "But I could use a golf tune-up. I'd love to take Walt's money for a change in our weekly game."

Shep's change in topic worried me. Was there a subliminal message here? Was he opening up to Rafe? Besides bringing Rafe back into the family fold, what was Shep's motivation to keep his son close at hand?

Rafe nodded. "Come out to Hogan's Glen anytime, Dad. I'd be happy to give you all the lessons you want."

"Perhaps I will," Shep said, a playful quality to his voice.

"That's true for everyone." Rafe gestured broadly. "You're all welcome to stay at my place and to play at my club."

"Of course we're welcome," Regina sneered. "You work at a public course. They let anyone play there." She turned to Hill. "When's the last time you played a public course?"

His sister's exaggerated eyeroll at *anyone* and subsequent glare my way shocked me. She didn't like me. I wasn't born with a silver spoon in my mouth. She couldn't have been more obvious about my lackluster lineage. I checked out the distance to the paneled door. About fifteen strides to exit this room, twice that many to the front door.

"That's not important," Hill said.

"Did you tell Rafe you moved back in with Mom and Dad?" Regina asked.

Hill huffed out a heavy breath. "What is this? Pick on Hill afternoon? I've done what you people asked. Rafe is sitting here in Dad's den. I want my principal released."

As Rafe studied his family members, the tension in the room thickened. He placed his empty glass on a cocktail napkin on the gold-inlaid coffee table. "What's the deal, Hill?"

"Your brother had financial setbacks again," Regina crowed. "He asked to tap into the principal of his trust fund. Dad wouldn't allow it until Hill helped us bring you to your senses."

"It isn't enough for you to run the company?" Rafe asked. "You have to run Hill's life, too?"

"He was being irresponsible," his sister said.

"He's a grown man. Stop bullying him."

"We have an image to maintain."

Rafe leaned forward. "So do I. Except my image involves hard work and supporting myself."

"You think you're different from us," Regina countered. "I've seen your car and your swanky condo. You didn't buy those luxuries with your weekly wages. You're as much a trust fund baby as Hill."

"How I manage my inheritance is my business, not yours." Rafe rubbed his temples and shot me a pained look. "Not quite a warm and fuzzy experience, is it?"

"My family isn't warm and fuzzy either," I said quietly, aware of everyone watching us. "But I still believe you have an opportunity here, if you want to pursue it."

"I came here today because I wanted to be part of this family." Rafe scanned the room and so did I. Amanda and Shep stood together by the mantel, Hill had joined Ashley over at the wet bar, and Regina had commandeered Shep's easy chair. The large seat fanned out around her, throne-like.

"What happened today was a detective followed a lead and questioned me," Rafe explained. "I didn't kill Starr. I don't know who killed her. My reputation is important to me, and I wouldn't dishonor the family by committing a crime."

He paused to take a deep breath. "Dad and Florie welcomed me home, and I thank them for their kindness. Cleo said something to me the other day, something that gave me hope we could be a family again. Now I'm not so sure about our ability to forgive and forget. It's been fireworks and drama ever since I arrived, and we haven't even started talking about Brenna."

"Leave my sister out of this," Regina said, leaping to her feet. "She's no topic of idle discussion."

"We've never talked about the shooting," Rafe said. "Golden money and Golden lawyers made the repercussions go away, but Brenna's death changed all of us. It's time we faced facts."

"You're mistaking this cocktail party for a therapist's office. Go blab to them, but leave us the hell out of it," Regina said.

Shep studied the amber-colored booze in the bottom of his glass. Ashley looked as if she'd rather be anywhere else in the world but here. Hill stared out the window. Reggie stood close to her mom. Brenna was clearly a sore subject here.

Beside me, Rafe cradled his head in his hands. "I don't feel so good.

"What's wrong?" Beads of sweat dotted his hairline. His color seemed off, too. "What can I do?"

"Dizzy," he said.

"Let's find you a place to lie down." I glanced at his family. "Anyone care to make a suggestion?"

Hill stepped forward. "I'll show you the way to Rafe's room."

"Thanks." I followed his lead, wrapping my arm around Rafe's torso to support him. Midway up the wide stairs, Rafe paled even more and clutched his stomach. "Need a bathroom," he said.

"Help me, Hill." Together we wrangled him upstairs and into a bathroom. I heard the unmistakable sounds of retching and vomiting. A while later, Rafe wobbled back into the hall.

"I need to lie down a bit before we drive back to Hogan's Glen," he said. "I don't want to stay overnight, but I'm too weak to drive."

"I can drive," I said.

"Thanks, but I need to prove to my family that I'm not weak. I can stand on my own two feet without them."

Hill helped me get him settled, and Rafe's eyes closed tight. I followed Hill out of the room, hugging my arms to my chest. "Thanks for the help. Poor Rafe. He's had a crappy day. I wonder if he picked up the flu or something from the police station."

Rafe's brother waved a hand dismisively. "He'll be fine."

"Oh?"

"He's had a weak stomach his entire life."

CHAPTER 26

Weak stomach?

That was news to me, but I mopped Rafe's brow and watched as the man I loved emptied the contents of his stomach over and over again. How did I miss this before? Rafe had eaten colorful and spicy foods at my house without any tummy aches.

Purple pork chops. Blue ricotta cheese. Spaghetti sauce.

My knowledge of Rafe's eating preferences was at odds with Hill's statement.

The sun set, and my concern for Rafe rose with each tick of the clock. He was still in the grip of a powerful bout of nausea and vomiting. His clammy skin and lethargy worried me. Other than Hill helping us to Rafe's room, the rest of the family had vanished. Mary brought some ice cubes and a wet cloth for his head, but that was it.

We were on our own in this well-appointed but impersonal room. Worse, I felt responsible for getting us in this mess. I'd insisted we come and mend fences with his family. I'd meddled, and I should've kept my mouth shut. I wiped his brow and then reached for his wrists to gently bathe them with the cool cloth. When I griped his arm, the skin stayed pinched together.

Uh-oh. He was dehydrating. I offered him ice chips. "They'll come back up," he said with a miserable moan. "My throat burns. My hands and feet keep falling asleep. If I could fall asleep, I'd feel better."

Each time he vomited, he seemed weaker and dizzier. With

his condition worsening, I needed to take action. He was too heavy for me to carry to the car. I didn't dare wander the halls of this place and leave Rafe alone for a minute with his heartless family. He needed medical attention. Intravenous fluids. Anti-nausea drugs. If I couldn't get him to the hospital, I could call an ambulance to come get him.

I called.

And loosened a shitstorm of Golden fury as I directed the rescue squad to Rafe's bedroom. "Good thing you called, ma'am. He needs fluids," the efficient Hispanic man said as Rafe was loaded onto a bright yellow transport.

"Thank you. I'll meet you at the hospital."

"He doesn't need medical treatment," Amanda said. "My son needs rest. I insist you leave him here."

The technicians looked at me for direction. Without sparing a glance at anyone, I nodded toward the door. "Hospital." To my relief, they rolled him out and drove away.

"We don't do this," Amanda said, as I shouldered my purse.

I held her level gaze. So what if fire burned in her eyes? It burned in mine, too. "Rafe is seriously ill. He needs medical attention."

"Everyone will know the ambulance came here. They'll know we had those people in our house. Our personal physician makes house calls, but there's no need in this case. Rafe will be fine in the morning. He's done this before."

I'd been sick with worry over Rafe for hours. I didn't have the patience to deal with a woman with no maternal instinct. "Excuse me. I have to get to the hospital."

She stepped closer and scowled. "He won't marry you."

Ah. A direct attack this time. "Whether he asks or doesn't ask is up to him. Maybe I don't want to marry into this family. Did you ever think of that?"

She shook her head at me. "Are you implying something is

wrong with us?"

"I'm implying that who I marry, for whatever reason, is my decision."

"Forget about the money. Shep won't let him lose control of his inheritance. You'll have to sign a pre-nup."

Money. I huffed out a breath of disgust. "Is that what's bugging you? I don't want Rafe's money. Until this afternoon, I didn't know he had a trust fund. I care about Rafe for who he is. He cares about me, too."

She held onto each side of the door frame, blocking my egress. "I can make sure he never sees you again."

"No wonder he doesn't want to move back home. This family is worse than a concentration camp. If the kids don't toe the Golden line, they lose their inheritance. You can control Hill and Regina that way, but Rafe has seen the light. He's his own man, and you can't stand that."

"Get out. You're no longer welcome in my house."

I half-laughed. "Was I ever welcome here? Charity begins at home, Ms. Woman of the Year, and from what I've seen, you've shown darned little charity to your son."

With that, I left. Not quite a grand exit, but it worked for me. Using the GPS system in Rafe's car, I found the hospital and Rafe. He was hooked up to an intravenous drip and resting when I arrived.

"How is he?" I asked the male doctor monitoring his vitals.

"His blood pressure is better now. He'll be good as new come daybreak. Can you describe how his illness progressed?"

"He seemed fine during the day, but late this afternoon he seemed restless and on edge with a headache. Then the nausea and dizziness set in. He couldn't stop vomiting after that." I recounted all of Rafe's symptoms. "Is a virus going around?"

"Could be."

The man's sharp tone and guarded posture put me on edge.

"Is there something else I should know?"

He studied me as if he were measuring his words. "I'm running tests on him."

"What kinds of tests?"

"Non-standard tests."

"I don't understand."

"It could be nothing. Or it might be something."

"You're scaring me. What do you suspect?"

"You say he was fine earlier in the day?"

"Yes. No vomiting. No signs of illness."

"Like I said. It could be a virus. But it might be something else. Either way, we'll know for sure when the test results come back."

CHAPTER 27

Hours passed. I sat beside the hospital bed, holding Rafe's hand. He dozed. I dozed. Then the nurse would come in, check his vitals, and I'd awaken. Rafe slept through several of these cycles, and I was glad he rested undisturbed. After two bags of fluids were administered, the hospital staff cleared us to leave.

The sun was shining when we left the hospital early Wednesday morning. I drove home on autopilot, grateful that the bulk of the traffic on I-270 was headed toward D.C. and not northbound in my direction.

The girls were in school by the time Rafe and I took the Hogan's Glen exit off the interstate. Mama and Bud should be at home still. Though Bud might have slept in my bed, my guess was that he was in Mama's room now.

"Take me home," Rafe said as we approached the turnoff for Manor Run Road.

I kept straight on Main Street. "Not a chance. Until you're back at full strength, I'm keeping an eye on you, at my house." I couldn't wait to get home. I might even kiss the ground of my driveway.

"I'm sorry about my buzz saw of a family," Rafe said, his eyes slitted against the daylight. "I can't say they mean well because I don't believe they do. They're set in their ways."

"In my business, I learned how to get along with many different kinds of people, but I found yesterday beyond strange. Your family never gave either one of us a chance. Your dad seemed to be the only one with an interest in you, and even that seemed conditional upon your returning to the family business."

"He thinks he's protecting me."

"From what?" My fingers tightened on the steering wheel. "From me?"

"Not from you. The world. He thinks he's protecting me from the world."

"I don't understand."

"I'll explain it better, but later, okay? I'm not up to a long, drawn-out conversation about my folks. I feel like I could sleep for a week."

"That's exactly what you need to do. Sleep the day away."

"I've got work."

"After the night you've had, you shouldn't go to work either. I'll call Jasper and let him know you won't be in today."

"Thanks. I'd appreciate that." He paused for a moment. "Will the board fire me?"

"Because you're out sick for one day? I should hope not."

"No. The other. Being questioned for murder."

"Now you're worried? Because of your job?"

He nodded, eyes wary.

I took a deep breath, aware that it would be easy to spin back up into super-Cleo mode. I looked at his tired face. He was barely hanging on, for goodness sake. This was no time to jump on him for being laid back.

I patted his arm. "That would be extreme, but you know what? Even if they act stupid about this, the world won't end. You can get another job in a heartbeat. You're that good."

"You're sweet," he said. "I don't deserve someone as nice as you."

"Yes, you do." I signaled for the left into my drive and made the turn. Bud's car slumbered behind Mama's Olds. I parked Rafe's car behind my Volvo. "But first you deserve an uninterrupted rest after the last twenty-four hours you've had."

"What will your family think?"

"They'll think I'm taking care of you. Come on."

He didn't move. "Can you figure out who killed Starr?"

"I will do my damnedest to find her killer."

"I changed my mind. I want you to dig. You're good at solving mysteries. After tonight, I'm sure you could do anything."

"I'm highly motivated to learn the truth. That's the real secret to my prior successes."

"I have a secret."

"I'm sure you do. I have several myself."

"Kiss and tell?"

"Not this morning. You need sleep, a shower, and mouthwash before you're getting near me."

"But I get to sleep in your bed?"

"You do. That's the safest place for you right now."

He shook his head. "I can't go in. Detective Radcliff will see my car parked out front. He told me to stay away from you."

"Britt will have to get over himself. He doesn't control whom I date. I don't mind people seeing your car at my house. Unless it's a problem for you. Will it ruin your reputation as a single golf pro to have your car here in plain sight of God and everybody?"

Rafe summoned a crooked smile. "Might enhance my rep. Let's go for it."

With that, we went inside, and I got him settled. He fell asleep before he hit the pillow. I shooed Madonna and her pups out of my bedroom, closed the door, and tiptoed down the hall to Mama's room, but it was quiet inside. I had enough walking-around sense left to leave the lovebirds alone.

I headed downstairs with my dog pack to make calls. Rafe's assistant was surprised about Rafe's sudden illness, but he said he could handle the Ladies' League on his own.

The Ladies' League? It was Wednesday, and I hadn't thought once about golf? Yikes. "Cancel me for the league today, Jasper. I won't be there."

"Jonette already took you off the list when she called to cancel first thing this morning," he said. "She said you two had too much going on to golf today."

No Jonette either? What would the league do without the two of us old faithfuls there? Probably dance the watusi.

The dishes were done. The house was tidy. Whatever Mama and Bud had done to take care of the kids hadn't left a mess. Good. I yawned big. I was too tired to deal with anything right now.

I curled up on the couch, Madonna flopped down on the floor beside me, and puppy Moses nestled in my arms. The other pups curled up next to their mom. I drifted off to sleep with the word *secrets* on the brain. Rafe had a secret. What was it?

"Wake up," Mama said, shaking my shoulder. "There's a man in your bed."

I started awake, heart racing. Sunlight streamed in through the sheer curtains. The room looked familiar. The smell was familiar. I was home and safe. I blinked away the mental cobwebs. "I put him there. It's okay."

"It's not okay. The man was questioned for murder. I understand you wanting to help your boyfriend. I even understand your offering to use our house for his bail money. What I don't understand is you bringing him beneath our roof. Impressionable young girls live here."

"Tell her, Bud," Mama prompted.

Bud shot me a desperate look. His face flushed. "Your mother worries your judgment may be clouded by your personal relationship with Rafe."

"Of course it's clouded. I wouldn't bring home every suspected murderer out there. Only the ones I'm in love with. What's going on here? Why the inquisition?"

Bud fanned the newspaper my way. Big headline on page one, above the fold no less: "Golf pro questioned for murder."

CHAPTER 28

I scanned the newspaper article. "Of course he was unavailable for a comment at press time. He was at the cop shop, his parents' house, and the hospital. Did they even try to call him? Nothing came in on his cell phone. I would have heard it ring. I ought to drive over to that newspaper and give Jack Graham a piece of my mind. This was biased reporting. He ought to be excommunicated or something."

"They don't do that." Bud settled into the rocking chair across from the sofa where I sat. "In fact, the more outrageous his story is, the more people buy papers, until he steps too far over the line and gets fired."

I smacked the folded paper against my knee. "Can't we sue him for libel?"

"He quoted from the police report. He didn't print anything libelous."

"If he was a local boy, I could call his mama and get him in big trouble," Mama said, sitting down where my feet were. "That's the trouble with these outsiders moving in here. People want progress but they don't know their neighbors when that happens. Accountability goes all to hell."

I dragged my feet out of the way in the nick of time. Rubbing the sleep from my eyes, I sat up and tried to think straight. "What can we do?"

"What do you want to do?" Bud asked.

"We can figure out who really killed Starr, and then write our own newspaper story," Mama said. "I want to help. I've seen plenty of detective shows on TV, so I'll more than carry my weight. Who do you like for it?"

The mental fog wasn't lifting. I shook my head fast to clear it. "I don't have a solid feel yet, but that's how I work. I keep asking people questions until I can piece the information together, and right now I need to question Rafe."

"Wake him up! Time's a-wasting," Mama yelped. "I've got a hair appointment in an hour."

I caught her eye and held it. "We're not waking him up. We spent most of last night in the emergency room because Rafe got dehydrated from a vomiting bug. He's sleeping until he wakes up naturally. He needs that rest."

"But still—" Mama protested.

"But nothing," I interrupted before she worked up to full steam. "He sleeps. Got it?"

"Yeah. I got it. I don't like it, but I got it." Mama huffed out a troubled sigh. "Let's get Starr's cell phone records and see who she called."

"Great idea. Except we can't do that. We're not a police agency. We're not even a real detective agency. We can't get anywhere near her phone records. Besides, Britt probably checked that."

"For a bright boy, he can be awfully dense at times," Mama said. "How about her credit card records? Can we check those?"

"Not unless they're in her trash can, and we sort through it." I glanced at Bud to be sure I was right. He nodded. "So far I haven't been desperate enough to dumpster dive, but there's always a first time I guess."

"No trash diving for me," Mama said. "That's not something a lawyer's wife would do." She and Bud exchanged lovestruck smiles, making me groan.

"I'll figure this out. Meanwhile, why don't you and Bud get

going on your day? I'll drink some coffee and decide how to proceed on my investigation."

"How about a stakeout? I could watch the Catoctin View Motel for you. Or any suspect you have in mind."

I needed to nip this trouble right away before it grew into a giant beanstalk. "Mama, you can't stake someone out for an hour. A stakeout takes longer than that, and there are bathroom issues to consider. You have to hold it for a very long time."

"You're right. I need a real toilet. I'm too old to squat in the woods."

"I should hope so."

My cell phone rang. Jonette. "You ready?" she asked.

"For what?" I asked, wishing I'd already guzzled two cups of coffee.

"Our door-to-door campaign this afternoon. I thought we'd hit Cloverdale and Hillside neighborhoods. Only four more weeks until the election."

Oh. That. "I forgot we were doing that today. It's been crazy here."

"I saw the paper," Jonette said. "What did his family say?"

"His family? That's more than a two-minute conversation." And much more than I wanted Mama and Bud to hear. "What time are you heading out?"

"I'm ready now."

"Give me twenty mintues and meet me at Rafe's condo."

"Roger that." I ended the call.

"Are you campaigning instead of investigating?" Disapproval laced through Mama's glare. "Should you be spreading yourself so thin?"

"I promised to help Jonette today. I'll help Rafe this evening. Not much I can do until he wakes up anyway. Let's synchronize schedules. You and Bud head out. The kids will be home at three-thirty. I'll take the dog and puppies with me so Rafe can sleep without interruption."

"What about his car?"

"I'm driving it to his place. No one will know he's here."

"Devious. And perfect." Mama's eyes twinkled. "I'm going to like being a P.I."

God help us.

The puppy leashes snarled no matter what we tried, but the Gordian knot slowed them down when we pulled up to houses. We worked out a system where Jonette held a puppy in her arms and rang the doorbell while I stood in the drive with the other dogs on leashes.

If anyone was home, the talk was lively over the squirming puppy and the dog park Jonette wanted to create. Moore for Mayor buttons went like hotcakes.

Between campaign stops, I held onto Madonna and Moses, while Jonette took charge of Arnold and Ariel. "What a great idea to bring the puppies!" Jonette exclaimed. "Who knew so many people loved dogs?"

"A lot of people know about the puppies now," I said. "We won't have any trouble finding homes for them."

"I still get first pick," Jonette said.

"You do. Decided yet?"

"Nope. I want them all."

I shot her a warning glance. I loved Jonette like a sister, but I had to be firm on this, otherwise I'd end up with all the puppies. "Only a few more weeks, then I start adopting them out."

"I promise I'll make my choice soon."

"You'd better."

"Where were we with Rafe's story?" Jonette asked as we strolled past several vacant lots in Cloverdale. "You told me about how odd his family is and how upset his mom was about the ambulance."

"I don't understand them. They're neurotic about the Golden money, and Amanda Golden is certain I'm a gold digger. They are some other adjectives that describe them as well, but I shouldn't trash Rafe's family."

"If they're anything like Regina, I feel your pain." Jonette shot me a questioning look. "Do you trust them?"

"You'd think the answer should be yes. After all, they're upper-class people with college educations, but I don't trust any of them. Regina and the mom are wired tight. Hill is blinded by his need for money. The dad's a piece of work, too. Comes across as caring because he's a hugger, but then he's adamant about the money, and even more so about Rafe moving home."

"Control freak, eh?"

"Exactly. I don't know who's in charge there, but something is very wrong in that house. Shep, the dad, made some comment to the tune of he'd fire everyone in the company if Rafe would come back to work for them. It was as if he dropped a nuclear bomb. Regina and her mom nearly lost it. And Regina's flunkie, Mary, remember her? Turns out, she's the housekeeper's daughter. Mary was so startled by our conversation, she turned over a drink and rushed out to change her clothes."

"I bet one of them killed Starr. Sounds like a huge cover-up," Jonette said. "What are they hiding?"

"Whatever it is, it isn't good. I swear they're all walking on eggshells."

"Guilty behavior, for sure. One of them has to be the murderer."

"Why would you think that? They knew Starr through her relationship with Rafe. Once he stopped dating her, she went away."

"Did she?"

Her question tripped me up. "What do you mean?"

"Did she stay away?"

"I saw nothing to indicate that any of them would associate with her. Rafe's mom is ultra class conscious. She probably wouldn't visit the grocery store with her own housekeeper. I don't see any reasonable connection. Starr lived an hour north of them. Judging by the trailer she occupied, she lived a modest life. She drank too much and had a gambling problem."

"Starr's sister then. Did she do it?"

"Jenny Kulp? Britt said she had an alibi. I'd like to talk to her again, but I need an angle."

"What about the kid that's the spitting image of Rafe? That screams *angle* to me. Why not demand a paternity test?"

My feet stopped moving, but the dogs didn't notice my lack of momentum. They tugged me forward. "That is a wonderful idea."

"I know. I'm good at being nosy. I had the best teacher in the world."

I ignored her slight on my character. "Rafe needs to prove the child isn't his. I shouldn't have any trouble convincing him to request a test. That'll be our ticket to see the sister and the daughter."

A mustard seed of hope sprouted.

Our plan sounded good.

Would it bear fruit?

CHAPTER 29

Macaroni and cheese with ham is one of my go-to meals when I want comfort food, and given Rafe's vomiting bout, this choice seemed eminently safer than spaghetti, my other comfort meal. Rafe ate the little helping of applesauce, a whole-wheat roll, and the tidbit of ham I served him. Moments later, he loaded his plate with mac and cheese, more ham, and a heaping spoon full of string beans.

"Feeling better?" I asked.

"Much better. I could eat everything on the table. Maybe even the table, too. Is it edible?'

My kids burst out laughing. "Do it," Charla said, her red curls bouncing with impish delight. "I want to see you eat the table."

Rafe leaned down and looked like he would take a bite of the table edge, but then he grinned. "I'll stick with the food for now. Better not invite too much trouble with my stomach."

Forks scraped plates as we ate. It felt nice having the four of us at the table. Mama was with Bud, and Charlie was thankfully elsewhere. Other than the potential murder charge hanging over Rafe's head, it felt like I had a family again. I know I don't need a man for completion, but the mathematical symmetry appealed to me. Four was a great number for a family.

Charla nudged Lexy. "Tell her."

Lexy bit back a smile. "Something nice happened today."

"Yes?" I asked.

173

"The yearbook staff selected random photos of kids around school to fill a bonus page, and they used more of my pictures than John Paul's."

John Paul? Oh, yes. The new boy who had the keen eye for pictures. Lexy's rival on the yearbook. "How wonderful!"

"That's not all," Charla said, egging her sister on. "Tell Mom."

"Well . . ." Lights danced in her eyes. Lexy wasn't her grandmother's daughter for nothing. She knew how to draw out the drama and suspense.

"Tell me," I urged, hoping that this secret was a good one.

"John Paul saw my pictures of the puppies. He liked them. He said they were terrific, Mom. Can you believe it?"

"I can. You are an excellent photographer. About time the whole yearbook staff recognized your talent."

"She has a date!" Charla crowed.

"Charla! You weren't supposed to tell. You promised," Lexy said, tears in her eyes.

"A date?" I choked on the word. I wasn't ready to hear it coming out of my baby's mouth. "You're thirteen. A date?"

"He asked if I wanted to go hiking with his family so we could take pictures together. I really want to go. Is it okay?"

"It sounds okay, but I need to speak with his mother first."

Lexy's eyes flashed in defiance. "I'm not a child."

"You are a precious teenager, and it's my duty as your mother to make sure you're in safe situations. I'm not singling you out. I called Charla's friends' parents, too."

Charla nodded. "She did."

"I guess that's okay," Lexy said. "But you won't embarrass me, right?"

I caught Rafe's curious gaze and nodded. "I'll be myself. That's the most I can promise."

★ ★ ★ ★ ★

While the girls were bathing and finishing homework after dinner, I drove Rafe home in my car. Dark shadows striped the road, bringing my fears for my boyfriend's long-term freedom back to the surface. I needed to pry into his family history without alienating him.

"You're good with them," Rafe said, as I turned off Main Street and headed to Manor Run Road.

"What?"

"Your kids. You listen to them, and you allow them to make their own choices."

I nodded, uncertain where he was going with this. Rather than let my imagination run wild, I held my tongue and waited for him to make his point.

"My mother wouldn't have allowed us to be on the yearbook staff. She didn't allow us to play with other kids, especially if their families weren't our social equals."

"Being a parent isn't an easy job," I began, hoping I was reading him right. "We make mistakes, but we do our best. I don't agree with your mother's choices for you now or in the past, based on your comments about your childhood. That doesn't mean she's wrong, though."

"She was wrong. I can't tell you how many times I wanted to strike out on my own as a kid, to walk out the front door and never look back. I packed up my stuff a few times, but I didn't go through with it. Instead I bided my time and left when I could support myself."

"I'm glad you found a way to be happy. That's important." I shot him an appraising look. Now that he'd rested and eaten, his color looked good. He'd been downright playful at the dinner table. Perhaps he wouldn't mind answering a few personal questions.

"Your stomach okay now?" I asked.

He rubbed his belly. "Feels better than it has in days. You're a great cook."

"Thanks." I navigated a few quick twists and turns in the road. "About your stomach—your mother implied you threw up a lot as a kid."

"I did. Thought I'd outgrown it, too."

"It struck me as odd, your having a weak stomach, given that I've seen you eat Mama's crazy meals and even my spaghetti with never so much as a burp. I've never seen you throw up before."

"It's a solo sport. It's not something I break out on hot dates."

"You know what I mean." I pursed my lips and drove.

"Maybe I'm allergic to my parents' house," he offered as an olive branch.

"Maybe."

"I hate it when you do that."

"What?"

"When you placate me like that. If you don't agree, say so."

"I don't know what to believe. I thought you had a bug or food poisoning, but the ER doctor spooked me. He's running extra tests. I don't know what that means, what he suspects."

"It means he doesn't know either. No point in worrying about a test. It's not like I flunked it or anything."

"Guess not." Though I drove at the speed limit, my thoughts raced. "I don't understand your family. Why do they act the way they do?"

"That's easy. Money. It's all about the Golden money." His sharp tone worried me. "My father's grandfather amassed a small fortune, set up trust funds for the family, and the money keeps growing. My father enjoys the things money can buy, but he still remembers how tight his family was. He wants us to be like that, but we can't. I can't. It's too hard. There are too many memories."

Finally. We were getting somewhere. "This goes back to your sister? To Brenna?"

"Yes. Everything goes back to that. My family changed after her death. We weren't close-knit before, but afterward we could barely spend time in the same room together. Everyone was so sad, so fragile. It's still there in that house, that tension. Did you feel it?"

"I did, and I wondered if it bothered you. I'm sorry I encouraged you to visit them. I thought you'd feel better with your family's support behind you in this trying time. I made the situation worse, and I apologize for that. And then to have you become physically ill while we were there only added insult to injury. I promise I won't make that mistake again."

"Don't beat yourself up over this. My family won't change. They're too rigid in their thinking, and they don't even see it. I'm lucky I got out, that I'm able to have a limited objective view."

"Care to share your observations with me?"

"They're chasing empty dreams. My father drinks too much and indulges himself with boats and golf. My mother's off doing her charity work. Reggie's burying herself alive in the company, and Hill's still a child in his attitudes and spending patterns. He may never grow up."

"Interesting." I had similar inclinations about his family. But there was something missing. "What about you? What do you see about yourself?"

"I'm chasing after independence, but it isn't enough. It may never be enough."

The way his voice trailed off alarmed me. I'd never heard him sound so sad. "Rafe?"

"I carry the burden and shame from Brenna's accidental shooting because I shot first. That knowledge is there when I wake up in the morning, it's there when I close my eyes at

177

night. I was part of that. I caused the death of a person I loved."

I parked the car outside his place and wished I could stop his pain. Poor guy. I couldn't imagine what that would feel like. I'd never killed anyone, and I hoped to high heaven I never would. The police. The mess. The guilt. I shuddered.

"I'm sorry. If there's anything I can do, name it."

"You can spend the night with me."

"Now I know you're feeling better. Mama's sleeping over at Bud's house tonight. I have to go home, and you know it. We had our big chance last night."

"Some fun that was." He kissed me on the lips, lightly. "I'm glad you're in my life. I don't know how I'd make it through this without someone strong at my side."

"Thanks." The things we'd spoken about tossed around in my head like damp towels in a clothes dryer. Certain aspects of his sister's death struck me as inconsistent. "Not to belabor a point, but did you ever see your sister's death certificate?"

He drew back, his eyes searching my face. "No."

"I've heard you speak about her death twice now, and I can't quite visualize the logistics. How'd your sister get down there? Did she often hide at the shooting range? Why didn't she cry out? Why didn't she move when she heard you guys talking or shooting? For her to have been struck the same as the paper target, she had to be standing at the same height. Didn't that strike you as odd?"

"Never thought about it before. Back then it was all about sorrow and loss. Still is, but I see your point. Why didn't Brenna help herself? Why didn't she stick to our routine? Why didn't she wait?"

"Did anyone else know of your plans?"

"We didn't confide in the adults, but it wasn't a secret. We kids had free range of the property back then."

My suspicion-o-meter spun into high gear. "I need to see

that death certificate. I'm going to request one through Vital Records."

"Why? What do you suspect?"

"I doubt it occurred as you were led to believe. We'll see what the death certificate says. Oh, and one more thing before you go, Rafe. That little girl, Kylie, we haven't talked about her."

"Starr's kid? Why should we talk about her?"

"The resemblance is strong. If I were you, I'd request a paternity test."

"Kylie is beautiful, but she can't be my kid. I'd stake my life on it."

"Hope it doesn't come to that. But a paternity test will clarify who her father is. That might lead us to someone with a motive to kill Starr."

"It will help clear my name?"

"Proving she's not your daughter will support my theory that the police rushed to judgment in labeling you a person of interest."

"All right, then. Let's demand a paternity test. I want to get out from under this cloud of suspicion."

As I drove home, I mulled the possibilities. The child shared the same coloring as Rafe. If he was wrong and Kylie was his daughter, the paternity test would add weight to the evidence against him.

But if the child wasn't his, that opened the door to another Golden being the father, another person who had a vested interest in Starr's life or death. After meeting Rafe's family and learning they all golfed at the club where Rafe met Starr, I had no doubt that his brother and father knew Starr. And there must be other Goldens in the extended family—Ashley's father, for one.

A Golden had fathered Starr's child, but which one?

CHAPTER 30

Deer Pines Mobile Home Park in Madeira had seen better days. A smorgasbord of worn-out vehicles accented the postage-stamp lawns and faded trailers. Last time I visited here, Jonette had helped lighten the tension, but my passenger today, Rafe, seemed underwhelmed by his lackluster surroundings.

But he had good reason, given the call he'd received from the golf course trustees this morning placing him on administrative leave. I'd hoped they wouldn't be so heartless, but I'd hoped in vain. Everyone wanted to be associated with a winner. With the negative press about Rafe, he'd changed from winner to loser in their eyes.

Ouch.

On the bright side, he now had time to help chase down leads. Good thing my accounting business was slow this time of year. I couldn't leave Rafe's future to chance.

I stopped on the street in front of the tan trailer and stared at it with growing unease. A maroon sedan with a cardboard passenger-side window sat in the one-car driveway. Would Starr's sister even talk to us? "This is her place."

"I've been here before."

"Oh. Right." Heat steamed up my collar. Of course he knew where his former girlfriend lived. "I knew that."

He craned his neck to scan the neighborhood. "Looks the same, except for the vehicle. Never seen that before."

"Must be the sister's car." The curtains inside the trailer

moved. I hoped with all my might we would find answers inside. "Someone's home. Let's go."

We walked up to the door and knocked. A television blared inside.

Jenny Kulp, Starr's sister, answered the door. Her bloodshot eyes and matted hair gave her a wild look, worrying me. Had we awakened her at eleven in the morning? Was she a fit parent?

"I'm Cleo Jones," I began. "I met you at Starr's memorial service. I apologize for dropping in unexpectedly, but I didn't have your phone number."

"I know who you are." Her narrowed gaze drifted over to Rafe and warmed. "I can guess who you are. Hello, handsome."

"May we come in?" I asked. "We'd like to talk to you about Kylie."

A little imp in clothes a size too small peered around Jenny's denim-clad leg. The Golden family resemblance appeared even stronger in person.

I knelt down to her level. "Hi. I'm Cleo." I reached into my purse for the small stuffed animal I'd brought and offered it to her. "Would you like this bear?"

Her eyes rounded like saucers. She nodded yes, but she didn't reach for the toy. My heart went out to the timid child.

Rafe knelt beside me and smiled. "Hello, Kylie. I'm a friend of your mother's."

"I don't want to do this outside," Jenny said, her reedy voice sailing over our heads. "Come on in."

She stepped aside, and I saw a jumble of clothes heaped on the sofa. Jenny-sized shoes and one cheap plastic doll were on the floor. I scanned the room as unobtrusively as possible. There were no other toys in sight. A whiff of garbage tainted the air.

"I'm glad you showed up," Jenny said to Rafe as she zapped the TV remote. "We can't make ends meet, and I'm plain worn out worrying over it. A thousand a month. That's what you paid

Starr, right? A thousand a month would put food on our table and keep our electricity turned on."

My God. This woman had never met Rafe before, and the first words out of her mouth were gimme gimme? That wasn't right. Though I wanted to blast into her, I held onto my patience. It wasn't easy.

Rafe didn't speak for the longest time. "Your sister told me she was going back to school. I loaned her tuition money to get her back on her feet. She signed papers saying she would repay the loan. I helped her so she could help herself."

"People like us don't ever get back on our feet. Don't you get it? I can't repay you the money you already gave her, but I can't take care of Kylie on the money she has coming in either. It isn't enough. Do you want the kid going to foster care?"

Rafe muttered something under his breath. He reached for his wallet. The big doofus. This woman was playing him, same as Starr had played him. Rafe had a big heart, but he wouldn't hang on to his money long with the likes of Jenny around.

I stayed his hand. "Let's think this through. How about if we head back to the discount store on the edge of town and buy some things to help out? That would be a start in the right direction. But, if we agree to help you, we want something in return."

Suspicion darked Jenny's pinched face. "What's that?"

"We need Kylie's toothbrush or a lock of her hair," I said.

"Why?"

"Paternity test."

"Wasting your money," Jenny said. "The truth is staring you both in the face."

My chin went up. "That's the deal. If you want our help today, we want something in return. Otherwise we're walking out the door and never coming back."

Jenny searched our faces. We must have looked formidable

because she agreed. "Deal."

I squatted down and offered Kylie the tiny bear again. This time she took it, hugging it to her tummy as if it would fill an empty spot. I rose with a sigh. "We'll be right back with items for the child."

With that we walked out. I wanted to take little Kylie home with me, but she was clean and didn't appear to be underfed or neglected. I didn't have any rights where the child was concerned, but I wanted an easier life for her.

Rafe hadn't said anything for a while. I cranked the car and pulled away from the curb. "What are you thinking?"

He scowled. "Kylie looks more like me in person than she did in the picture. How can that be? It isn't possible she's my kid, but she sure looks the part. Why didn't Starr tell me she had a kid? The kid wouldn't have changed how I felt about Starr. Her daughter can't be my kid. Because of Brenna, I've always taken precautions and have used contraceptives. I've never thought I'd make a good parent."

"Don't sell yourself short," I said. "You've a lot to offer a child and a family. You're kind and compassionate. You care about people."

"Starr pulled the wool over my eyes. I'm still a dumb jock."

"You trusted her, and you wanted to help her. Nothing wrong with that. The fault lay with Starr—she wasn't honest with you."

He gazed over at me. "How do you cut to the heart of the matter so easily?"

"Analytical thinking is one of my strengths." I cleared my throat. "Speaking of figuring stuff out, you mentioned yesterday you had a secret. Is it relevant to Starr or Brenna's deaths?"

His lips twitched. "Not that I know of."

"Are you going to tell me what it is?"

"We dumb jocks need a few aces in the hole when it comes to smart chicks. Wouldn't want you to think you know every little thing about me." He eyed me critically. "But you could try guessing."

What was he doing? Was he trying to put me off or to intrigue me? Either way, I didn't like it. With so much at stake I needed an exact answer. I wasn't buying his dumb jock schtick any more than me being a smart chick. If I was so smart, why couldn't I figure this out?

I shot him a frosty look. "Guessing is an inexact science. I've got my hands full trying to solve Starr's murder. Maybe we'll get back to this later."

He nodded. "Definitely later."

CHAPTER 31

Not knowing Jenny's cooking skills, I selected child-friendly, easy to prepare groceries. My shopping cart brimmed with whole milk, juice, cereal, cheese sticks, animal crackers, bread, peanut butter, jelly, bananas, and frozen dinners. I tossed in a new toothbrush for good measure.

I hurried down the clothing aisle, wishing I'd thought to shop for Kylie's clothes first so that I wouldn't worry about the frozen items defrosting. I grabbed jammies, undies, shoes, socks, a jacket, jeans, and several long-sleeve shirts. I also threw in several beginning readers, a large teddy bear, crayons, and a coloring book.

Rafe tagged along without saying much. At the checkout counter, he helped place the items on the belt. When I pulled out my credit card, he said, "Put that away. I'm getting this."

I shook my head. "I volunteered to buy this stuff without consulting you. We didn't discuss a budget, so I bought what I could afford. I'm prepared to pay for these items. I'll foot the bill. I want to help little Kylie."

"You're helping by knowing what she needs. I couldn't have done this without your help. Your money's no good here. I've got this." With that, he swiped his card through the machine.

I wished I could do more to help the child, but solving her mother's murder would help a little. I contented myself with that knowledge. We carried the shopping bags to the Gray Beast and headed back to the trailer park. The lack of conversation weighed on me. Was Rafe stunned at the thought he might have a daughter?

"She's a cute kid," I began.

"I didn't know about her."

Though I was driving, he stared straight ahead. What was he thinking? Was he avoiding eye contact with me for a reason? I dithered in that place of *do I push him to open up or wait and see if he said something else.* Why was dating so complicated?

After awhile, he huffed out a breath and looked my way. "Why did Starr keep her a secret from me?"

"You got me. I don't understand it either. But Kylie is a lead we can't ignore. She has needs for food and shelter, and I'm not sure her aunt is able to take care of her. I was appalled at the lack of toys and the outgrown clothes. Kylie is too precious to be poorly treated."

"Thank you for knowing what to buy for her. I would have bungled it."

I shot him a sidelong glance. "No, you wouldn't. I have more confidence in you than that. But you would have thrown money at the problem. It's better to make sure the child has clothing and food, better to make sure your money is going toward her care. We're doing the right thing by taking this one step at a time."

"I hope so."

Since Starr had taken great pains to hide Kylie's existence from Rafe, I was intrigued by the possibilities. Had she been protecting Kylie or Rafe? "Kylie is part of this. I'm sure of it."

"This?"

"Starr's murder investigation."

"How do you know that?"

"Female intuition. Starr kept secrets, and those secrets got her killed. We have to figure out what she knew and who didn't want that information to come to light."

"Kylie was a secret. At least from me."

"Why? Did Starr think you wouldn't like her if she had a kid?"

"Starr had issues. She was friendly and smart, but she rarely showed initiative. She stewed about things and missed opportunities. To put it in context of schoolwork, Starr wasn't an A student, though she had that capability. She skated by on her looks and personality."

"Maybe Kylie was her ace in the hole. As long as she could get money out of you without telling you about the daughter, she didn't have to answer any questions about the child's welfare." She didn't have to share custody of the child either. Had Rafe considered that?

"She knew what to say to make me feel sorry for her. She sounded so excited about becoming a nurse because she wanted to help people. I wanted her to improve her quality of life. I never thought of myself as her meal ticket. I thought I was helping her."

"You were, but you helped Kylie at the same time. Don't forget that. No telling where Kylie might have ended up without you stabilizing Starr financially."

"Good point." He lapsed into silence again. "About what you said a few minutes ago, that Kylie was somehow connected to Starr's death—is the child in danger?"

I ran through what I knew. "I hope not. Starr's been dead nearly two weeks now. Jenny or Britt would have mentioned if someone had tried to hurt Kylie. I mean, how threatening can a five-year-old be?"

"I hope you're right."

I slowed for a pickup loaded with hay bales turning left. Little drifts of hay swirled past my windshield. I hoped I was right about the child's safety, too. I hadn't thought my theory all the way through, but if Kylie was the reason for Starr's death, then

187

an obvious suspect would be her aunt. Jenny's motive would be to have custody of Kylie.

Was Jenny a killer? I wish there was a way to visually recognize a killer, but I'd been fooled before. Killers didn't necessarily give off a tangible vibe until they were in a deadly mood. Should I mention my theory to Britt? He'd already told me to butt out. He had to know I wouldn't do that.

"She has Brenna's eyes," Rafe said.

His statement jolted me back to the present. "Kylie isn't Brenna. Don't feel guilty about recently learning of her existence. That's what Starr wanted, to leave you out in the cold. You didn't know."

"I had to be pretty dense to miss something this big."

"Again, not your fault. Starr hid the child from you. But what if you knew? What would you have done differently if you'd known Starr had a daughter?"

"I don't know."

My hands jerked on the steering wheel, and the tires edged over on the grassy shoulder. I muscled the car back on the two-lane road. "Excuse me? You don't know? You have to know."

"I'm not family material. We had this discussion on the way here."

"But, but, but," I sputtered. "You were engaged to be married. I don't understand. Why get married if kids weren't in your future?"

"Tiffany didn't want kids either. We agreed on that."

"To say I'm surprised is an understatement. You're good with kids. You'd be a terrific dad."

"It's not for me."

Was that why Starr kept Kiley's existence a secret?

Because Rafe thought he might be a deadbeat dad? Oh, brother.

★ ★ ★ ★ ★

Back at the trailer, we shelved the groceries and cut the price tags off Kylie's new clothes. She glanced at me with a tremulous smile. "Is it Christmas?"

"It's a day for making new friends," I said, heart on my sleeve.

The child pointed to where Rafe stood talking to Jenny by the door. "Is he my lost daddy?"

"I don't know, but we're gonna find out. Did your mom say your daddy was lost?"

She nodded, rocking the large teddy bear in her little arms.

I knelt down beside her. "I promise you I'll find your lost daddy, don't you worry."

"I heard what you promised Starr's daughter," Rafe said on the ride home. "Should you be making promises you can't keep?"

I glanced at my purse where Kylie's toothbrush was bagged securely. We'd agreed to send it with Rafe's toothbrush to be tested. "What will you do if she's yours?"

"She isn't," he stated flatly.

"How can you be a hundred percent certain? Birth control methods fail all the time. Humor me. If she's yours, will you integrate her into your life? Would you seek custody?"

My skin prickled the longer he remained quiet. In all my dealings with Rafe, I'd never seen him back down from a challenge.

He'd wined and dined the golf club board to smooth out problems. He'd pitched in with childcare when I'd had emergencies. He'd taken charge of the puppy birthing.

"She's Jenny's daughter now," he said.

"And?"

The weight of my expectations hung on that single word. Our past and our future met at that instant. I glanced down at my bare fingers on the steering wheel. I wanted a man who wasn't afraid to stick up for what was right. For what was his. I didn't understand why he hesitated.

"And," he began slowly, "no matter how crappy a parent Jenny will be, there's no reason to think I'd be better. I'm sure I'd be worse."

My foot slid off the accelerator. My stomach dipped to my toes. "You can't believe that."

"I do."

Funny, I'd longed to hear him say those very words, but not in this context. How could I even think about one day marrying a man who thought he'd be a bad father? My girls were everything to me; I couldn't imagine not being part of their daily lives.

I couldn't picture Rafe walking away from Kylie either, not after the way he'd put himself out to help Starr. His words didn't jive with his past actions. Granted, he was under a lot of stress right now, what with being a murder suspect, having his golf job put on hold, and now a kid that appeared out of nowhere.

Even so, I couldn't give him a pass on this.

Family mattered.

CHAPTER 32

"Thanks for helping me, Mrs. Jones," Zoe Lapinski said as a dark-haired baby boy cried in her arms. Britt's sister-in-law patted the child's back and bounced him a little, quieting him. Two other little boys pushed toy dump trucks around the office. Tears brimmed in Zoe's eyes. "I knew money was tight, but I had no idea about our debt. Justin promised things would work out, and I believed him. Now he's gone, and I don't know what to do."

"Call me Cleo." I waited as she collected herself. Zoe's troubled face reminded me of little Kylie and the uphill battle she faced in the world. Oddly, I wanted Rafe to be her dad so that the child would have adequate food and shelter. And love. Couldn't forget that.

"Your brother-in-law told me about your situation," I said once it looked like she wouldn't dissolve into a puddle. "I can file the paperwork for an extension. After that, we can open a negotiation with the Internal Revenue Service, but we need to understand your finances first."

Zoe wailed, setting off the baby, and bringing the little boys rushing to her side. "All the papers are jumbled. There are trash bags of unopened bills. I'm overwhelmed. My credit cards are maxed out. Britt and Melissa buy my groceries and pay for my gas, but I'm terrified the kids will get sick. Will the IRS take my house?"

I was tempted to fuss at her for trusting so completely in a man, but we'd all been there, at one time or another. "They don't take your home, but the bank might. Did you pay your mortgage?"

"My husband died three weeks ago, and I've been trying to cope since then. There's no money, and bills are coming fast and furious. A debt collector knocked on my door yesterday."

"Do you have any sources of income?"

"Like what?"

"Like a job. Or a retirement account. Or an insurance annuity. Or a home business."

"No. We don't have anything like that. My job is taking care of the kids. The two oldest are in school, but I can't make enough to put the youngest three in daycare and have anything left over."

"What about life insurance? Did he have a policy?"

"I don't know."

"Do you have a local insurance agent?"

"I don't think so. This is all so much to take in. My head is reeling," Zoe said. "I want to wake up from this bad dream."

I sympathized. Ever since I'd learned of Rafe's connection to the murdered Starr Jeffries, I wanted the trouble to go away. But it wouldn't. And trouble would bite both of us in the butt if we weren't proactive. I found the form she needed and printed it out.

"Sign this." I placed the form and a pen near Zoe. "This authorizes me to represent you."

Zoe shifted the baby to her left side and dashed off her signature.

I scanned the paper into my files, pushed a few buttons, and sat back. "Done. That gives us a little breathing space. But this is only the first step."

The young mother's eyes filled with tears. "Tell me what to do."

"Go home and take charge of the bills the same way you take charge of the children."

"I'm scared."

"Life's scary, but we manage. Start small. Open a stack of envelopes and sort them by due date and amount. Create a spreadsheet if you have a computer. Find out if you own your vehicles, or if they have loans or leases. Focus on one step at a time."

She stood and her children followed her lead. "Thanks. I appreciate your help. I'm embarrassed I can't pay you."

"Don't be. Everyone needs a helping hand now and again."

After Zoe left, Mama scurried in from the outer office; her scarlet pumps were muffled on the carpet. "I thought she'd never leave," Mama said. "What's the latest on our case?"

I took a deep breath to transition from the client's crisis to my own. I hadn't told Mama about Rafe's sister's shooting, so I withheld the info about the death certificate we'd requested. "Rafe took the toothbrushes to a lab today and requested a rush DNA analysis. It cost him an arm and a leg, but he can afford it."

"You think the little girl is his, don't you?"

"The resemblance is even more striking in person. The child is a Golden, of that I have no doubt. But Rafe insists Kylie isn't his daughter."

"You believe him?"

"I believe him, but he's having doubts. By my count, there are at least three other Goldens who could have fathered that child—Rafe's brother, father, and uncle. I'm not sure the child's aunt is taking good care of her. I wanted to bring Kylie home with me."

Mama snickered. "You need a five-year-old like you need a hole in the head."

"I know. But even with an alibi, the aunt is a possible murder suspect in my book. She might have hired someone to murder her sister to gain custody of Kylie. And the trailer. She moved right into Starr's trailer. She profited by Starr's death."

"Can I stake her out?"

The world wasn't ready for Mama on a stakeout. I wasn't either. "No. You shouldn't stake anyone out. Don't you have wedding details to work out?"

"I'm good on that. I owe you for keeping me out of prison, and I need to pay off the debt while I'm still in my right mind."

"You don't owe me anything, and there's nothing wrong with your brain." I guided her to her office and beat a hasty retreat.

My cell rang. I hurried back to my desk to catch the call. "I need to talk to you privately. Meet me at the park?" Rafe asked.

"Will do." Madonna bolted from under my desk where she'd been hiding from the children. Had she heard the word *park*? I wasn't sure, but I could tell she needed to go out. I clipped a leash on her. "Mama, I'm taking the dog out for a walk."

I hugged my sweater tighter, wishing I'd taken the time to grab a jacket as the wind blew right through it. The weather forecast had called for mild temperatures today, but the stiff breeze made it quite chilly. As I rounded the corner to enter the park, I saw Rafe pacing around the granite marker in the center. The rest of the park was deserted.

Madonna picked up Rafe's scent and hurried forward. I tagged along, glad I was going her way.

Rafe strode over to meet us and wrapped me in a hug. I felt warmer immediately in the boyfriend-wrap, but the way he clung worried me. Had something terrible happened? "You okay?" I mumbled into his shirt.

"Thanks to you, I am," he said. "The hospital called. The reason I threw up so much the other night is beyond belief."

A knot formed in my stomach. I stepped back to search his

face, nearly tripping over the dog. Rafe steadied me, but I still felt off-kilter. I stumbled over to a wooden bench and sat. Madonna leaned into me, her head on my lap.

"What are you saying?" I asked, not sure I could put my worst fears into words. "Someone made you ill on purpose?"

He perched next to me on the bench, hands clasped together. "Someone poisoned me."

My breath stalled. "Are they sure?"

"They ran the test three times. Positive for arsenic every time."

"Arsenic?" I went cold all over. "Do you use rat poison at the golf shop?"

"Not to my knowledge. But even if I did, I wouldn't be poisoned by touching it, which I would never do. The hospital said the poison was in something I ate or drank. To be on the safe side, I threw out all the food and liquids in my house. Even the squirt bottle of mustard."

The stomach knot doubled in size. "I'm stunned. I don't know anything about arsenic except that it's historically been used to kill people. Someone tried to poison you? I can't believe it, but it must be true if they tested three times. Dear Lord. How? When?"

"That's the tricky part. They can't narrow down the timeline of the dose. It could have been at the Pro Shop. It could have been before I went to the police station or while I was there. It could have even been at my parents' house. They said I could have had a reaction in as little as thirty minutes after ingestion. I keep thinking about that diet soda I drank in Potomac. My doctor wants hair samples and fingernail clippings to test to see how long this has been going on."

"You're going to do that, right?" He nodded, and I finally felt it was safe to gulp in autumn-scented air. "Good. We need to understand if this is a one-time deal. Wait—you think your family might be involved?"

"It's a strong possibility."

"No way." What kind of family would poison a son? That went beyond the pale. "There has to be another explanation."

Rafe's eyes bored into mine. "While the hospital can't be specific about a timeline, I know for a fact I didn't feel sick until after we arrived in Potomac. When you couple that with the knowledge that I had similar episodes in my teens, we have a pattern. Someone in my family hates me and wants me dead."

Needing to touch him, I reached for his arm. "I-I-I hear what you're saying, and I'm worried sick about your health. I don't want anything bad to happen to you. Whoever did this should be punished. But, Rafe. Your family? That's a strong accusation. We should approach the matter with caution."

"Why the hell should we do that? Someone tried to kill me. I've already called the county cops. They've sent a search team to scour the house for arsenic."

Hell hath no fury like a poisoned Golden. My lungs tightened. "That's a bad idea."

"I hope they all rot in jail."

"I never knew you felt this way about your family."

"I do." He blew like a winded thoroughbred. "It's my turn to hit them where it hurts. Even if the cops find nothing, my parents will be embarrassed and humiliated by the investigation. That doesn't balance out years of their crap, but it's a damned fine start."

"This is shocking. I'm usually the one jumping in headfirst and you're the cautious one, but you've flip-flopped so far the other way, I'm alarmed. You've convicted them in your mind without a fair hearing. Even if, God forbid, one of them did this terrible thing, do you want to punish the entire family? I urge you to think about the larger picture. Be cautious."

He rose and resumed pacing the central monument. "To hell

with being cautious. I'm done giving my family the benefit of the doubt."

Madonna and I watched him, not knowing what he'd say or do next. His take-no-prisoners attitude floored me. I couldn't wrap my mind around his vicious need to strike back at his blood kin. I'd heard of people who responded passively to aggression until they snapped. Is that what happened to Rafe? He simply couldn't take it anymore?

Or was he the kind of man who kept track of slights? Did he keep a virtual tally of each injustice, real or perceived?

That kind of thinking didn't cut it with me. Sure, Rafe's family could've been warmer and more sensitive to his needs and nicer to me, but tarnishing everyone's reputation wasn't equitable.

How could I fix this?

Terrible things had been done to him, in the past and the present. I ached for the injustice of it all, and I wanted Rafe to be vindicated, but we didn't need to go nuclear in the process. We needed a plan and, for that, we needed cooler heads.

"Why aren't you agreeing with me?" he demanded.

"I am."

"You're scowling at me. And arguing. Those aren't supportive actions."

How could he doubt me? I loved him. I'd stood by him throughout this entire process. With my pulse going wild, I struggled to remain poised, but his accusation hurt. "I'm concerned about your strong reaction. In my experience, people who poison their enemies don't react well to pressure. If, and that's a big if, a family member is responsible for this crime against you, we have no way of knowing which person is responsible without a police investigation. You're not thinking clearly. We're not prepared to deal with this alone."

"I don't need this. I thought you were on my side."

"I am on your side. Take a few deep breaths, and give your mind time to clear. Head back to the condo. Get some perspective on this."

He stared down at me, an ice storm in his gaze. "On this? Or on us?"

"On this." I rose, dislodging Madonna who was all scrambling paws and flying fur as she huddled next to me. Taking a chance that we hadn't passed the point of no return, I leaned forward and kissed Rafe's chiseled lips. "Call me if you hear anything more."

CHAPTER 33

I couldn't face Mama yet. She'd take one look at me and know something was wrong. Instead of heading back to my home office, I left the park and sauntered downtown with the dog, numb to the cold, my thoughts in a heated jumble.

Why would Rafe's family target him? He wasn't integral to running the family business. He wasn't a financial kingpin. He didn't even want to hang out with them. It made no sense, though I'd be the first to say his family wasn't the warm or fuzzy type.

I could easily imagine his imperial sister Regina, his reputation-conscious mother, or his controlling father trying to manipulate Rafe into falling into lockstep with them, but poison? That went beyond the pale.

Who else had been there? His brother, though Hill didn't appear to be competing with Rafe over anything. Mary had been there. As the housekeeper's daughter, she'd grown up with the family, but she'd never been an insider. The housekeeper had been present, too. And Rafe's designer cousin Ashley.

Both the housekeeper and Ashley had expressed some warmth toward Rafe. I had no personal read on Mary. She'd been an emotional zero.

Our visit to their household had been spontaneous. No one knew we were coming. No, that wasn't right. Hill, Regina, and Mary were at the jail. They knew of our intent to drive down to see Rafe's parents. They could have called ahead.

Come to think of it, they probably alerted the family of our impending arrival. Was that enough time to prepare a killer drink for Rafe? Had my water been poisoned as well? I had been too nervous to drink any of it, thank goodness.

Speculating wasn't getting me anywhere. I needed information. I stopped to wait for the traffic to clear at the intersection of Main Street and Burkittsville Road. Fortunately, Madonna stopped, too. The familiar downtown buildings helped ease the chill of murder out from my heart.

Madonna veered left, and I followed her lead, right to the door of the bank. Charlie's bank. And the bank where Madonna's late owner had worked. Did she recognize the place?

The bank. My brain made a connection. Charlie had volunteered to run credit checks on Rafe's family. What had happened to that information? Usually credit checks took a few days. I hadn't seen my ex-husband in over a week. I should go in for a status update, but I had the dog.

I couldn't leave her outside. What if someone stole her? Hogan's Glen wasn't the sweet little place it used to be. The dog or the info? With Rafe's freedom and potentially his life on the line, I needed that information.

I squared my shoulders and opened the door. Two of the four tellers rushed over. "I know dogs aren't allowed," I started, "and promise I'll take her right out. Would someone please ask Charlie to come outside for a moment?"

"We wouldn't dream of letting you take her away without us saying hello," Norma said, dog biscuit in hand. "You leave Madonna right here with us, and we'll take good care of her, won't we, girls?"

Air whistled softly through my teeth. "I don't want to get anyone in trouble."

"It's no trouble at all. Hello, my beautiful doggie," Ellie said, taking the leash. "We've been hoping you'd bring her by. Dudley used to bring her in all the time."

"Thank you. I'll just be a minute, then." I edged away, certain Madonna would bolt toward me any minute, but she seemed to enjoy being the belle of the ball.

Charlie's face glowed with satisfaction when I knocked on his door. "I'm glad you came by."

"I haven't seen you in a while. You been doing okay?"

"Sure. Thought I'd stay away, and let you come to me. My plan worked." He leaned out and told Karen to hold his calls. Then he shut the door, motioned me over to his guest chair, and sat beside me. "What can I do for you?"

He hadn't tried to kiss me or compliment me or even propose again. Was that his new strategy? What was he up to? "Did you have time to run those credit checks for me on the Goldens?"

"I did."

He breathed deeply and slowly exhaled, as if he savored my fragrance. I patted my windblown hair self-consciously. "What did you find out?"

"In a minute. First, I read the newspaper story about Rafe and the Madeira woman. I don't want him around our daughters."

"He didn't kill anyone."

"You're sure of that?"

"As sure as I am of anything. Please, tell me what you found out on the money front."

"All three Golden children inherited multimillion-dollar trusts from their great-grandfather. Rafe's mother and father have substantial real estate assets and not much else. The brother already ran through all his money. The sister's trust is heavily invested in risky ventures. Golden Enterprises is generating low returns for investors and losing clients right and left."

"All of them need money?"

"Looks like it."

"And Rafe's trust fund has liquid assets?"

"He has a great credit rating, unlike his family members. Why's he out here in Hogan's Glen pretending to be a golf pro and working for pennies? I don't trust him, Clee."

"He's not *pretending* to be a golf pro, he *is* a golf pro. He wants to be his own man."

"People with that much money think they walk on water." Charlie reached over and took my hand. "I don't want you to get hurt."

His touch felt warm, familiar, and comforting, which confused me. "I don't want that either."

He drew a little closer, his thumb caressing my hand. "You're a good person to care for others and to help them. I didn't appreciate what I had until I lost it. I'm so sorry for everything. I was a fool. Can you forgive me?"

The ceiling didn't fall in, nor did the floor collapse. But tears sprang to my eyes. "Not now, Charlie. I can't handle this now."

"Nothing to handle. I'm not going anywhere. Bud Flook waited nearly forty years for your mother. I figure I can take things slow the second time around. I messed up. No one knows that better than me."

"I'm involved with someone. Look elsewhere."

"Nope. I know the real thing when I see it. I'll wait for you. Meanwhile, I stand ready to assist you in any way possible."

"Thank you. I appreciate your help. And I should be going. I left Madonna in the lobby."

We rose, Charlie still clinging to my hand. "Thanks for the financial information," I said. "I don't know how that helps yet, but it will."

"Any time."

I glanced down at our connected hands. Unconsciously, I'd interlaced my fingers through his, like we used to do. Oddly, it didn't feel wrong. I felt grateful for his help. I leaned in to give him a kiss on the cheek. He turned, and our lips met, dead-on.

Startled, I pulled back. He looked at me with woeful, puppy-dog eyes, and damned if I didn't let him lean in and kiss me again. On the lips.

Both of us stepped apart, and he opened his office door. There was nothing to say. I walked out, maneuvered through the tellers, and picked up Madonna's leash. At the door, I glanced over my shoulder. Charlie stood watching me, speculation in his vibrant blue eyes.

Damn.

CHAPTER 34

Talk about confusing. I berated myself over and over again as I marched home with the dog. I knew better than to let Charlie get the upper hand. He'd not taken any liberties; no, I'd allowed the kiss to happen. Twice.

Double damn.

For a minute there, I'd flashed back to my old comfortable life with my ex-husband. He'd been everything I wanted. We'd had so many good times together, they all ran together like a highlight reel in my head. Times where I'd known he'd be there for me, times when I'd carried him.

Neither of us had appreciated how fragile that trust was. It had seemed as boundless as our love. Then Charlie had chased after vitality and youth. He'd been so enamored of another woman's attention, he'd broken trust with me. Once I learned of his betrayal, I'd walked away, and the heartache nearly killed me.

Now Charlie wanted me back. He admitted he'd made a terrible mistake. A year ago, I might have leaped at the olive branch he offered. It floored me to know that I had any charitable feelings for him. Charlie and me. Was it possible?

What did I want?

I thought I wanted to build a life with Rafe, but he'd hidden so much from me. He'd kept his family from me. He'd kept his past a closely guarded secret. When I'd asked him pointed questions about his childhood, he'd deflected the conversation. How could I build a future with a man who wouldn't share his life or his thoughts with me?

Rafe had made it clear he wanted an affair. Nothing more.

Not much future in that.

Charlie would put a diamond ring on my finger today if I let him. He'd make a legal commitment in a heartbeat. Only he'd already shown by his past actions that being married and committed to one woman didn't equate with faithfulness in his mind.

My passion for Rafe sparkled with lusty excitement. I didn't feel an elemental connection when Charlie walked into a room. I'd never felt that way before I began having an affair with Rafe.

One of Mama's cliched sayings flashed through my mind. If you play with fire, you will get burned. Rafe was fire all right, and my self-preservation instinct urged caution. I'd been burned before by a man, and I didn't care to repeat the experience.

"Mrs. Burnside, you need a trust lawyer to set that up for you," I stated loudly. Darby Burnside didn't wear her hearing aids half the time, and I needed to make sure she understood. She'd been one of Daddy's longtime clients, so when she called this afternoon and asked me to come over, I hadn't hesitated. "Steve Saunders over in Frederick is who I recommend. He's very competent, and he's helped a lot of folks establish trust funds. He knows his stuff."

"I know you must think poorly of me, dear," Mrs. Burnside said from her deluxe motorized wheelchair. "But my Johnny would blow his inheritance in a week. I have to think of my grandchildren."

"Steve can discuss the ins and outs of trusts for children." I studied her pain-dulled eyes and saw a spark of the old Darby Burnside in there. "Are you certain you want to go this route? It will pit your grandchildren against their father."

She nodded. "I'm sure."

"All right. I'll have Steve contact you. If you need anything else, call me." A few sips of tea and a little polite conversation later, I was free to leave. My elderly client had a clear mind I envied. A clear mind. I used to love gazing off the overlook up here and staring into the valley. The fresh air and the elevated perspective helped me sort through my troubles time and again. Given the state of my love life, a little clarity would be much appreciated.

I listened to the radio as I drove across the ridge to Overlook Park. Traffic was picking up now that the sun was lower in the sky. Long wispy clouds floated overhead. The air blowing in my window brimmed with the rich aroma of fall leaves.

When I pulled in, only a Jetta and a Ford pickup were parked in the lot. I exulted when I passed two couples on the mulched footpath walking back to their cars. I would have the place to myself. It didn't get any better than that.

I made my way to the point and stared out over the wide swath of valley. Twenty years ago the land had been neat rectangles of farm fields, but now the landscape resembled a chaotic sea of houses. Hogan's Glen's reputation for good schools and quiet neighborhoods had spawned a glut of housing choices.

I soaked in the sun's rays and admired the play of light and shadows across the populated valley. The mountain ridge beyond beckoned my attention. Solid and awesome and firmly rooted.

Roots. I needed them. These days I felt like chaff in the wind, blowing every which way. Change was in the air, and I didn't deal well with change. Mama was moving on with her life, the girls were growing up. Two men wanted me, and their interest made me feel desirable instead of washed up.

Daddy used to say that time healed all wounds, but time

hadn't healed the wound Charlie had inflicted on my heart. Time had eased my anger level. Had my ex-husband truly changed his stripes, or had this romantic pursuit been prompted because I'd told him flat-out no?

And my boyfriend. Rafe was walking around on borrowed time. Granted, there was no smoking gun in Starr's homicide case, but the circumstantial evidence against Rafe looked bad. He'd been seen with Starr on the evening of her death. He'd routinely called her and given her money. He'd been involved in a fatal shooting accident years before. He was familiar with guns.

I shivered at the thought of Rafe pointing a gun at anyone. No matter how I tried, I couldn't match his face with that action. It couldn't be real. It didn't seem probable, though it appeared to be possible.

When I looked at Rafe, I saw a man bewildered by all the fuss, a man who proclaimed his innocence.

In the three months I'd known him, he'd eaten Mama's crazy dinners, dealt with squabbling teenagers, accepted my limited availability for recreation, and even delivered puppies. Any one of those things might drive a person to extreme measures, but he'd kept his cool under fire.

He'd given me a key to his house, and I'd given him my heart.

But the child.

I kept coming back to little Kylie, Starr's daughter. Though Rafe claimed to be unaware of her existence, she was living proof of an intimate liaison. He swore Kylie wasn't his daughter, but she looked like a Golden to me.

My temples ached. I massaged them, closing my eyes to clear my head. *Think, Cleo.* If Rafe was right, and I believed him, then Kylie had been fathered by another Golden. Possibly Rafe's dad, brother, or uncle. They all patronized the country club where Starr had worked. They might have known her.

Did they *know* her in that other sense? And why would it matter now, years later? Was Kylie a motive? Did a Golden want custody of her? Or, worse, was Kylie in physical danger? Surely, no one would harm a child.

But another child had been hurt. Rafe's baby sister. His brother and sister had been part of that death. Their parents had covered up the matter.

His family was up to their blue-blooded necks in this.

One of them could have poisoned Rafe with arsenic. Rafe claimed he'd thrown up a lot as a kid, leading both of us to think that the poisoning had been habitual.

Come on, Cleo. Put it together.

Rafe. If I shifted the focus from Starr to Rafe, what did I get? Someone wanted to hurt Rafe.

He was the only financially solvent Golden.

Did the killer want him dead? Was this about his money?

His brother was broke, his sister heavily into risky ventures. His parents were over their heads in real estate debt.

But to kill your own flesh and blood? For financial gain? That was cold.

In the distance, a car backfired, startling a lone crow from nearby shrubs. The bird's eerie squawking echoed down to the valley floor. I blinked against the strong sunlight and tried to re-arrange the order of facts, hoping to make a new connection.

Starr died of a gunshot wound to the head. Her secret child might be a motive.

Rafe had been poisoned.

He was rich.

Starr and Rafe's sister were shot to death.

Rafe's poisoning wasn't a single incident.

This rock was hard. I shifted my weight, bringing one leg up underneath me so I could sit on it. I kept coming back to Rafe and his family. What did I know about his blood kin?

I started with his parents, Amanda and Shep Golden. They'd kept a lid on their youngest child's tragic death. They were land poor. Since they had a shooting range on their property and encouraged their children to shoot, I believed they knew how to handle guns. They had the means. They might have a hidden motive in protecting their family, but did they have the opportunity to kill Starr?

His older sister, Regina, knew how to shoot, and she'd staked her entire inheritance on a risky venture. How desperate for money was she? Would she and Hill inherit Rafe's assets? She definitely had the intellect and the calculating personality to be a ruthless killer, but I didn't know about her whereabouts the night Starr died.

Hill. The smooth-talking, fun-loving brother. What secrets lurked in those mischievious blue eyes? How had he blown his inheritance? His liquid assets included a sports car and a five-thousand-dollar monthly stipend from Golden Enterprises. He lived at home and was engaged to Rafe's former fiancée. Was that by chance or choice? Had he gone after Starr when she was Rafe's girl? Could Kylie be his child? Did Hill resent his brother? Or did he envy Rafe's independence?

It galled me that I couldn't answer those questions about his immediate family, but I hadn't covered my entire suspect pool yet.

His cousin Ashley had been at the house when Rafe was poisoned. She had a daughter of her own who was the first official member of the next Golden generation. Her family's estate adjoined the property where Rafe's family lived, so she had ready access to Rafe and the household. What motive would she have to hurt Rafe? She'd decorated his place in Hogan's Glen and kept his secrets. Gauging by her upscale business location, she wasn't hurting for clients, but I didn't know for sure. Even if she was a killer, I could see her going after another Golden for financial gain, but why kill Starr? It didn't make any sense.

Mary and the housekeeper had been in the Golden house when Rafe was poisoned recently and in the past. Both women had handled the glassware for the drinks. One of them could have put something in Rafe's diet soda glass. Except Mary and her mom depended on the Goldens for their income. If they brought the Goldens to the point of ruin, they'd hurt themselves and gain nothing. Another dead end of information.

Clearly, I didn't have enough facts.

The only way to get them was to make a pest out of myself with Rafe. From previous conversations on this topic, I knew he valued his privacy. Would he hate me for putting his family under suspicion?

I couldn't get answers sitting here on a rock. Time to go home and call Rafe.

But when I walked back to the car, my orderly thoughts once more dissolved into chaos. My Volvo sedan commanded the empty lot, but something had happened to it. Something bad.

I tried to speak. No words came out. Shuddering, I crouched to the ground and glanced around. Each tree seemed dark and threatening.

I knew two things.

Someone watched me now from the woodline.

My windshield had a bullet hole in it.

CHAPTER 35

The hair on the back of my neck prickled. I fumbled for my purse strap on my shoulder, couldn't manage the zipper to open it up. Should I run? Should I hide?

Was I the shooter's next target?

I crouched beside the car. The shot must have originated from the direction of the path I'd trod. That was the only way the hole could go straight through the windshield and into the driver's headrest.

I listened for rustling in the bushes, but I couldn't hear anything over the roar of blood in my ears. Finally, my fingers closed on my cell phone lifeline.

Detective Britt Radcliff's voice came on the line. I cried out my need, "Help."

I hugged the fuzzy blanket around my shoulders as the tow truck hauled my car down the mountain. No matter how I tried, I couldn't warm the chill in my marrow. Someone shot my car. If I'd been sitting in the driver's seat, the bullet would have gone right through my head.

Britt had confirmed the bullet was a .22, the same caliber that killed Starr. He'd collected the bullet from my car as evidence and stuffed me in a squad car.

"You didn't see or hear anything?" he asked for what seemed like the hundredth time.

"Nothing. Except for the car backfiring and the crow taking

flight. That backfire was the gunshot, right?" At his nod, I shuddered. "I needed time to think about the case. Overlook Park seemed like the perfect place."

"Thinking almost got you killed."

The condemnation in his eyes caused my voice to hitch. "Ya think I don't know that? I can't stop thinking about where they shot my car."

His thick brows arched. "You believe it was two shooters?"

"I don't know anything. *They* was a slip of the tongue. But this incident was no slip up. They meant to shoot my Gray Beast. They were sending me a message."

"It's the same message I've been giving you since you started acting like you were a crime fighter. Stay out of this. Whoever this is, he or she plays for keeps."

"I don't understand why I'm a target. I don't have much in the way of information."

"Tell me what you know."

"Rafe didn't do it. You know that, right? If Rafe had killed Starr, there'd be no reason for anyone to come after me."

"Unless Rafe is the shooter."

"You're wrong. Rafe wouldn't shoot anyone." Too late I remembered the tragic shooting death of his baby sister, Brenna. "He wouldn't shoot me."

Britt's stern visage didn't relax. His silence weighed on me.

"Okay, okay." I told him about the credit history search, the DNA test for paternity, about the arsenic discovered at the hospital, and my list of Rafe's potential poisoners.

"Stay away from Rafe," Britt said. "Stop poking around in his life. It's full of scorpions."

"I can't."

"Cleo."

"I can't. I believe he's innocent. If he didn't kill Starr, someone else did, and that someone else is scared because we're getting close. Where were Rafe's family members when Starr was killed? Do you know? Did you even check them out as potential suspects?"

"I can't answer those questions."

"You should. And you should be prepared to move forward on other persons of interest when the DNA test rules out Rafe as Kylie's father. I don't know what the motive for Starr's murder was, but I'm guessing greed, since so many people in Rafe's family need money."

"You can't guess about homicide. You need facts. I have no evidence leading to any of those people. The evidence points to Rafe. He's also the only one with clear opportunity."

My teeth clamped together at Britt's insistence on Rafe as the killer. How could a police detective be so blind? "We don't know that. Any of them could've had an opportunity. Starr kept her daughter a secret from the Goldens. Was she paid to keep quiet? Would a Golden born out of wedlock be worth killing for in this day of unwed mamas?"

"Jenny Kulp got custody of the child, not the Goldens. Kulp has an alibi. I checked her out."

My chin jutted out at his pat answer. "If I were you, I'd double-check her alibi. Starr's sister profited from her death. Whether it was Jenny who killed Starr, or a Golden or a stranger, Rafe's been framed for the deed. I'm certain of that. He didn't kill Starr, but someone went to a lot of trouble to make him appear guilty."

Britt shook his head, his lips turning down. "Hon, I know you mean well, but you're stirring people up. You've hit a nerve. Murderers come in all shapes and sizes, but there's only one Cleopatra Jones. Your mother would skin me alive if anything happened to you."

I waved off his concern as another idea occurred to me. The brazenness of it warmed me, and I shucked off the blanket. "We need to strike back at his powerful family, now, while they think I'm helpless. They won't be expecting an offensive move."

"You need to go home to Dee and the girls."

"That's what the Goldens expect, but I won't roll over and play dead. That house in Potomac is where I need to be. I'm gonna drive down there and shake the family tree."

"Now I know you're nuts. Stay away from the entire Golden family."

"Not happening." I studied him for a long moment. "But you could go with me."

He studied me back, as if he were deciding something important. "You can go with me, but I have something to show you first."

Britt drove me to the police station and parked me at his desk. "Stay put. I'll be right back."

The Law Enforcement Center bustled with buff-looking young men. Three officers had people sitting at their desks, as I was doing. A female officer strolled by. All of these people risked their lives every day to keep the peace.

Kudos to them for that. One bullet hole in my car, and I'd fallen apart.

But I shared with them a need for justice, a need for the real story to be told. Would I have made a good cop? My head said yes, but my gut said no. I couldn't get past the whole shooting thing.

Give me an accounting nightmare any day. The cops could keep the armed criminals.

Britt returned, manila folder in hand. He withdrew a page. "Take a look at this."

I read the first line of the formal-looking document with growing interest. "Brenna's death certificate? How'd you get it?"

"I requested it, same as you. Only my request got bumped to the head of the line."

I read the coroner's statement describing the death of Brenna Golden. It wasn't pretty. Over fifty wounds. My stomach turned at the words.

"Poor kid," I whispered. "What were you doing behind the target?"

Britt nodded. "Valid question. One I wondered myself, so I also requested the coroner's detailed report. I didn't learn much except to see a schematic of the wounds."

"I don't need to see that." I had a perfectly good imagination. "What about a photo of Brenna? Was that in the coroner's report?"

"If there was, it was removed before I accessed the file."

Not that I wanted to see the corpse, but the omission seemed downright odd. "What does that mean?"

He held up his palm. "Before you go getting crazy ideas, it might have no meaning at all. The picture could have been lost or misplaced. Happens all the time."

Chagrined, I studied the death certificate again. "The time of death is given as seven in the morning. That's precise. How'd the coroner pinpoint it so exactly?"

"I believe he took the time from the police incident report. The kids began firing at the range at that time."

"Does this seem right to you?"

Britt leaned closer. "Everything seems neatly tied up, but it feels off for some reason."

I felt a flicker of hope. "You don't trust the report?"

"Never said that. But I'm willing to hear more from the family about this cold case."

That was something, at least. If I couldn't flush Starr's killer from the field of suspects, perhaps understanding Brenna's death would shed light on how the Goldens operated.

CHAPTER 36

Britt drove us to Potomac. Knowing I wasn't alone bolstered my courage. Deep in my bones, I knew this was the right thing to do. There were answers in that house, answers that had been kept secret for way too long.

Florie opened the paneled door. In her tidy uniform and owlish-looking glasses, she seemed like a caricature of a housekeeper. "Yes?"

"I apologize for coming unannounced, but I need to speak with the family," I said in a rush of words, hoping against hope she wouldn't slam the door in my face. "My car's in the shop, so an old friend drove me down. This is Britt Radcliff."

Florie bobbed her head in Britt's direction as she clung to the front door. Indecision crossed her face like a passing shadow from a hawk's wing. Then she invited us into the foyer.

"Please wait here," Florie said before melting into the house. Her soft-soled shoes made no sound on the ceramic tile floor.

"Kinda like a tomb in here," Britt said, hands jammed in his pockets.

"Keep your voice down," I warned. "We don't want to get thrown out before we even begin."

He grinned. "You have no idea, do you?"

His question caught me off guard. Was he talking about the killer's identity? I brazened it out. "What do you mean?"

"The Goldens will treat you with kid gloves. You've got something they want."

"The truth?"

"No. They don't care about that. They've got their own version of the truth. They want Rafe."

"They're not going to get him. I mean he doesn't want to be gotten. Oh dear, that still didn't come out right. He's never felt comfortable here. He won't return to the family fold."

Britt rocked his weight forward onto the balls of his feet.

"He won't," I asserted. "He told me about growing up here, about what it was like to be different. I understand what that's like. He may have the same last name as them, but he's his own man."

"Blood will tell."

"Hush. You sound like Mama."

"Delilah is right. I've seen it over and over in my work. No matter how dysfunctional a family is, they band together to face an outside threat. Your action to come down here and prove Rafe's innocence is a wonderful, loyal gesture. However, Rafe won't see it that way, and it's likely his family will resent the intrusion. You should at least call your boyfriend, and tell him what you're doing."

"I didn't want to call earlier because he might tell me to turn around, but now that we're here, I don't mind texting him." I pulled out my cell phone and entered a brief message.

In Potomac with your family. Will prove you are innocent. Love, Cleo

Message sent, I turned off the ringer on the phone. "Satisfied?"

He shrugged.

I was saved from replying as Florie hurried back. "Mr. and Mrs. Golden will receive you in the library."

Britt's head swiveled to take in the jewel-toned artwork, the crystal vases with freshly cut flowers, the elegant drapes, and the upscale furniture. Shep Golden stood by the wet bar, drink in hand. His white polo had a large sailboat logo, his trousers looked as if they'd just come off the ironing board. Amanda Golden stood beside the crimson and gold drapes, the sun radiant on her lithe body. Next to her was Ashley, the supermom cousin who lived next door. They both turned at our approach.

I introduced Britt, declined a drink, and got right down to business. "I'm here to talk about Rafe and Starr."

"What now?" Amanda Golden said. "Isn't it enough that the local police have crawled through our lives and home all afternoon?"

"I had nothing to do with that," I countered. My hands went up, palms out to show my lack of threat. "I'm trying to help your son prove his innocence. I need to know what happened between him and Starr all those years ago."

"That's in the past," Shep said. "We have an unwritten rule to never look back. It's our family policy."

Amanda's sharp eyes bored into me. I'd had a crappy day as well. She didn't frighten me.

"That's unfortunate, because we need to find out who else beside Rafe had a connection with Starr. I understand she worked at the country club. Did you know her, Mr. Golden?"

"I didn't know her. She worked there, for goodness sake. No one pays attention to staff."

"She didn't look familiar when Rafe began dating her?"

"I suppose."

"Did you ever date her?"

"That's absurd," Rafe's mother snarled. "He's a married man."

"Not as absurd as you think. There's a child. Rafe says the child isn't his. But I have to tell you, Kylie looks exactly like a Golden."

"A child?" Shep repeated in a flat voice.

"Do you know something about Starr and her daughter?" I

asked, glancing around the room. Ashley had retreated to the bar and was fooling around with the glasses. I wanted to shout at her that one of them might be laced with arsenic, but I didn't. She could be the poisoner.

Regina walked in with Mary on her heels. "Stop this at once," Regina said. "You have no right to be here. We've been through enough today."

I drew myself up to my full height. Granted, I was four inches shorter than Rafe's high-powered executive sister, but I felt tall. "Someone in this house has it in for Rafe. They're making sure he will pay for Starr's murder."

"She was a hustler. A greedy opportunistic hustler. I told him that from day one," Regina said. "He laughed at me and said she had an honest face. All she ever did was lie to him."

"Please continue."

"Starr wanted what Rafe had—money and connections. She used him, and he let her do it because she made him feel good. She wasn't worth his time. She liked to make men feel good."

"How do you know about that?"

She shrugged. "You hear things."

"Things about Starr dating another Golden?"

Regina blinked furiously. "I've said enough."

Hill walked in holding hands with Tiffany. "That's a first, Reggie," Hill said. "You always have more to say. Hey, Cleo. What's this about?"

I noted Florie hovering by the door and waved her in. "This is about clearing Rafe from police suspicion. He's very close-mouthed about the past."

"He's a Golden. We guard our secrets," Shep said.

"Our private affairs are none of your business," Amanda Golden added.

"Rafe has been punished enough for his secrets." I took a deep breath. "Someone in this library is a killer."

As if the movie had stopping rolling, everyone froze in place. Ashley stared at me. I accepted her unstated challenge. "Let's start with Ashley. She knew the ins and outs of Rafe's place from designing it for him. I'm sure she has access to his place today because Rafe is highly trusting. She lives next door to this house. She could have poisoned Rafe last week and throughout his childhood."

"Poison?" Amanda leaned toward me, her voice shrill. "My son was poisoned?"

"He was. And not just once. He recalls similar vomiting events throughout his childhood, and you claimed he had a weak stomach. It's weak for good reason. Someone has been poisoning him for years."

"That's outrageous," Regina snapped. "You don't have any proof."

"I have the hospital report from the night he was poisoned, and I trust Rafe's recollection of his childhood. You don't forget vomitting episodes. Someone here gave him arsenic. Someone who wants him out of the way. They say poison is a woman's weapon. Maybe it wasn't Ashley who poisoned Rafe. Maybe it was Regina. Maybe she couldn't stand the competition from her younger brother."

"Liar," Regina shouted. "I didn't poison anyone."

"But you know where the arsenic is, don't you?"

"There were rats in the poolhouse years ago. We put out arsenic to kill them. Wait. Is that why the cops were here today? Looking for our rat poison?"

I nodded. "How many people knew about the arsenic? Show of hands?" Mary and Florie didn't raise their hands. I waited until they looked my way. "How about you ladies? Did you know about the poison?"

Mary gave a slight nod but kept quiet.

"I would never hurt Mr. Rafe," Florie said. "He's so sweet to me, always coming to my kitchen for ginger ale for his upset tummy."

"What about you, Hill?"

"I'm no poisoner, but I knew about the rats. I didn't know we had arsenic on the premises, still don't, and I don't care. I've got better things to do than to sit around rehashing the past."

The blonde at his elbow started. I turned my attention to her. "The answers are in the past, aren't they, Tiffany? You used to date Rafe and now you're with Hill. What does that say about you?"

The model-thin woman quivered. "That I know a good thing when I see it?"

Her lame quip fell on deaf ears. What had Rafe ever seen in her? I dismissed her and turned back to Hill. "Did you date Starr?"

His face colored. "Not cool. My fiancée is in the room."

"This is exactly the time to talk about it. Let me be more specific. Did you sleep with Starr?"

All eyes turned to him, and he shrugged. "Sure. She put out for anyone. Once Rafe found out about her equal opportunity humping policy, he dumped her."

"You dated her while she was dating your brother?"

"We hooked up a couple of times."

His cool tone gave one impression, the fire in his eyes another. My curiosity surged. "Did she ask you for money?"

"That's none of your business."

"She did, didn't she?" A piece of the puzzle snapped together in my mind. The big picture became clearer. "You didn't blow your inheritance gambling. You blew it on Starr. Did she blackmail you?"

"Wait a minute," Regina said, pointing at Britt. "I recognize your voice. You're the police officer who called with questions about Rafe and Starr. The one I saw with Rafe at the police station."

"I'm a detective," Britt said, "but I'm here in an unofficial capacity with my friend Cleo."

"This isn't a police matter?"

"Only if you think it is."

"This is very confusing," Regina said.

"Not as confusing as the layers of secrets around here," I said, focusing on Rafe's sharp-tongued sister. "It's my guess you encouraged Hill to go after Starr to prove to Rafe she wasn't faithful."

Shep groaned and sat down too hard in his chair. Booze sloshed over the side of his glass. Mary brought him a handful of napkins.

"Damn," Hill said. "She's right. You did tell me to go after Starr."

"I did it for Rafe's own good," Regina said. "He's always been too gullible, too trusting. Starr was a nasty user. I didn't want her sinking her sharp claws into Rafe."

"Instead she sank them into me. Thanks for nothing, big sister," Hill said.

"I can't believe the two of you," Amanda Golden said. "You should be ashamed of yourselves. Rafe's your brother."

"He doesn't act like he's a member of the family," Regina grumped. "He doesn't want anything to do with us or Golden Enterprises. He walked out and never looked back."

"Can you blame him?" I asked. "Someone in this room, in his family, set him up for a murder rap. Someone wants him to pay for a crime he didn't commit, and I think it dates back to an earlier tragedy in your family. To Brenna's death."

CHAPTER 37

Ashley gasped. Mary and Florie stared at the floor. Hill and Regina caught each other's eye. Tiffany looked like she'd rather be any place but here. Shep drained his whiskey glass.

"We don't talk about Brenna," Amanda said, frost dripping from her words.

I walked across the room toward Rafe's mom, needing to closely gauge her reaction. "You should. There were irregularities in the investigation of her accidental death, things you kept out of the police record."

"Dredging up the past won't help my son," Shep said.

"I know how hard a loss can be, but the more I think about how this family reacts, the more I believe the present trouble stems from the past. Consider how it looks from my perspective. Shep hides from the truth, Amanda orchestrates her own truth, Regina runs interference for the company, and Hill escapes by playing the bad boy. Brenna's death affected everyone in this room, even Mary, Florie, and Ashley. No one has said this out loud, but at least one of you blames Rafe for her death."

Stunned silence met my ears. No one protested. No one denied it. I was on the right track. "You think he did it because he feels such shame and responsibility for the incident. I've got news for you folks. It's his nature to care for the people around him. He feels terrible about the incident because he failed to protect Brenna, not because he murdered her. Need I remind you that three Goldens shot that day."

Ashley's nose went up. "His bullets were clustered around her heart."

"How do you know that?" Amanda asked.

"My guess is that she asked someone to pull the autopsy record. How many different guns were involved?"

"Three," Hill said. "Mine, Rafe's, and Reggie's."

"It's my belief someone killed Brenna elsewhere with one of those three guns. Then they placed her behind the target at the range. It's the only thing that makes any sense."

"Who would want to hurt Brenna? She was the sweetest child," Florie said. "She had a kind word for everyone."

This was the first I'd heard from the housekeeper. I'd always wanted to say "the butler did it" on one of my cases, but she wasn't a butler. Worse, petite Florie didn't seem strong enough to carry a teenager's body all the way to the distant gun range.

"According to Rafe, Brenna was everyone's favorite. He mentioned she was the best and brightest of you all. As the youngest, I imagine she got the most attention. I imagine Brenna's shining star made the other children fade into the background. She could have challenged Regina for the Queen Bee slot in the family. She was younger than Hill, but she outshone him in every way. She could have ruined Ashley's chances at being the prettiest of the next generation. Even Mary could have felt threatened by this bundle of perfection. Someone in this room murdered Brenna, and they're doing their damnedest to bury Rafe alive."

A roar of denial swept through the room. Everyone spoke at once. I couldn't keep up with so many angry conversations. I'd wanted to stir things up, and I'd done that. The kettle was officially at full boil.

Rafe stormed into the room, eyes blazing. His voice rose

above the fray. "What's the meaning of this?"
His question was directed at me.

CHAPTER 38

The fury in Rafe's voice stunned me. I'd never seen him this angry at me before, never seen how cold his eyes could become. The room fell silent. Britt stepped to my side, placed his beefy palm on my shoulder, and I edged closer to him for safety.

"Cleo—" Rafe demanded from the center of the room. "Explain why you're here, and why everyone is at each other's throats."

I'd expected him to be irritated by my meddling, but his caustic tone erased the explanation from my mind. I stood there mute, unable to respond.

Sensing an opening, Regina stepped into the power void. Her voice shook with rage. "Your tramp of a girlfriend is accusing us of murder, that's what. She dared to bring up Brenna. Said one of us killed Brenna. One of us here in the library."

Others joined in the finger-pointing fray. The decibel level rose to a crescendo again. "Enough!" Rafe roared.

In that moment, I knew what Rafe didn't. He was the natural leader of this family, the prodigal son they all knew should head Golden Enterprises. That he'd turned his back on them, that he'd lost them millions of dollars in potential deals, was eating holes in someone's craw.

"Cleo, explain yourself," he demanded again.

He doesn't know about the car, I reminded myself. *He's torn between protecting his family and hearing me out. He hasn't condemned me out of hand. He's asking for an explanation.* I could work with that.

I cleared my throat, squared my shoulders, and met his icy glare. "It's as Regina said. Someone in this room killed your sister all those years ago. I'm sure of it. Others here blame you for her death because you shouldered the responsibility of her loss. Your family is hurt by your choice to walk away from them. Because of your defection, and because of Starr blackmailing Hill for years, the killer decided to tie up loose ends. The killer took Starr's life and arranged for you to be blamed. Someone in this room, someone you know and love, despises you. Because for all intents and purposes, you're a threat to whoever that person is. You've hung on to your money and your soul, something the killer lost all those years ago."

His eyes bored into me, then his steely gaze swept across the room, resting on each person in turn. They looked away from him, as if they were afraid of what he might do.

"Hill?" Rafe asked.

"That's the jist of the matter, but I disagree with Cleo's conclusion," Hill said.

"Starr blackmailed you?"

Hill glanced at Tiffany before facing Rafe. "She did."

"Why? I don't understand."

"Because Starr knew something about me, something I didn't want to come out."

"Why didn't you tell me you were in trouble? I would've helped you."

He hung his head. "I couldn't."

"You can always talk to me. We're brothers."

"No one can live up to your high standards. I'm not the man you are, and I didn't want my taped sexcapades to be headlines in the Washington press. I've made a lot of mistakes, but those days are in the past. I've got a second chance. With Tiffany. She loves me despite my flaws."

Rafe stared at Hill before catching his father's eye. "Dad?"

Like me, Shep appeared at a loss for words. He took a deep breath and spoke in a voice laced with regret. "We should have told you kids the truth about Brenna years ago."

"What truth?" Regina said.

"We made sure the family was protected," Shep said. "We couldn't take the chance one of you kids would spend your life in jail. On the original autopsy report, it was as Cleo said. Three guns, three kinds of bullets in our precious baby girl. Indications were that the shots at the range were fired after her death. Your mother and I figured her death had been an accident you kids covered up. We made sure it stayed covered up. The coroner helped us out by omitting that the range bullets were postmortem, for a price of course."

"You thought I killed Brenna?" Rafe asked.

Shep didn't say anything. His silence was worse than an outright accusation.

"I didn't kill her," Rafe said. "I swear by all that's in me. If someone killed her, it wasn't me. I didn't shoot anyone on purpose. Not Brenna. Not Starr."

His ebbing strength energized me. I wouldn't give them another opening to hurt him. "I know who did it," I blurted. "I know who poisoned Rafe, and I know who committed the murders."

"Cleo," Britt growled.

I ignored the fireplug of a man at my side and charged wildly ahead. "I have the proof at Rafe's place. Turn yourself in by tomorrow morning, or I'm giving my evidence to my detective friend."

"She's bluffing," Regina said.

"She's leaving," Rafe said, his hand clamped on my arm. "With me. I don't care if I ever see any of you again. Stay away from me. Don't call. Don't write. You're all dead to me."

With that, we swept from the room on a stormy tide of emotion. Britt belted me and my purse in Rafe's sports car, and we drove off into the sunset. Too bad there was no scriptwriter ready to type out "and they all lived happily ever after."

I could have used a good fairy tale ending right about then.

CHAPTER 39

"Rafe," I began as the mile marker posts flew by us on the interstate. "I can explain."

"I don't want to hear it," he muttered.

"Someone framed you for murder. I couldn't let that stand. Not while there's a breath in my body."

"You're nosy, insensitive, and downright bullheaded."

"And those are my good qualities," I quipped, hoping to lighten his dark mood.

He barked out a laugh. "What am I going to do with you?"

"What you should have done all along. Trust me to find the truth."

"This is my family we're talking about."

"So it is. Your family is angry with you."

"Thanks to you," he broke in.

"Thanks to your noble attitude. You saw your father. He believes you killed your sister all those years ago. He's believed it from day one. He doesn't know you at all."

Rafe accelerated into the far left lane of the interstate. "I can't believe he thought so poorly of me."

"He thought there'd been an accident. It still might have been an accident, we don't know. All we know for sure is that you weren't involved in the shooting."

"You think Hill or Reggie shot Brenna?"

"Them, or any of the others."

"Not my parents. They doted on Brenna. Neither of them

230

would have gotten up in the middle of the night, shot their daughter, and pretended it didn't happen. You didn't see them, didn't see how none of us mattered that day, how their dead child was the only one they thought about. Hill and Reggie and I huddled on my bed all day and into the night. It was terrible. I never thought her death was anything more than Brenna hiding out down there between the bales of hay behind the target. I never considered any other possibility. I can't wrap my brain around it."

"Had she ever hidden in the hay bales before?"

"No."

"Why didn't anyone question her out-of-character action at the time?"

"We couldn't. Brenna was everything. She was our heart and soul. For her to be gone so abruptly, we couldn't think straight. We were numb. Still are."

Though his voice broke, I continued to push through his barriers to learn the truth. "Did Hill or Reggie act different that day?"

"How?"

"I don't know exactly, different. More edgy, more morose, more guilty."

He fell silent for a bit. "Nothing stands out in my mind, but I was so torn up I couldn't stop crying. My sister wasn't killed on the gun range. I can't believe I'm finding that out now. I can't believe my parents had the autopsy report scrubbed. It's too much to process."

The car swerved onto the shoulder, and he yanked the wheel back. I wanted to pat his arm or stroke his head, but I was unsure of his reaction to comfort. My grip tightened on the strap of my purse. "Do you want me to drive?" I asked.

"No. I need to stay focused. Driving helps. Suppose you were right all along, that Brenna and Starr's deaths are connected—

what's the link? I don't see it."

"I've been struggling with that aspect as well. Here's what I have. Both are female. Both were killed with a gunshot. Both promising lives were cut short."

"That doesn't get us anywhere. We knew that before you went to my parents' house and stirred the hornet's nest."

"I'm not finished, but these next thoughts require a leap of faith. Brenna was the apple of everyone's eye. She received all the attention."

"She deserved it."

"Maybe someone else thought they should have the limelight."

"Not Hill or Reggie."

"Slow down, I see flashing blue lights ahead."

He slowed until we passed the motorist getting a ticket, and I took a moment to gather my thoughts. "It could be Hill or Reggie, even though you don't want to consider them, but there were other children around. Mary and Ashley. They were closest in age to your baby sister."

"Why would one of them shoot Brenna?"

"I'm not certain. I'm just guessing, mind you, but attention seems significant. If everyone noticed how wonderful Brenna was, another child, one who was less sure of herself, might have felt overlooked."

"That's a stretch. Why didn't they push her down, muss her hair, or whatever the hell girls do when they fight?"

"I can't answer that because I don't know much about your sister. How did she feel about the other kids being around? Did she act a certain way to stay in the spotlight?"

"Brenna's goodness wasn't an act. She always shared her toys and games. Mary and Ashley played with Brenna's dolls. One time she choreographed a dance, and the three of them performed for us after dinner. She didn't fight with other kids.

She loved everyone."

"Someone didn't love her. Maybe it was the housekeeper."

"Florie? No way. Brenna was her favorite. She was always cooking with Florie and helping her with the chores. Brenna wanted to do everything with everyone."

I'd never known anyone like Brenna. She'd excelled at everything. "No wonder you were all so devastated."

We drove a few miles in silence. A child paragon. That was Brenna's defining characteristic. It felt relevant. "I keep coming back to resentment or envy. It could have been Florie. For all her tenderness toward the girl, maybe Florie felt Brenna took attention from Mary. Tell me about Mary as a child."

"Not much to say. Her mom made sure she was dressed nicely, and she played by herself in the kitchen a lot. She was shy around us, but not around Brenna. My sister had a way with Mary."

"Mary fits my idea of someone who is insecure and might have been jealous. What about Ashley? What was she like as a child?"

"She was always over at our house. Hill and I hated her tagging along with us, so we played soldiers, cowboys, or pirates when she came over. She was okay, but she was a girl."

"Ashley played with Regina and Brenna?"

"Reggie always had her nose in a book or was at the stables. Ashley was Hill's age, but she hung out with Brenna."

"So an older child played with a younger, more popular child." I massaged the facts, feeling my way. "Ashley seems very appearance conscious now. She might have resented the attention Brenna received."

"This sounds far-fetched."

"You're in denial, but you can't afford that luxury. You're the killer's target now. Because you're certain of your siblings' innocence, I'm leaning toward Mary, Ashley, or Florie as key suspects in Brenna's death. Since they'd killed once, they thought nothing of killing Starr, who was a threat to the family. If I'm right, one of those women is a killer. One of them poisoned you."

Rafe shuddered.

I slipped into my thoughts again. It felt like we were on the edge of a breakthrough with the case. I believed Mary was guilty. I hoped my risky move would pay off.

My investigation had paid off in other ways. I had a better picture of Rafe's past and of his family. I had a better overall picture of the man I loved. I admired the boy who'd forged his own way in the world.

"Why'd you take Britt Radcliff with you?" he asked. "Did you think you'd need police protection against my family?"

His cutting tone aggravated me. The truth boiled out. "Someone shot my car on purpose."

He stared at me in shock. "What? Your car?"

"Eyes on the road, please. I didn't tell you about it because I didn't want to alarm you. Britt took care of the report and getting my car towed. The more I thought about it, the more I knew I needed to confront your family and force the issue. I couldn't do that with you along."

He grunted. "Tell me about the car."

I gave him a detailed report of my stop at Overlook Park and the bullet hole in my car. "That incident told me I was on the right track with finding out who the real killer was. Britt pried my intentions out of me. He wouldn't let me go down to Potomac alone."

"I'm glad. I don't want anything to happen to you."

"Me either." More miles rolled past. "Is there anything else that comes to mind? Any other family secrets that might be relevant to the killer's identity?"

He didn't say anything.

Since I was striking out on finding Starr's killer, I might as well try a different line of questioning. "What about sex?"

He shot me a smoldering look. "What about it?"

"A member of your family is Kylie's father. I'm certain of that. As far as I can tell, that limits the potential donors to you, Hill, your dad, and Ashley's dad. Who else in your family had sex with Starr?"

He grimaced. "Hill admitted sleeping with her."

"And the others?"

"I don't know."

I could needle him about the morals of the men of his family, but it was bad enough accusing the women of murder. I decided to rest my case. We cruised over the rolling foothills of suburban Maryland, and I admired the brightly colored fall foliage.

"What evidence is at my place?" he asked. "What links the two killings?"

"Regina was right," I said. "I was bluffing. I'm banking on the killer believing me."

"That's a long shot."

"I wish I had more, but this killer knows how to cover his or her tracks. The killer doesn't know if Starr might have implicated her in either a conversation, letter, or other communication. If I'm right, and I believe I am, the killer will break into your place tonight to destroy the evidence."

"Where does Britt stand in all of this?"

"I laid my plan out to Britt before we drove to Potomac. Without solid evidence to the contrary, he's unwilling to consider he was wrong. You're still at the top of his suspect list. If someone breaks into your place and we catch him or her, he might reconsider his stance."

"Risky."

My teeth clamped together. Rafe didn't know the half of it.

CHAPTER 40

Rafe and I ate a veggie pizza with Mama and the girls at my place. With the wedding in two days, Mama and the girls couldn't stop talking about their clothing and the artificial flowers. I smiled and nodded at appropriate intervals, but throughout the meal I felt Rafe studying me. The questions in his eyes worried me.

"You okay?" I asked at a lull in the conversation.

His gaze swept the others at the table. "Fine."

I got the message. He didn't want to talk about his concerns in front of my family, which was a good thing. If Mama knew we were staking out his condo tonight, she'd insist on coming along.

After dinner, I cornered Mama in the kitchen. "I hate to ask this again, but would you stay with the girls? Rafe and I need some time alone at his place."

Mama grinned. "Sure thing. You take that new black nightie Jonette found for you. The man won't know what hit him."

"Good idea. I'll toss a few essentials in my purse. Thanks."

Once we arrived at the condo, Rafe checked to make sure no one had entered his place before we'd arrived. While he checked the closets and under the bed, I deposited my purse on his living room table and my insurance policy under the sofa.

The two of us hunkered down in his bedroom, sitting on the floor and leaning against the bed.

My thoughts were in turmoil. Would my gamble pay off?

Would the killer take the bait? Would Rafe forgive me for unearthing his family secrets?

"I can't believe you're spending the night at my place, and we're not ripping each other's clothes off," Rafe grumbled.

"I can't believe you would even think about sex at a time like this. Someone's trying to kill us."

"Hey, I can multi-task."

"Maybe you can, but I can't. Not when my car was used for target practice. Not when you've been framed for murder."

"I didn't do it."

"That defense will go over great in court."

His teeth gleamed in the near darkness. "What's our plan? If a killer breaks in here, how will we stop them?"

"Besides that baseball bat next to you?"

"Yeah. Besides that."

"I thought about bringing one of my guns," I began.

"No guns." His deep voice boomed in my ear. "I don't want any guns in this house."

I couldn't believe he didn't see the gaping flaw in his logic. I matched his commanding tone and volume level. "What if the killer doesn't know your rules? What if said killer brings a gun in here? Can you smack her with the bat before she shoots us?"

He whipped out his cell phone. The display illuminated the dark bedroom. "We need to get you out of here. I'll call Britt to come take you home."

Though I was flattered by his concern, I stayed his hand. "Leave Britt out of this. I'm not going anywhere. Neither are you."

Rafe picked up the bat. "You think the killer will walk in the front door?"

"Not like there are any other entrances. I doubt she would come through a window. That would be too messy."

He was silent for a while. His breathing sounded loud in the darkness. "You think it's Florie?" he asked.

"Never said that, but Florie spent her life cleaning. She wouldn't create a mess."

"Neither would Ashley. She threw out lots of my stuff when I moved in here. Said I needed to wipe the slate clean with my fresh start. Said I was becoming a hoarder."

"Were you?"

"Not by the world's standards. I'd saved a bunch of junk from school. She was right. I didn't need that old stuff. I haven't missed it at all."

"She shouldn't have made you get rid of your mementos. That was mean."

"She was doing her job."

As the conversation trailed off, his words echoed in my ear. He'd mentioned Florie and Ashley, but not Mary. Was that intentional? I probed a bit. "Mary works all the time. Doesn't Regina give her time off?"

"I can't say. Every time we see Reggie, Mary is with her. That should mean Mary is off the hook for the crimes. She can't murder anyone if she's at my sister's constant beck and call."

Grudgingly, I admired his logic. However, I remained open to outside possibilities. Mary topped my list of suspects. You had to watch out for those quiet, repressed types. "There's still a chance it's Hill or Reggie."

"No way." Rafe placed the bat on the carpet and wrapped an arm around me. "When this is over, you and I need to have a long talk about boundaries."

This was the most we'd talked about his family ever. I felt like we'd barely scratched the surface. I tipped my head back to look at his silhouette. "Why wait?"

"Because we have opposing views about boundaries, and I need to be at the top of my game to discuss this with you."

"I don't mind a boundary here or there, but I can't abide

secrets. I know you don't want to be compared to my ex, and God knows I don't want to be compared to your knockout ex-fiancée, but secrets regarding other people are dangerous. We wouldn't be where we are with your case if I hadn't pushed through your boundaries. You'd be facing the death penalty for murder otherwise. That outcome is unacceptable to me."

"How would you feel if I pushed into your private life?"

"I'll tell you anything you want to know. All you have to do is ask."

"Why did you marry Charlie Jones?"

His quick question stunned me for a moment. "Ouch. Went right for the jugular, didn't you?"

"Doesn't feel so good, does it?"

"It's uncomfortable, but I don't mind sharing the truth. I trust you with my darkest secret. Charlie and I were an item in high school. One thing led to another. We married because I was pregnant."

"You had a shotgun marriage?"

"It wasn't like that. Charlie's mom was alive back then. She was delighted to have a grandchild on the way. My parents supported my decision to keep the baby and marry Charlie, but they pushed hard for me to continue my education. It wasn't easy, but I did both."

"This is a secret because?"

"Because I'd never want to hurt Charla's feelings. Lexy came early, so the fact that I had Charla eight months after I was married isn't significant to the girls. I'll tell Charla the truth if she asks, but she needs to bring it up. I won't volunteer information that might hurt her feelings."

"I see."

I drew in a deep, satisfied breath. It felt good sharing confidences. Heady with success, I took a turn at the truth wheel. "Why Tiffany?"

"Obvious physical reasons. But it turned out we weren't compatible."

"Got news for you. Few couples are one hundred percent compatible. Lots of speed bumps on the road to marital bliss."

"Figured that one out for myself."

Time passed as we sat there by the foot of the bed. I don't know what Rafe was thinking, but I believed there was more to the Tiffany story than he was telling. It made me wonder what other secrets he had.

Being still, full of carbs, and warm, it wasn't long before I dozed. A while later, I swam out of sleep as Rafe's body tensed. "Shh!" he whispered. "Someone's at the door."

"Don't confront her until she's inside," I whispered back, my pulse quickening. "We want to catch the killer red-handed."

From our prime vantage point on the bedroom floor, we saw a flashlight beam enter the living room. I heard a faint snick as the door closed. I glanced over at the digital clock by the bed. Midnight. The witching hour.

Rafe and I had agreed—well, he'd insisted and I'd finally quit protesting—that he'd crawl on hands and knees in the living room before he turned on the lights, while I dialed 911 in the bedroom. I was keenly aware I was seven feet away from a locking bathroom door.

Recklessly, I edged closer to the bedroom door.

The living room lights flashed on, blinding me. I blinked furiously, wishing I was out there and Rafe was in here. That bat was no match for an armed intruder.

"What are you doing?" Rafe said.

"What I have to do," a muffled female voice said. "Why couldn't you shut up and go to jail like you were supposed to?"

"Put the gun down." Rafe's flat voice sent chills down my spine. "I won't go to jail for a crime I didn't commit."

Gun? Uh-oh. I'd better act fast if I wanted to save us. With fear-thickened fingers, I keyed in the emergency number. "This is Cleopatra Jones," I whispered into the phone. "I'm at fourteen eighty-six Manor Run Road. A woman with a gun just broke in here."

"Please stay on the line," the dispatch operator said.

"I can't." I tried to shiver away the mantle of black fright. It didn't budge. "I have to save Rafe. Sorry."

"Put the bat down," the intruder ordered. "What evidence do you have against me? What did Starr tell you?"

"Why'd you kill my sister? Answer me, Ashley."

Ashley?

My heart jumped. I'd been thinking Mary all along. Over-worked, overlooked Mary. Britt was right. Guessing got you nowhere. "I gotta go. The intruder's name is Ashley Webber." I placed the open phone on the rug by the door.

"Come on out, Cleo. I know you're hiding in there," Ashley said. "Keep your hands where I can see them."

I edged out the door, hands raised above my head. My breath came in shallow, quick pulses. This was one of my worst ideas ever. Rafe's designing cousin wore black from head to toe, including a scarf over her nose and mouth. Her eyes blazed pure fury. In her hands was a .22 with a silencer on the barrel. Her weapon of choice, if you discounted her hobby of poison-ing people.

"You won't get away with this," I shrilled, wincing at my high-pitched voice. "If I figured it out, so will the cops."

"No more head games," Ashley said. "Since there are two of you, I'll set the stage for a murder suicide. Given Cleo's aggres-sive behavior in Potomac, the police will believe Rafe silenced her to protect his family, felt remorse over his action, and killed himself."

To my horror, Rafe rushed his cousin, and the gun discharged. The shot was so quiet, you'd barely know a bullet had been fired, unless you overlooked the hole in the lampshade and the gouge in the drywall. Couldn't think about that now. I had to save Rafe.

I ducked behind the leather sofa, reaching underneath for the .38 revolver I'd hidden there earlier. My hand clenched around the engraved grip. Rafe might have a policy against guns, but I didn't. Guns evened the playing field.

"Damn you!" Ashley shrieked.

Where was the cavalry when you needed them? This wasn't supposed to happen so quickly. I crouched with my weapon and saw Rafe and Ashley rolling on the floor. Ashley's pistol went flying. She kicked, bit, and bucked, but she couldn't shake Rafe. I straightened from my defensive crouch, but I kept my gun trained on her as I edged closer. I'd confronted killers a time or two.

They were never predictable.

"Why?" Rafe's voice broke with emotion. "What did Brenna ever do to you?"

"Everything. I was the family's darling before she came along. It was always Brenna this and Brenna that. No one gave a damn about Ashley. I fixed that problem. With Brenna out of the picture, I became the family's poster child for success. I was prom queen. I was the head cheerleader. I won the shooting tournaments. I won the most riding trophies. I even built a business based on my good looks and great taste. All thanks to Brenna."

"Tie her up, Cleo. She disgusts me," Rafe said.

"Can't do that, but help is on the way."

He glanced over at me and recoiled. "You brought a gun into my house?"

"I believe in protection," I said. "Ashley's killed twice now. I knew the baseball bat wouldn't be enough. You're lucky she didn't shoot you."

Ashley studied me. Then she summoned an enormous amount of force and headbutted Rafe. He went down, and she pushed his still body aside.

Horrified, I kept my gun trained on her as she scooted backward. "Stay put," I said, matching her progress.

"You won't shoot me," Ashley sneered. "I know your type. You're all talk and no guts. You don't have any evidence here. There isn't any. Starr never made notes about our meetings. She tried to blackmail me about a mistake I made after Hill's well ran dry. Only I never had your kind of wealth. Daddy lost our stake when the high-tech market went south a few years back."

"Starr was another problem you took care of? Like Brenna?"

"Yes. That little upstart tried to worm her kid into the Golden money machine. Her fate was sealed once I realized her intention. My Dahlia is the only true Golden child. She will inherit all the Golden money, not some trailer trash kid. I'm protecting my family, same as Shep and Amanda did all those years ago."

"You're in for a surprise. The Golden family fortune has fallen tremendously in recent years. Regina isn't the business manager that Brenna might have been, or that Rafe could be. Rafe has more money than all the rest of his family combined. You won't see a dime of his money."

Ashley shrieked and kicked her cousin. "Why didn't you die already? I've fed you enough poison over the years to kill a mule. Die, dammit."

"I researched poisonings online," I continued. A siren warbled in the distance. I had to keep talking. I had to beat this woman at her own game. "Rafe developed a tolerance to it, and he got away from you and your poison. That's why you framed him for Starr's murder, right?"

"Rafe's a dumb jock. He got what he deserved." Eyes on me, Ashley groped for her gun.

"Stop," I said. My heart thrummed in my ears. "Don't make me shoot you."

"Bitch."

As she spoke, I aimed at her gun and fired. My bullet sliced through her extended palm, and she howled, clutching the injured hand to her belly and crooning nonsense. Blood dripped from her fingers onto the carpet.

Knees trembling, I walked over, collected her gun, and jammed it in my waistband. "Don't move." She didn't appear to hear me, but she obeyed my command. Keeping her in my field of vision, I knelt beside Rafe, checked for a pulse, and found one. Relief surged and ebbed. Why wasn't he waking up?

Heavy footsteps clomped up the stairs. "Cleo?" Britt yelled. "You okay?"

"I'm fine, but I can't say as much for this murderess."

"We never saw her. She must have been already inside the building," Britt said as he huffed inside the condo. Uniformed police officers swept into the room and took Ashley away. Britt took the guns from me and parked me on the sofa. Two paramedics charged in and worked on Rafe. "She headbutted him," I said.

Things happened in freeze-frame shots. I watched a step out of phase with the rescuers. *Please let him be all right.* A vial snapped open. They waved it under Rafe's nose. He shook his head. His eyes blinked open. "What happened? Who are you? Cleo?"

Tears filled my eyes, clouded my vision. I scooted as close as I could get. "I'm here."

He craned his neck up. "Did we get her?"

"Sir, remain still until we finish your health assessment," the bulky attendant said.

I nodded and fought the lump in my throat. "Yeah. We got her. Your sister's murderer will be brought to justice. Ashley killed Brenna and Starr, and she tried to kill us. She'll be locked up for a very long time."

"Thank God."

They rolled him out on a gurney. I sagged against the wall, out of gas. Options swirled in my head. Should I blot the blood out of his carpet? Was it evidence? Should I race to the hospital? What?

Britt touched my arm. "You recorded everything?"

"I did." I unbuttoned my shirt to reveal the mini digital recorder he'd attached earlier to my bra. "Take it. And the backup recorder in my purse. You should have enough to convict Ashley for both murders."

"You didn't tell Rafe about the recorders?"

"Not yet."

"Rafe didn't know about the gun either?"

"Nope."

"I'd say you two have some trust issues to work out."

I buttoned myself back up. "That we do."

CHAPTER 41

Britt kicked me out of Rafe's place, so I drove to the hospital. Rafe was okay, I reminded myself. He was crazy for going up against an armed assailant, but okay. We'd set the trap and caught the killer. Funny how clear events seemed at one in the morning.

Men and women in blue scrubs buzzed in and out of the nurse's station in the emergency room. I shielded my eyes against the bright light and scanned the motley group assembled in the lobby. No Rafe. Guess they'd already taken him back to an exam area.

A cheerful nursing assistant directed me down a hall in the back of the facility. My shoes squeaked on the highly polished floor. A noise sounded behind me. I whirled and half-ducked, worried that I might still be dodging another bullet, but there was only a young man pushing a wheeled machine past me.

"Sorry if I surprised you," he said. "We've got a full house tonight, and I had to break this squeaky cart out of cold storage."

"It's okay," I managed, though my heart raced. I continued on to exam room eleven, knocked, and entered.

Rafe rested on the bed, his eyes closed. They opened at my entry. "It's me," I said, easing to the side of his bed and taking hold of his hand. "How're you feeling?"

His fingers closed around mine as if I was his anchor. "Dumb. I should have remembered all those martial arts classes Ashley took. She was always so driven as a kid. I thought I had her pinned to the floor tonight, but she outmaneuvered me. My head hurts like a sonuvabitch."

I covered his hand with my other one. "If it's any consolation, her head must ache, too."

He thought about it. "Nope, it doesn't make me feel better. I'm having trouble taking this all in. I've never run into anyone who's hated me so much. The worst part is I didn't see it. Ashley presented a loving front to me. I thought we were good friends."

I nodded. "I've been in your shoes. When someone you know does bad things, it's a complete shock. One of the unfortunate side effects of sleuthing is I became less trusting of people in general."

"That I understand. I don't like being blindsided. How did I miss her true feelings about my family and me for all those years?"

"She's an acomplished liar. Had to be for her to get away with murder for so long."

"I hope there's enough evidence to convict her."

"Don't worry. The police have what they need. I taped her confession."

"You did? How come I didn't know about it?"

"You're hearing about it now."

"You brought a gun into my house."

His surly tone rankled. My chin rose. "I did, and I'd do it again in a heartbeat to defend someone I love. Guns aren't evil, but people can be evil."

"That's a point I'd like to debate when I don't have a raging headache." He rubbed his thumb over the back of my hand. "Thank you. It hardly seems adequate to say those two words, but I'm grateful. You saved my life and cleared my name." He tried to grin, though it came out a grimace. "I'll make it up to you when I get out of here."

"Sure, but first let's get you doctored up. What did the doctor say?"

"Concussion. They want to hold me for observation overnight, but I want to go home."

I heaved out a breath and realized that's what I wanted, too. I'd been away from home a lot lately. Mama's wedding was in two days, and God only knew what disasters were waiting to unfold there. "I'll take you home with me tonight. That way I don't have to leave you alone in the morning to get the girls ready for school."

"No offense, but your place isn't restful. I want to go home-home to recuperate. To Potomac. You were right about that. It's time I made an effort to be part of my family."

Unsure of his intent, I leaned forward, searching his face. "You're moving back to Potomac?"

"Not in the near future. I like my life as a golf pro in Hogan's Glen. I like dating you."

I smiled. "That's a relief. I thought I'd lost you to the family business."

"I'm staying put. But I'm keeping an open mind about the future."

I dared to hope I would be in his future. "Reconciling with your family is important." I cast about for a new subject. "Any word yet on the DNA test to determine Kylie's father?"

"Nothing. I'll let you know as soon as I hear something."

There was a commotion in the hall. Mama and Bud Radcliff sailed into the exam room. "What's going on in here? Did you go on a stakeout without me?" Mama asked, worry stamped in her amber-flecked eyes. She had a death grip on her triple-stranded pearls. Bud's normally pressed slacks looked distinctly wrinkled. I tried not to think about what they'd been doing.

Rafe's hand jerked in mine, sending out a fresh wave of alarm.

"Keep it down, Mama," I said. "Rafe's got a screaming headache and a concussion."

"Sorry," she whispered.

Bud's smile stretched across his craggy face. "Good news, Rafe. With the murder solved, your name has been cleared. And your job at the course is there if you want it. You're a free man."

"Thanks to Cleo," Rafe said, trying to smile. "She kept the pressure on, and she believed in my innocence from start to finish."

"It hardly seems fair to applaud my pigheaded, stubborn qualities," I said.

"You are who you are," Mama said, reaching up to pat my shoulder. "Don't apologize for that."

Another commotion sounded in the hall. Regina, Hill, Amanda, and Shep Golden filed in. Hill strode to the opposite side of the bed from me, his handsome features ashen. "Damn, bro. You're going to have a shiner. Little Ashley did that to you?"

"Little Ashley has at least one black belt in martial arts, and God knows what else in her lethal arsenal," Rafe muttered. "I'm lucky to have survived our encounter. If not for Cleo here, I'd have at least one bullet hole in me."

Shep Golden nodded. "Well done, Cleo."

As I flushed under his praise, Mama elbowed Bud toward the door. "We'll wait for you outside, dear," she said.

Regina edged in front of Hill and nodded my way. "I apologize for the awful things I said about you. None of us knew the truth about Ashley. None of us had an inkling she'd killed Brenna. We tried to brush that 'accidental' death under the carpet, and that was the wrong thing to do."

I hardly knew what to say, but good manners never went out of season. "I accept your apology."

Amanda wormed her way in front of Shep. She worried her

hands together, but her eyes were on her son. "All those years we thought you had a bad stomach, and it was your cousin poisoning you. Can you forgive us for not protecting you?"

"It's okay. Looking back, I wasn't the only one with a bad stomach," Rafe said. "Who would have suspected a killer in our home? If not for Cleo's insistence on clearing my name, I wouldn't have a future or my freedom. I'd be planted next to Brenna. I owe her."

"We all owe Cleo," Shep said. "She's a fine young woman."

I blinked back tears.

A male nurse and an orderly came in. "There are too many people in this room," the nurse said. "Three of you have to leave."

Knowing Rafe wanted to be with his family, I rose. "I'll step out." With care, I kissed the side of his face. "If you change your mind about tonight, call me. I'll come get you wherever you are. Love you."

He nodded, his large pupils dulled with pain.

I walked out of there under my own power, but fatigue bent my shoulders. I wanted to crawl into my bed and sleep round the clock. Mama and Bud stood up in the lobby as I entered.

"There you are," Mama said, as if I'd been lost for weeks in the woods. She swooped me into a big hug.

Tears brimmed in my eyes and spilled onto my cheeks. "Here I am," I said.

"What's the plan?" Bud asked.

"Rafe wants to be with his family, and I want to go home."

Bud nodded. "I'll drive you."

As welcome as that idea was, it wasn't practical. "My rental car's here."

"Dee and I will pick up the car in the morning and rescue the Gray Beast from the body shop," Bud said. "You're running on fumes. Come on, let someone else take care of you for a change."

"Fine." I was too tired to argue, too tired to do anything more than trudge to Bud's car and sit down. Mama sat in the spacious back seat with me.

"Tell us what happened," she said.

I recounted the story, hitting the highlights. Mama crowed about Ashley's downfall. "Britt should hire you to be a police consultant. You're smart as a whip."

"I'm not feeling smart right now. Exhausted is more like it. Who's with the girls?"

"Charlie," Mama said. "He came right over. Sure is handy with him living next door."

I drew in a full breath for the first time all evening. Rafe would heal. Ashley would go to jail. My girls were safe. The puppies were growing up and would have good homes. Sure, I didn't have all the answers, but I'd restored order to Rafe's life. Hopefully, my life would settle down again as well.

Despite my optimism, a question of a different nature worried at my thoughts. The wedding. Britt was Mama's escort down the aisle. "I've been meaning to ask. Why did you ask Britt to walk you down the aisle?"

Mama and Bud exchanged glances in the rearview mirror. "Tell her, Dee," Bud said.

His terse instruction clanked around in my brain. "Tell me what?"

"I've been meaning to tell you. I always wondered if this was the case, but Bud helped me find out for sure."

"What?" I sat up straighter, sensing news of great import.

"Britt's my nephew. He's the son of my sister Ruthie."

I shook the cobwebs from my head. "Aunt Ruthie? I don't understand. She died when you were a junior in high school. I

251

remember you saying she died in childbirth. I thought the baby died, too."

"My mother thought she was doing the right thing. She put the baby up for adoption. I wish I'd known of Britt's existence back then. I could've had him all this time, but I am lucky to have him now. He's your first cousin. Heck, he's your only cousin."

Britt was related to me? My hand covered my open mouth. Mama gazed at me expectantly in the faint light of the car. I slowly lowered my hand. "I hardly know what to say. How did you know?"

"Britt reminded me of my sister from the first day he walked into my Sunday school class. His eyes, the way they flash when he's crossed. His sense of humor."

News this big could take days to sort out. As tired as I was, I couldn't manage it in the dark. Tomorrow. I'd think this through when I was good and rested. I yawned and sat back. "He has one of those?"

"He does. Anyway, I suspected he was kin all along, and I'm not denying I favored him for years because he reminded me of Ruthie. I didn't have any way to approach him about it, not until recently, anyway."

"What changed?"

"His adoptive parents died. The Radcliffs were so proud of their adopted son. So proud Britt made something of himself. I couldn't diminish their bond in any way, but once they both passed, I decided to take action. Bud helped me cut through the red tape. I discovered the truth a few months ago."

"Does Britt know?"

"Yes. Bud and I visited him and Melissa one Sunday afternoon and showed them the papers. I asked him to keep quiet about it until I told you."

"You knew for months?"

"Well, we have been busy," Mama said. "Between the puppies, the crime solving, teenaged girls, and everything else, there's hardly been a moment to spare."

And with both of us trying to find time to be with the men in our lives, that didn't leave any spare time for the two of us to chat about long-lost relatives.

Britt Radcliff.

My cousin.

No wonder he'd acted like a big brother to me for so many years. He must have suspected the truth long before Mama tumbled onto it.

"Forgive me?" Mama asked. "I know how you feel about secrets, but I wanted to wait for the right moment."

I barked out a laugh. "You waited until the night I confronted an armed serial killer? How is that the right time?"

"It just is." After a moment, Mama spoke again. "There's more."

"I don't think I can handle too much more tonight."

"You can handle this. I forgive you for the house."

"The house?" I didn't have to fake my confusion.

"Stealing the house out from under me."

I groaned at the topic. There was no way I could win this argument. She'd won it every time she'd brought it up after Daddy's funeral. It had gotten to the point where I wished Daddy had left the house to Mama.

"I can see how unstable I must have looked to Joe," Mama said. "I was such a mess in those days, it's a wonder he didn't divorce me."

"He loved you. He wouldn't divorce you."

"I'm grateful to Joe for his love and trust, and I'm trying to say that now I realize he was acting in my best interest when he deeded the house to you. I'm not mad about it anymore. I don't think you tried to swindle me out of something that was mine. I know he trusted you to keep it safe for me."

"That house will always be your home, Mama. I've told you that repeatedly over the years. Do you finally believe me?"

"I believe you, but it doesn't matter. I'm moving out. Bud and I will live in his house."

"You're full of surprises tonight. Anything else I should know about? Did Charla elope? Did Prince Charming wander in off the streets? Did the dog start passing gold-plated poop?"

"None of that stuff. What secrets I have left are mine and mine alone."

Secrets. I hated them. But for once I felt grateful that I didn't know everything. My eyelids drifted shut, and I stopped fighting exhaustion.

Sometimes a gal's gotta go with the flow.

CHAPTER 42

The beaming bride and groom twirled past, she in an elegant froth of blush chiffon, he adorned with a bow tie the same shade and a dapper charcoal gray suit. The love they felt for each other filled the entire parish hall.

Truthfully, I felt relieved to have a moment to relax. The ordeal about a killer on the loose was over. Rafe had reconciled with his family.

Francine and Muriel, Mama's longtime friends, waltzed by with small trays of appetizers. Rafe and I both settled on the mini apple tarts. My mouth watered at the first bite. These ladies were onto something when they talked about a catering business. Once word got out, they might be able to buy back the deed to their home. I vowed to do everything I could to help them become profitable.

"Yum," Rafe said, looking at me.

I'd splurged on a new dress for the wedding. New spiky heels too. I couldn't complain about the cost because how often could a daughter dance at her mother's wedding? It was a reasonable expense given the circumstance.

"You're feeling better?" I asked hopefully.

"I still have a headache, but overall I'm starting to feel better. You look amazing in that dress."

His roughened voice gave me very nice chills. I preened. "That's me, Miz Amazing."

He took my hand. "Walk with me?"

We slipped out of the noisy room and eased onto the loveseat in the empty counseling room. "Much better," Rafe said, drawing me close for a kiss.

I gave myself to the moment, but despite both of our intentions, I didn't melt in his arms. I was disappointed and hoped he couldn't tell the difference in my response.

"I've got something to tell you," he began.

"Oh?" Given the revelations of the last few days, I expected something monumental. The president was an alien, or Mary was a secret opera singer, or he had three wives in Morocco. Whatever it was, I was certain it would be unsettling. I clutched my hands together and summoned a vague smile.

"The DNA results are in."

I couldn't breathe. "And?"

"I'm not Kylie's father."

Air eased from my lungs. I nodded. "You said as much all along. I believed you."

"The thing is, they were able to determine parentage based on our similar DNA profiles. You were right in saying the child is a Golden."

"Is Hill the father?"

"That's what I thought. We know Hill slept with Starr. But the child isn't his."

"The suspense is killing me. Who is Kylie's dad?"

His expression hardened. "My father."

I blinked. And blinked some more. My instincts had been lousy with this case. I'd assumed Mary was the killer and Hill was the sperm donor. Both assumptions had been wrong.

Wait. This wasn't about me. It must be tearing Rafe apart that his former girlfriend slept with his brother and his father. Ick.

"You okay?" I asked.

"I was upset at first. Mad at Starr. Mad at my father. But

then I thought about that little kid. Cleo, I have another chance at being a big brother. Kylie's my new baby sister."

"Will your dad seek custody?"

"Yes. He's had the firm's lawyers on the matter ever since yesterday morning when the results came back. My mother's furious, naturally. My father confessed he and Starr had casual sex a few times. He wasn't as conscientious about condoms as he should have been, hence, the unexpected offspring."

Inside, I deflated. The news had come in yesterday, and he didn't tell me until now? I edged back in my seat. "Hill must be relieved."

"Yes and no. Having another Golden in the family involves slicing the company into another segment. Dad wants Kylie to be a full member of the family."

"Starr's sister may object. Jenny planned to raise Kylie."

"We're working that out. Dad's going to build them a cottage behind the big house, so Kylie's address will be Potomac instead of a Madeira trailer park."

"Has anyone told her yet?"

"Soon. Florie is delighted at the thought of having a little one underfoot again. She loves kids."

"Kylie is in good hands, then. I'm glad." And I was. Kylie deserved to be loved by both sides of her family.

The reception hall doors opened and shut. Lexy and her photographer friend walked out, each with cameras around their necks, deep in conversation. She grinned at me. "Hi, Mom. Mr. Golden, have you met my friend John Paul Delong?"

Rafe stood and shook the gawky boy's hand. "My pleasure."

"Can we take your picture?" Lexy asked.

"Sure." Rafe sat down beside me, his arm draped casually along the back of the loveseat. The kids snapped picture after picture until I called a halt. "Enough! Go hound Mama and Bud. This is their shindig."

Lexy and John Paul exhanged a sheepish glance.

My maternal radar pinged. "What?"

"You said hound. Did you know about the dogs?"

She had my attention now. "What dogs?"

"Charla and her girlfriends smuggled the puppies into the reception. They were sleeping in the kitchen, but now they're running around the parish hall."

"Oh, dear!" I bolted into the reception room, Rafe following. Puppies were scampering underfoot. The sixty-somethings were nimbly stepping over them and dancing the afternoon away. Jonette sat on the floor, a vibrant pool of blue with a squirming Arnold in her arms. Her Moore for Mayor sash looked as if it had been chewed in half. With a few weeks to go before the election, she had time to order another sash.

"Charlie was right," I said.

"About what?" Rafe asked.

"The puppies. He knew Jonette would choose Arnold."

As I watched, Dean leaned down to hug them both. The puppy licked his face, and the deal was sealed. Arnold belonged to Jonette and Dean. Now I needed good homes for Moses and Ariel.

I caught sight of Charla dancing with her friends and hurried to intercept her. "The puppies don't belong here."

She didn't look the least bit repentant. "They wanted to come. They're part of our family."

"They're going to have new families, Charla," I said gently. "You need to get used to that."

"I don't want to think about it."

"Round the puppies up, except Arnold. Jonette's taking Arnold home with her. I don't think you could pry him out of her arms with a crowbar."

"Oh, Mom. You're no fun at all." Charla stomped off, her red curls bouncing with outrage. Oh, to be fifteen again and to have so much passion.

"Wanna dance?" Rafe said.

I did. The slow number suited us both. I tried to let the music take me away, but I couldn't relax. Rafe and I weren't on the same sheet of music relationship-wise. I'd risked my life to save his neck, but he couldn't pick up the phone to call me yesterday about the DNA test? Something wasn't right. Our level of give and take wasn't equitable. The debits outweighed the credits.

I trusted and believed in him. Why didn't he reciprocate?

At the end of the number, he gave me a squeeze and a peck on the cheek. "My headache isn't going away. I need to go home to peace and quiet. Do you mind?"

"No. I understand."

"You could surprise me later. In your birthday suit. Or that black nightie I missed out on the other night."

"We'll see," I hedged, not sure if I wanted to jump in the sack with him. What I wanted was a heart-to-heart talk about the speed bumps we were experiencing.

Rafe left, and, perversely, my mood improved. I walked over to talk to Britt's wife, Melissa.

"You know!" Melissa said.

I nodded.

"I've been wanting to hug you ever since I heard the news about Britt's biological mother." Melissa threw her arms around me and held on tight. She nodded toward the dance floor where Britt danced with his daughter in his arms. "He's so proud and happy to have family again."

"I'm happy about the news. Britt's a good guy. He already feels like family. It's awesome news."

She nodded. "The best. And thanks for helping my sister. Zoe never would have known to look for a life insurance policy if you hadn't cued her. She said you're her new accountant."

"I'm glad she's doing okay and happy to have her as a paying client."

I continued around the room, talking to folks, hugging old friends, and ending up in the corner where my ex-husband sat. I plunked down next to him. "How's it going?" I asked.

"Great, now that you're here," he said.

I searched his blue eyes to see if he was telling the truth. For most of our married life, I'd been able to read him. As I gazed into his eyes now, I felt the sincerity of his emotions. He wanted me more than anything. No doubt about that.

He smiled, the freckles on his nose scrunching up as his entire face beamed with happiness. With elegant ease, he rose and bowed. "Mrs. Jones, may I have the honor of this dance?"

It would be in my long-term best interest to keep Charlie Jones at arm's length. I didn't want to give him the slightest impression that I was softening in my stance toward him. That old saw echoed in my ears: fool me once, shame on you; fool me twice, shame on me.

That's what I thought, but my hand found his. "Of course, Mr. Jones. I'd be delighted to dance with you."

As the slow dance progressed, I closed my eyes and relaxed in his arms. What did the future hold for me? Would Rafe and I work out our communication issues? Would I give Charlie another chance?

Dime if I knew.

Rather than answer these hard questions, I counted my blessings. I'd solved another complex case, found a cousin, enjoyed a good relationship with my kids, gained a stepdad, and settled my differences with Mama about the house.

In all the ways that counted, I was truly rich.

ABOUT THE AUTHOR

A scientist by training, a romantic at heart, **Maggie Toussaint** loves to solve puzzles. Whether it's the puzzle of a relationship or a whodunit, she tackles them with equal aplomb and wonder. Maggie's previous cozy mysteries from Five Star are *In for a Penny, On the Nickel,* and *Death, Island Style.* Her other published works are romantic suspense books, one of which won Best Romantic Suspense in the 2007 National Readers Choice Awards. She freelances for a weekly newspaper. Visit her at www.maggietoussaint.com.